Lestrade and the Deadly Game

Volume V in the Lestrade Mystery Series

M.J. Trow

A Gateway Mystery

REGNERY
PUBLISHING, INC.

Since 1947 • An Eagle Publishing Company

Copyright © 1999 by Regnery Publishing

Published in the United States by
Regnery Publishing, Inc.
An Eagle Publishing Company
One Massachusetts Avenue, NW
Washington, DC 20001

Distributed to the trade by
National Book Network
4720-A Boston Way
Lanham, MD 20706

Printed on acid-free paper.
Manufactured in the United States of America

10 9 8 7 6 5 4 3 2 1

Books are available in quantity for promotional or premium use. Write to Director of Special Sales, Regnery Publishing, Inc., One Massachusetts Avenue, NW, Washington, DC 20001, for information on discounts and terms or call (202) 216-0600.

International Standard Book Number:
0-89526-312-2

The character of Inspector Lestrade was created by the late Sir Arthur Conan Doyle and appears in the Sherlock Holmes stories and novels by him, as do some other characters in this book.

FOR DAD

As flies to wanton boys, are we to the Gods;
They kill us for their sport.

King Lear Act IV Scene i

1

One To Get Ready . . .

The Greeks had a word for it. It was a short one and it translated rather well into Anglo-Saxon. Someone had pinched their Games.

But in other ways, the year was set fair. The Congo was annexed by Belgium. Bosnia and Herzegovina, the terrible twins of those tiresome Balkan States, were annexed by Austria. There was even a new annexe at Scotland Yard. The British Army of course excelled itself by devising a new pattern sword with a pistol grip hilt of gutta-percha. To the Yeomanry who had served so well on Veldt and Nek, it declined to give any swords at all. And weary gentlemen, then abed, shook their heads and muttered as they read their morning papers. That buffoon Haldane had introduced a new part-time soldier he called a 'terrier'. The country was of course going to the dogs.

Mr Edward Henry crossed again to his window, the only one that permitted a decent view of the river, sparkling now in the morning sun. He looked at the grandmother on the wall.

'Yes.' He heard the monotone behind him. 'Half-past. It's certainly getting on.'

He turned to Inspector Gregory and gave him the old Pukka Sahib's look which had decimated the natives of Ceylon. But Gregory was too white-skinned to notice.

'You'd think they'd be here by now,' he said, trying to fix an air of even average intellect on to his bovine face.

'Indeed.' Henry's temper, no longer than he was, was within an ace of snapping. He flicked open the silver box and cut himself into a new Havana.

'Ah,' said Gregory, with the air of a man about to be offered a smoke. 'Ahhmmm,' and he had the grace to turn disappointment into a cough as he fidgeted on his chair. 'Did I ever tell you about that case in Piddletrenthide, Chief?' he asked hopefully.

'Yes,' said Henry.

'The old pedlar with the monkey?'

'Yes.'

'The one with the missing third finger, left hand?'

'Yes.'

'Well, it was back in '96. Or was it '97 . . .?'

Mercifully, Henry was not to find out, for the knock at the door heralded the arrival of Inspector Mungo Hyde of the River Police.

'Sorry, Mr Henry,' he blustered, struggling with his forage cap. 'Lighter broke loose at the East India. My boys and I have been out since dawn.'

'Thank you, Inspector. Take a seat.'

In the event, Hyde took two. It had to be said that the bacon buns of Mrs Squatt of Rotherhithe had done immeasurable harm to the good man's waistline. It was rumoured in the River Police that he had to take soundings to make sure his feet were still there, for even in a strong nor'westerly, he'd lost sight of them years ago.

'Did I ever tell you, Mungo, about that case in Yorkshire last year?'

'Yes, Tom,' the River Policeman answered.

'Right in the centre of Arndale, it happened.'

'Yes.'

'You'd have thought he'd have been past it, wouldn't you, a man of his age?'

'Yes.'

'But not a bit of it. He . . .'

The door crashed back and a tall, square policeman stood there, a bridle draped over his shoulder.

'Sorry I'm late, Assistant Commissioner,' he said in a bluff accent from somewhere north of Watford. 'Dray horses bolted along Fleet Street. Must have got a whiff of a mare, I suppose. At least those lazy bastards of reporters had a jammy time. All they had to do was to lean out of the window for a story.'

'Gentlemen,' said Henry, 'I don't believe you know Inspector

8

Edgar-Smith of the Mounted Division. Inspector Hyde of the River Police and Inspector Gregory of . . .'

'L Division, sir.' Gregory rose and shook the man's hand. 'I used to ride a horse, you know . . .'

'Really,' grunted Edgar-Smith, a little less than captivated by the admission. 'Well, I never.'

'Oh, but surely.' Gregory was surprised. 'You being in the Mounted Division, and all . . .'

He met six hostile eyes in his usual blank manner, but they were quickly joined by two more.

'Ah, Abberline.' Henry gestured the newest arrival to a chair. 'Gentlemen, I believe you all know Chief Superintendent Abberline.'

There were nods and rumbles all round. Then Abberline realized that Henry was looking at him for an explanation.

'Ah,' he said, adjusting the gardenia in his buttonhole. 'Minor derailment at Penge.'

'But you live in Norwood, Mr Abberline,' Gregory said innocently.

Abberline withered him and noticed that Mungo Hyde's left eye was flickering with a life of its own. His head began to dip towards his shoulder. When he realized everyone was looking at him, he began to tug at his collar. 'Damned thing,' he said. 'This patrol jacket seems to have shrunk in the wash.' He could help Abberline no further.

Henry was altogether less concerned. 'You appear to have a lipstick smudge on your cheek, Chief Superintendent,' he said blandly, sitting back behind his desk.

Abberline rose sharply, glancing behind him. Quickly realizing all was well, he produced a monogrammed lace handkerchief and dabbed his face. 'Mrs Abberline,' he grinned sheepishly. 'You know what women are.'

As he dabbed, the lacy scrap floated to his feet. He bent to retrieve it – and what he could of his dignity – and his eyes met a pair of less than reputable boots. He followed up the matching trousers and was within a whisker of snatching the handkerchief when the owner of the boots did it for him.

'M,' said the owner, reading the ornately embroidered initial. 'That must stand for Mrs Abberline. How is Ermintrude?'

'Lestrade . . .' Abberline began, but the Assistant Commissioner cut him off.

'We're already forty minutes late, Lestrade. Mr Gregory has been here since ten.'

Lestrade crossed the room and shook Henry's hands warmly. 'How can I ever forgive myself?' he asked solemnly. He looked deeply into Henry's eyes. He knew what those forty minutes had cost him.

'May we please begin?'

All eyes settled on Henry as he leaned forward in his leather chair. Simultaneously, all legs except Hyde's crossed at the knee.

'Gentlemen,' said Henry, his eyes dark and serious through the smoke of his cigar, 'we all know that the Congo has been annexed by the Belgians. Rumour has it that Bosnia and Herzegovina will, after all, be annexed by Austria. It is not of course for us to question the machinations of the Government in creating the Territorial Army. By the way, Edgar-Smith, have your chaps had a crack at this new pattern sword yet?'

'Sword be buggered!' snapped the man from the Mounted Division, slapping his shoulder anew with the bridle. 'Give my boys six inches more on their hardwood truncheons, that's all I ask. We'll crack these suffragists' skulls . . .'

'Yes, thank you Inspector,' Henry interrupted. 'Gentlemen, you've seen my memoranda to your various departments. All leave is cancelled forthwith. Rest days will be suspended until the matter in hand is passed.'

'The . . . matter in hand, sir . . .' Lestrade twitched his moustache. As usual, he had seen no memorandum at all.

'Haven't you seen my memoranda?' Henry quizzed him.

'No, sir, I confess not,' said Lestrade.

'Imbert!' roared Henry. 'Get in here.'

A curly-haired constable stuck his head round the glass-panelled door. 'Sir?'

'Did you or did you not place my recent memoranda on Mr Lestrade's desk?'

'Yes, sir,' the constable replied. 'In his In tray.'

Henry turned to Lestrade again. 'Do you remember an In memoranda?'

'No, sir, I'm afraid not,' Lestrade admitted.

'Tsk, the Olympic Games, man,' Henry snarled. 'Imbert, get out!'

'Yessir,' and he was gone.

'Within the fortnight, thousands of foreigners will descend on London like bees to the hive. Superintendent Quinn of the Special Branch is not with us this morning because even now he is combing his files on Undesirable Aliens. He tells me they are bulging. We shall have the scum of Europe on our doorstep, gentlemen, as surely as if there were a tunnel under the Channel itself.'

'Heaven forbid!' gasped Mungo Hyde, who perhaps saw his trade dropping off.

'I'm sure the athletes aren't that bad, sir,' Gregory proffered.

Henry scowled. The morning was not going well. 'I was not referring to them,' he still had the patience to explain. 'Their presence will attract thieves, vagabonds, swindlers and confidence tricksters by the yard. Our job is to be ever vigilant. I need hardly remind you that the Entente is, at the moment, a little less than Cordiale. Then of course, there are the Germans . . .'

'Why *are* the Americans coming, exactly?' Abberline asked.

There was a silence. Clearly, there was no answer to that.

It was luncheon, that day or the next. Chief Inspector Walter Dew, Criminal Investigation Department at Scotland Yard, was looking into the matter of the misappropriation of a number of old-age pensions. To be more precise, he was looking into the bowels of the upright Remington which had worn a permanent groove into his desk. The capital L was playing up again. It was the one he used most, by virtue of his guv'nor's name, and the thing had clashed with the exclamation mark and a number of other careless keys to grind right through the headed notepaper with the unusual watermark and into the impossible-to-reach little void behind.

'Rosie Lee, guv?' a cheery voice called.

Dew cursed anew. 'I should have been at the Collar by now, Hollingsworth. The last thing I want is a cup of gnat's pee I've got to blow on for half an hour. Know anything about typewriters?'

'I've had a few in my time, Insp.' The constable winked.

Dew turned to face him.

'Ah, you mean *machines*?' Hollingsworth said with a broad grin. 'Nah. I always use me old Dirty Den.'

11

Dew had been more years on the Force than he cared to remember. Twenty if it was a day. And all of it more or less within tinkling distance of Bow Bells. But this man's professional Cockneyism got right up his doublet and hose. 'Dirty Den?' he repeated with all the patience at his disposal.

'Pen, Insp,' Hollingsworth smirked. 'Well, never mind. I'll drink it, then. 'Ere, do you know, I do believe . . . yes . . . yes, there it is.' He put the cup down quickly, staring intently at the top of Dew's head.

'What's the matter?' Dew instinctively felt his parting.

'Grey, Insp,' Hollingsworth whispered in his ear. 'The old grey hair's a-lying in the meadow. First of many, of course.'

'In my day, Hollingsworth,' Dew fumed, 'young constables were expected to be seen and not heard. Now get out. I'm busy.'

'Very good, Mr Dew sir.' Hollingsworth tucked the cup in the crook of his arm and made for the door. 'Oh, by the way.' He paused. 'There's a bloke out 'ere. To see Mr Lestrade.'

'Who is he?' Dew asked.

'I dunno. He gave me his card somewhere.' Hollingsworth fumbled in his waistcoat pocket. ''Ere. The Marquess of Bolsover. Funny 'andle, ain't it?'

Dew sprang to his feet. 'You blithering idiot! Don't you read the papers? The Marquess of Bolsover is a nob of the first water. How long has he been waiting?'

'A few minutes.' Hollingsworth shrugged.

'A few . . .' Dew was speechless.

'Do you know,' Hollingsworth grinned, 'when you're annoyed, a little lump comes and goes in your neck.'

'When I'm *really* annoyed, Hollingsworth, there'll be lots of lumps coming up in your neck because it'll have my fingers round it. Show the Marquess in – and put your jacket on, man. This is Scotland Yard.'

'Right, Insp.' Hollingsworth sensed the urgency. 'But don't worry. I gave him a cup of Rosie.' Dew waved him out. He pulled on his best serge and adjusted his tie in the foxed grime of the mirror. With one last desperate swipe he dislodged the typewriter keys and flicked the dust off the depositions neck-high in the corner.

'His Excellency the Marquess of Bolsover,' Hollingsworth announced as though at the Lord Mayor's Show.

A stumpy little man in tweeds brushed past him. 'Lestrade.' He thrust out a martial hand.

'Er . . . no, sir. Chief Inspector Dew, sir.'

'Eh? Well, where's Lestrade?'

'Er . . . at luncheon, sir.'

'Luncheon? Good God. Police force. Going to dogs; country. You.' He rounded on the beaming Hollingsworth. 'Smirking.' He cuffed the lad around the ear. 'There. Something to smirk about. Lestrade; where d's he eat?'

'Er . . . the Collar, sir.' Hollingsworth's cheek smarted.

'Collar?'

'The Horse and Collar, sir,' Dew explained. 'It's a public house in . . .'

'Damn and blast it. Fetch him. Send your chappie here.' Hollingsworth looked at Dew who looked in turn at the Marquess. 'Now!' Bolsover roared and Hollingsworth scarcely had time to grab his bowler before he was hurtling along the corridor as though his tail was on fire.

'Please your Grace,' Dew bobbed, 'won't you have a seat?'

'Got one,' snorted Bolsover. 'Berkshire. D'you know it?'

'Well, I . . . er . . . don't leave London much, I'm afraid.'

Bolsover sat heavily on Lestrade's new swivel, the one he'd managed to misdirect by a bit of nifty paperwork before it reached Abberline's office.

'Should. Spot of rough shooting. Nothing like it. Soon be the Twelfth.'

Dew looked at Lestrade's calendar. It was June the fourteenth. The old boy must be a little confused.

'Rank?' Bolsover snapped.

'Er . . . Chief Inspector,' Dew admitted.

'Name again?'

'Er . . . Dew.'

'Urdu? That's a bally language, isn't it? Nigger.'

'May I ask the nature of . . .?' Dew ventured.

'No. Private. Go to top. Best man. Always have. Always will. Unfortunately, best man out. Got to make do with Whatsisface.'

'Lestrade.'

'Rank?'

'Chief Inspector,' Dew repeated. Obviously the old man was a little Mutt and Jeff as Hollingsworth would have it.

'Is that all?' Bolsover lowered. 'No bally good. Been sold a

13

pup here. Thought he was bally Assistant Commissioner at least.'

'Oh, I see, sir.' Dew realized the error of his ways. It was not a first for him. 'You mean Mr Lestrade's rank? Oh yes, he's Superintendent.'

'Age?'

'Mr Lestrade? Oh, I don't know. Er . . . fiftyish.'

'I'd killed seventy-six tigers when I was fiftyish. What's he done?'

'Er . . . well, he's solved . . . helped to solve several cases.'

'*Exempli gratia*?'

Dew's tongue protruded in the effort of remembering. 'No, I don't think that was one of his. That was one of Abberline's.'

'Abilene? That's a town in the colonies. In Kansas. This Lestrade. Any good?'

'Very, sir.' Dew was sure. 'As you say, the best.'

'Not what I said.'

An uncanny silence descended. During it, Dew's stomach, cheated of luncheon, gave a gurgling lurch and lay there, mutinous and growling.

'Hot, isn't it, Your Eminence?' he said at last. 'For June, I mean.'

'Flaming,' said Bolsover. And the silence fell again.

It came as the most exquisite relief to the Chief Inspector when the door crashed back and a bowler came whistling through it to ricochet off the green-painted pipes and land squarely on top of the pile of faded paper.

'This had better be good, Dew. I gave up a couple of pints of winkles. Oh.'

'The Marquess of Bolsover, Superintendent Lestrade,' said Dew. 'Superintendent Lestrade. The Marquess o. . .' and realizing his sudden superfluity, crept away.

'My lord.' Lestrade extended a hand. 'I'm sorry, my constable is rather new. I had no idea you'd been kept waiting. I trust that Inspector Dew has been helpful.'

'Doesn't know the meaning of the word.'

'Quite.' Lestrade gestured to a chair and found that Bolsover returned to his, leaving him to perch like a crippled parrot on Dew's, 'Er . . . my Chief Inspector's rather new as well.'

'Come to the point, Lestrade. Busy man. Son. Eldest son. Dead. Shot himself, y'see.'

14

There was no trace of emotion, no faltering in the Maxim gun delivery of the words.

'I'm sorry,' said Lestrade, reaching for a notepad.

'In the papers. Bally things. Thunderer's not been the same since Buckle. Who is this Harmsworth chappie?'

'Who indeed?' Lestrade stroked his chin ruefully.

'Wanted to do a bally story on me. Cheeky blighter. I sent his man packing.'

'Quite.'

'Wasn't suicide, Lestrade. Not my boy. Not a Fitzgibbon.'

'Quite.' Lestrade was grateful for small mercies at least. Nobody could make a monkey out of him. 'My lord,' he said, 'I shall look into the matter, of course, but I fear, with the Olympic Games so imminent, the entire Yard has its hands full.'

'Damn foreigners!' Bolsover snapped, getting smartly to his feet. 'Bally fool Gladstone. Should've sent a gunboat. Palmerston now, there's the chappie.'

'Yes, indeed. But until the Games are over, I fear I must place your son's demise on file.'

'File be damned.' Bolsover reached the door. 'He'd have beaten all those blighters. He was nimbler than all my boys. Fastest thing on two legs I've seen. Apart from a wallaby on heat, of course.'

'Of course . . . my lord, forgive me.' Lestrade's nostrils began to twitch. 'But do I understand that your son was an athlete?'

'The best,' Bolsover told him.

The words of Mr Edward Henry rang anew in Lestrade's ears – 'The scum of Europe . . .'

'Please, my lord, sit down. Have my chair.' He hopped off Dew's. 'You'd better tell me all about it.'

The two bowler-hatted gentlemen were shown into the bedroom of the late Anstruther Fitzgibbon, eldest son of the Marquess of Bolsover.

'I believe you know Inspector Bland. I am Superintendent Lestrade,' said the shorter of the two, 'You are . . .?'

'Overwrought, sir,' slurred the manservant and he swayed a little as he spoke.

'Yes, of course.' Lestrade wandered the thick pile. 'But what is your name?'

'Botley, sir. Hinksey Botley. I am . . . I was the master's manservant, man and boy.'

'How old was the master?' Lestrade found a silver-framed photograph of a boy in tasselled cap and white knickerbockers showing just a hint of knee.

'He was twenty-seven, sir.' Botley produced a handkerchief and trumpeted into it. 'A mere boy. I had tended him since he was a baby.'

Lestrade mechanically checked the bed.

'You found him?' he asked.

The manservant nodded.

'Tell me, Botley.' The Superintendent placed an avuncular arm around the old man's withered shoulders. 'Would you say the master was the type to take his own life?'

Botley straightened, as cut to the quick by the slur on the family honour as the Marquess had been. 'Never!' he said.

Lestrade smiled and patted the man. 'Well, well. Would you wait outside please? We'll send for you if we need you.'

Botley hesitated, swaying a little, then pivoted on one leg and made a determined bid to reach the door in a straight line. Lestrade followed him, eyeing the moulding intently.

'Again then, John,' he said.

Bland threw his hat on the bed and sprawled on a *chaise-longue*. He consulted the black notepad, bereft of its gold embossing now that economies were in vogue in C Division. 'Anstruther George Hartlepool Fitzgibbon. Third son of the Marquess of Bolsover.'

'Third? I thought he was the eldest?'

'Eldest surviving.'

'What happened to the others?'

'Er . . . eldest died of pneumonia as a child. Second fell prey to a hunting accident. Horse rolled on him.'

'Ah, you don't get that problem with a Lanchester,' Lestrade commented.

'Two other siblings, we think, but somewhat the other side of the blanket. One was a girl born to some American Amazon. She lives over . . . there. Bolsover never married the mother, although he was unencumbered by a wife at the time. The other was a lad, some years older. I got this from old Botley after a lot of haggling. Son of a serving gel. He seems to have been kept on as a boot boy until he was ten or so. Then he ran away.'

'What do we know about Anstruther?' Lestrade asked.

'Educated Harrow. Seemed to be some nonsense involving the games master. Went to Rugby. Some trouble there with the riding instructor. Went up to Cambridge. Some trouble involving a mathematics professor. Gonville and Caius.'

'There were two of them?' Lestrade checked.

'Apparently. Did a short spell with the Durham Light Infantry.'

'No Sandhurst?'

'For three days. There was some trouble with the fortifications lecturer. Don't quite know how he got a commission.'

'And in the Durham Light Infantry?'

'Yes.' Bland flicked over a page. 'Couldn't get much on this. Seems there was some bother with the chaplain and the regimental mascot.'

'Really?'

'Ah, I know what you're thinking,' smirked Bland. 'But it's all right, Sholto. It was a female goat.'

'I'm relieved to hear it. And since the army?'

'Well, he always had this poncho for sport. Quite a good hurdler. Would have got a Blue at Cambridge if he'd been there longer.'

'How long has he lived here?' Lestrade lit a cigar.

'This is the family's second town house. The old man lives in Grosvenor Place. He seems to own half of St James's.'

'No money worries, then.'

'Not judging by the look of this place. Anstruther had been living here on and off since he was eighteen.'

'Tell me about the Night in Question.'

'Last Tuesday. June the ninth. Anstruther had been over to the new stadium at the White City. Before that he'd done some running in the park.'

'Hyde?'

'Regent's.'

'What time did he come home?'

'Ah, now there Botley wasn't sure ' Bland said. 'It must have been after he went to bed. Around ten thirty.'

'So we don't know if he was alone?'

'No. The next thing we know for certain is that Botley knocked on his door as usual at ten o'clock.'

'This door?' Lestrade was drawn to it again.

'Yes. There was no reply.'

'What did Botley do?'

'Nothing. He couldn't get in.'

Lestrade's eyebrows knotted. 'Locked?'

Bland nodded.

'Where's the key?' Lestrade couldn't see one.

'Lost. Years ago.'

'Ah.' Lestrade wandered to the door again. 'The bolt.' It stood an inch or two away from the keyhole. Brass. Highly polished. He touched it with his fingers and it slid back easily. 'Odd,' he said, 'a bolt on a bedroom door.'

'Sholto.' Bland crossed the room to join him. 'I think we must assume that the late Anstruther was not as other men.'

Lestrade narrowed his eyes in the direction of his colleague. 'A Mary Ann, you mean?'

Bland nodded. 'God knows who he was entertaining on that very bed.' The policemen turned collectively to stare at it. 'The bolt was essential.'

'All right,' Lestrade said. 'What happened next?'

'According to my information,' Bland told him, 'Botley got a couple of tradesmen delivering in the street and they took the door off its hinges.'

Lestrade ran his fingers over the jamb. He withdrew them sharply as a couple of splinters got him. 'And not put back with any expertise either.'

'Ah, sorry, Sholto. That's my boys. C Division was never very hot on carpentry.'

'Once they were in, Botley and these tradesmen, what did they find?'

Bland read his book from where he was. 'Anstruther was sitting at his desk.' Lestrade took the same chair. 'He was slumped forward, his head by that paperweight thing.' Lestrade slumped forward.

'Like this?' he asked, in a muffled sort of way.

'Like that,' said Bland, twisting his head. 'Sunny side up. Gunshot wound to the left temple.'

Lestrade sat up. 'You've got the photographs?'

'Ah, well, Sholto.' Bland was realizing this was not his morning. 'I'm afraid my boys in C division aren't really on top of photography. They're a bit blurred.'

Lestrade looked at his man. 'How many came out?'

'Er . . . none.'

Lestrade sighed. 'All right, John. Tell me about the weapon.'

'Ah.' Bland crossed to the far wall and removed a chased box from the sideboard. He lifted the lid to reveal a green velvet lining and a single flintlock pistol. 'The partner to this one,' he said. 'Expensive piece. Made by Egg. We've got the actual one at Vine Street.'

Lestrade took the proffered pistol, letting the silver butt rest in his hand. 'Left temple?' he asked.

Bland nodded.

Lestrade held the gun to his head. 'Awkward bloody thing,' he commented. 'I'm sure your boys in C Division know more about these things than I do, John. How does it work?'

'Buggered if I know, Sholto. I think the bullet thing comes out here.' Bland waved his hand in the general direction of the gun. 'You pull that thing back, don't you?'

'The trigger?' Lestrade was on alien territory.

'Yes, but that curly thing. At the top. No. The other one. Yes, that's it.'

Lestrade clicked back the serpentine. Once. Twice. It would no further go.

'Does it fire bullets?' he asked.

'Well, the doctor dug *something* out of his head,' Bland observed.

Lestrade squeezed the trigger and the serpentine fell with a click. 'Hey presto,' he said.

'I should put it down, Sholto. Bloody thing looks dangerous to me.'

Lestrade glanced to his right. 'John,' he said suddenly, 'was the desk in this exact position?'

'Yes, I think so. Why?'

Lestrade stood up. 'Sit here,' he said, vacating the seat.

Bland did as he was told. 'What?' he asked.

Lestrade squatted beside him, cracking his knee on the desk corner as he did so. 'Agghh!' he screamed.

'A clue?' Bland asked excitedly.

'A minor dislocation,' said Lestrade. 'I'll be all right. Sit upright as though you're smoking. Oh, you are.'

'Like this?'

'Yes.' Lestrade closed one eye, concentrating on the wall beyond Bland's head. He clicked his teeth.

'Now lean forward, as if you're writing. That's it.' He frowned. 'Do you always write like that?'

'Well, in C Division, we haven't quite got the hang . . .'

'Yes, I know.' He lined up the wall again, shaking his head. 'All right. Now put your head down on the desk. No, nose down.'

'Sholto,' Bland muttered, 'this isn't very comfortable.'

'Don't move!' Lestrade hobbled across to the far wall. 'Ah ha!' he said.

'What?' mumbled Bland. It wasn't easy to talk through blotting paper.

'What do you make of this?'

Bland joined Lestrade in the corner. 'Wallpaper. Flock. Chinese, I'd say. We're quite good on Oriental wallpapers in C Division.'

'I knew you would be,' nodded Lestrade, 'but I'm talking about this brown stuff.'

Bland pressed his nose against the flock – a slight improvement anyway over blotting paper. 'Camp coffee?' he guessed.

'Blood,' said Lestrade.

'Good God, so it is. I wonder how I missed that?'

'I wonder,' sighed Lestrade. 'What do you make of it?'

Bland looked bland. Clearly he made almost nothing of it.

'Admittedly,' Lestrade helped him, 'I'm not very O'Fay with guns like that, but if I know my gunshot wounds, part of Anstruther's head would have been blown out sideways with the impact. And I think it's a ball, by the way, not a bullet. More or less in a straight line with the angle of the shot.'

'So?'

'So get back to the desk again.'

Bland did.

'Assume the position.'

Bland did.

'Now, pick up the pistol. No. As you were, nose on the desk. Right.'

Bland sat there, his nose back on the blotting paper. 'All right?'

'I don't know. Are you?'

'Well, it's a bit uncomfortable,' admitted Bland.

'Yes, you said. So why do it?'

Bland sat up, a little hurt. 'Because you asked me to, Sholto.'

'No, I mean if you were Anstruther, why do it? Why not sit back in the chair? Or sprawl on the *chaise-longue*? Or lie on the bed? Or stand by the window? This thing' – he took up the pistol again – 'must be over eighteen inches long. Why sit with your nose on the desk in order to blow our brains out?'

'What are you saying, Sholto? That Anstruther was murdered?'

Lestrade nodded slowly. 'It had occurred,' he said.

'Impossible,' said Bland. 'You're forgetting one thing.'

'Oh?'

'The locked door.' Bland was triumphant.

'Ah,' said Lestrade. Collapse of stout party.

'Are you seriously saying to me,' Bland was in full flight, 'that the murderer got into the room – yes, he could have been let in by Anstruther without Botley knowing about it. That he killed Anstruther – yes, he could have done, I grant you that, but what then? Did he arrange for Anstruther to get up with half his head missing and neatly lock the door behind him?'

'The window.' Lestrade stumbled to it.

Bland joined him and they peered down. A sheer drop of three storeys, no ledge; and bars six inches apart.

'Joachim the Human Fly?' Bland smirked.

'The walls?' Lestrade began tapping them furiously, listening for a hollow, a concavity that promised a secret passage. All he got was the disappointing pat pat of solid, Georgian brick.

'There's always the chimney, of course.' Bland was in his element. 'Perhaps it was the orang-utan from that bloke's Rue Morgue story. Rather apt, isn't it? Monkey jumps down chimney in Berkeley Square, loads antique gun and kills Fitzgibbon, returning whence he came. The *Daily Mail* will have a field day!'

'You're enjoying this, aren't you?' Lestrade muttered.

'I'm sorry, Sholto,' Bland laughed, 'but you can't pin a murder on this one. It's open and shut. Anstruther took his own life while the balance of his mind was disturbed. And if it wasn't before, it bloody well is now.'

'Where's the body?'

'Vine Street Mortuary. Want to look?'

'I'd better. If this hot weather goes on, he'll be walking to the funeral by himself.'

Lestrade limped painfully to the door. His fingers strayed again to the polished bolt and he shook his head. 'An open and shut case,' he said. And he was gone.

2

Two To Be Steady

'Bourne, sir,' said the young constable, standing rather awkwardly in front of Lestrade.

'Years on the Force?' the Superintendent asked.

'Nearly three.'

'What's this?' Lestrade perused the paperwork. 'Julius?'

'Julian, sir.' Bourne giggled.

Lestrade glanced at Dew whose eyebrows arched a little. 'Married?' said Lestrade in an unusually dark brown voice.

'Bless you, no,' giggled Bourne. 'Who'd have me?'

Lestrade could think of several people, from Cleveland Street to the Dilly.

'That shirt,' said Lestrade. 'It's a particularly nasty shade of pink. Here at the Yard we're a little more conservative than that. And that check . . .'

'Gingham, sir,' Bourne corrected him.

'Yes, well, it's got to go. A detective must blend into the background, so to speak. Merge with his fellow man.'

'Ooohh.' Bourne frowned and pursed his lips.

Lestrade threw down his pen. 'Rookies,' he muttered. 'Tell me, Bourne, can you make tea?'

'Certainly, pet . . . er . . . sir. Learned it at my mother's knee.'

'Yes, I thought you would have. Dew, show him the ropes. I'll give you a week's trial, Bourne. At the end of that time, we'll review you. If I'm not satisfied . . . er . . . with your progress, it's back to Lost Property with you.'

'Thank you, sir, I'm so grateful. You won't regret it. Now,

Chief Inspector,' the tall, blond lad said, 'where do you keep the pinnies?'

The body of the late Anstruther Fitzgibbon was lying on marble slab four in a particularly unprepossessing corner of the Vine Street Mortuary. Above, at street level, the myriad sights and sounds of a busy city, the largest in the world. The well-to-do shopped in the expensive arcades between Regent Street and Piccadilly, while Eros, slowly turning green from the exhausts of the new motor buses, aimed casually at them. The *haut monde* took tea at the Trocadero and liveried flunkeys ran hither and thither, colliding with scurrying errand boys and street pedlars. A hundred yards or so to the south-east, the *demi-monde* plied the shady side of Jermyn Street and both sides of the Haymarket, studiously ignored by constables and clergymen alike.

Yet down here, in the basement of C Division, in the busiest police station in the world, all was curiously silent. The only sound was the ticking of the clock, its massive institutional face the only object to break the dark, institutional green of the wall. From somewhere, a fly droned, heavy with the meals of an Edwardian summer.

A ferret-faced man in a brown suit and an unseasonal bowler peered over the corpse.

'Can I help you, Superintendent Lestrade?' A voice rang around the echoing marble corridors.

The ferret-faced man glanced up, briefly, and continued his inspection. 'Dr Hillyard, is there to be a post-mortem?'

'Tricky one, that.' Hillyard took off his spectacles and polished them with the grubby hem of his white coat. He spat copiously with a perfect aim into a nearby slop bucket. 'Coroner says yes, father says no.'

'What do you say?'

Hillyard smiled, revealing a row of broken, brown teeth. 'As we medical students used to say at the Scalpel and Haemorrhoid, "He who pays the piper calls the tune."'

'Meaning?' Lestrade looked up, tilting back the bowler. Old English proverbs were not his *métier*. No doubt C Division were well versed in them.

Hillyard closed to him. 'Meaning, Lestrade, that I was a Poor

23

Law doctor until your dear Commissioner took pity on me and gave me a job for which I actually got paid.'

'So there will be a post-mortem?' Lestrade was better on inferences.

'No. Probably not. You see, Lord Bolsover is one of the richest men in England. He's promised me a pension for life if I release this body for burial, no questions asked.'

Lestrade looked sourly at his man. 'The law's the law,' he reminded him, with that dazzling gift of erudition for which he was famous the length and breadth of the snug at the Horse and Collar. 'Whether it's suicide or murder, it is an unexplained death. There has to be a post-mortem.'

Hillyard smiled. 'I know,' he said. 'Just testing, Lestrade. What would I need with a pension from Bolsover when I can get one only one thousandth of the size from Lloyd George? Actually, of course, there's no need for one – a post-mortem, that is.'

'Your views then?' Lestrade circled the naked corpse as the doctor spoke.

'Shot to death.' Hillyard growled in his throat to summon up his next deathless aim. 'This damned sputum.' He spat. 'With this.'

The partner of the Egg pistol appeared from a side drawer which was full of false teeth and glass eyes.

'You'll know more about this than me,' the doctor confessed, 'but this is what it puts into people.'

Another side drawer scraped open and, hidden amongst jars which seemed to contain people's grey bits floating in brine, was a misshapen lead ball, about the size of a small marble.

Lestrade caught it expertly, for a man with an inflamed knee joint, and held it to the light. 'Some bullet,' he murmured.

'Ball,' Hillyard corrected him.

Lestrade saw no reason, in this sickly silence, to raise his voice merely on the suggestion of a rather-less-than-successful Poor Law doctor and he continued to murmur. 'Do I gather from your remarks earlier that the Marquess of Bolsover has been to see you?'

'He has. Or rather to see Superintendent Hawkins. They both came down here to see me.' He spat volubly again. 'Tell me, Lestrade, is the sun shining up there? I'm like a bloody mole these days. Haven't seen daylight in a fortnight.'

'Tsk, tsk and it is,' Lestrade commiserated with him. 'So Bolsover wants his son buried quickly, then?'

'Wouldn't you? Only son, heir to the estate. Old family name. Oh, God. I'm even talking like the old aristocrat now. Funny old cove, isn't he? Didn't show any emotion at all.'

'He saw the body?'

'He insisted on it. We'd already had three people identify him positively – and one negatively; rather odd that – so formal identification wasn't necessary.'

'Did the old man make any comment?'

'None. Except that he said he wanted the boy's body out of here by nightfall and he was going to the Yard. I thought old Hawkins would explode.' He spun sideways to spit into a container. 'It's that bloody pipe. I've got to give it up, Lestrade.'

'Try a cigar,' the Superintendent said. 'They're better for you.'

'No thanks,' Hillyard declined, unaware what a rare opportunity he was passing up. 'I'll suffer in silence,' and he hawked again.

'So he shot himself in the temple,' Lestrade muttered, running his fingers over the neat, circular hole near the hairline. The other side of the head was a mass of matted hair, dark brown with congealed blood. But there was no disguising the fact that a large section of the cranium had gone.

'Occipitally speaking, it's a mess,' Hillyard shrugged. 'You'll note the blackening around the hole?'

To Lestrade, the whole body was blackening.

'Powder burns,' Hillyard explained. 'Because the muzzle was pressed against the skin.'

'And if the gun had been fired from further way?' Lestrade was exploring every avenue.

'That depends on how much further,' Hillyard said. 'If it was more than a few feet, there'd be no traces of powder.'

'Doctor,' Lestrade tilted the bowler back into position. 'I have reason to believe that young Fitzgibbon here may not have been as other men. Is there any way of proving that, medically, I mean?'

Hillyard frowned. 'Well, not really, Lestrade. Even a dose of the clap could have been picked up from a doxy.'

'Did he have the clap?'

'No, I was merely postulating.' He spat again. Postulation

was obviously a habit of the good doctor's. 'Of course, I haven't checked his sphincters. But this long after death, well, I don't hold out much hope.'

Lestrade tipped his bowler and hobbled for the stairs that led to the light.

'I'd get that seen to,' Hillyard advised him. 'And that limp.'

'Powder burns!' Lestrade suddenly shouted. Only Hillyard in that basement was mildly surprised by the outburst. The others were past caring, in their labelled lockers with tags tied to their toes.

'I doubt if that's the cause of it.' Hillyard peered at him over his glasses.

Lestrade hobbled back to the slab in the corner. 'This pistol,' he said. 'It works with black powder, doesn't it?'

'I believe so,' Hillyard said. 'Why?'

Lestrade took up the dead man's hand, dangling limp at his side. 'Shot himself in the left temple, did he?' He was talking to himself. 'Take a good look at this – the space between his thumb and forefinger. What do you see?'

Hillyard rubbed his lenses again, peering intently, twisting the hand this way and that. 'Nothing,' he shrugged.

'Precisely.' Lestrade tapped his nose, tipless though it was. 'Nothing. No powder burns. Wouldn't you say, doctor, that if a man fired one of these, he'd have black powder all over his hand?'

'Er . . . yes, I suppose I would.'

'Let's try it. Got any gunpowder?'

'Well, I . . . er . . . here, I think.' And a little drawer produced a bag of the stuff.

'Right. Now if I remember my Antique Gun Classes, as well as what John Bland reckons you do, you put some of this in here, then you pull this back and press this down. At all times, of course, remembering to keep this . . .'

Suddenly there was a deafening explosion, enough to wake the dead. Lestrade stood transfixed to the spot, invisible in a pall of smoke, while plaster rained down on the head of Dr Hillyard.

'You bloody fool, Lestrade,' the good doctor snarled, coughing and gurgling in a mixture of terror and asphixiation. 'You might have killed us all.'

'Well, you and me perhaps, doctor.' Lestrade was more

accurate in his summation of the situation. 'But you see, it doesn't really matter. As we rookies used to say in the Truncheon and Cly Faker, you can't break a few eggs without making omelettes. Look!'

He thrust his right hand under the quivering doctor's nose.

'What?' Hillyard asked, still visibly shaken.

'Nothing!' said Lestrade. 'Except black powder.'

'Which tells us what, precisely?' Hillyard snapped, pulling masonry from his tousled hair.

'That whoever pulled the trigger on the late Anstruther Fitzgibbon, it was not the late Anstruther Fitzgibbon. Unless of course he got up and washed his hands afterwards.'

'How do you know I haven't washed the corpse?'

'Come on, doctor, this is C Division. Good-day.'

Lestrade made again for the stairs where a bevy of constables almost collided with him.

'What is it, sir?' the first one asked, truncheon rampant. 'Fenians? Suffragettes? Anarchists? Members of the Boilermakers' Union?'

Lestrade patted his arm. 'There, there, constable. Only one of Dr Hillyard's little experiments.' He reached for his half-hunter. 'But well done. Only one minute and thirty-eight seconds for you to respond to the noise.'

The constable beamed, pocketing his truncheon. 'Well, sir, here in C Division . . .'

'I know, old chap,' Lestrade beamed back. 'I know.'

And he heard the metallic tang of the spittoon as he reached the door.

That was the hottest June that Durham city had known. Lestrade had rarely ventured that far north and it had taken all his powers of persuasion to get Mr Edward Henry to let him leave London at a time when the predicted scum of Europe were arriving by the cartload. Their first heralds were the *hommes* and *herren* of the Press, bulging with notepads and stubs of pencils. They made exclusively for Fleet Street as though to eye up the opposition among home-grown reporters. They also took up valuable elbow space along the mahogany of several printers' taverns. But, as Lestrade pointed out to Henry, there had been no punch-ups yet and there was still not a single athlete in sight. Henry had said very well, but Lestrade was not to be accompanied by the usual swatch of sergeants and clutter of constables, the entourage that normally befitted an itinerant Superintendent. Young Bourne alone could be spared.

Lestrade tried to ignore the constable's jaunty boater in French grey raffia and the waistcoat of organdie. He could not however ignore the constable's tendency to wander into haberdashers' and milliners' as they crossed the Framwellgate Bridge. The flies droned heavily around the hansom ranks and the sun shone white and blinding on the solid towers of the cathedral, silent on its Norman granite. In the market-place the giant statue of Lord Londonderry glowered at them in his hussar finery of yellow stone. Bourne stopped to admire the cut of his pelisse and the svelteness of his Nankeen boots before being reminded by his guv'nor that they were here on business.

The Adjutant of the Durham Light Infantry was of little help. A man from the ranks, rather like Lestrade himself, he did not suffer fools gladly – and constables in objectionable mufti, not at all. He was cagey about Second Lieutenant Fitzgibbon, deceased, but he felt sure that a military funeral was out of the question. After all, he'd only been with the regiment for three months; barely time to cut cards with everyone in the Mess. The regimental chaplain whom Inspector Bland had mentioned was on sick leave and in retreat. Lestrade was given to understand that he was prey to nervous disorders and cried a lot in an Anglican, soldierly sort of way. Chances were he would not be back. The regimental goat was saying nothing. She chomped loudly on the lush, green grass of Northumbria, her blue eyes cloudy and shifty. She shook her hairy head at Lestrade and when she saw Bourne, spread her hind legs and peed up the wall of her compound. Lestrade walked away. He had learned to be wary of nannies.

Their next port of call was altogether more promising. And for this one, Lestrade went alone. He left Detective Constable Bourne window shopping in Margery Lane while he made for Ward's Waterloo Hotel, still vying, after all these years, with Thwaite's Waterloo Hotel. It came as a source of irritation to him and fury to the management, to know that his quarry was in fact staying at the other one.

'The Hero of Mafeking!' thundered the manager. 'At Thwaite's? I always said he was overrated. I'll tell ye summut,' his Geordie was showing in his anger, 'I shan't Mafick again, I can tell ye.'

The Hero of Mafeking stood square on to a billiard table in Thwaite's games room.

'Polo's my game, of course,' he said, absent-mindedly chalking his cue. 'Never could get the hang of this.' He crouched suddenly, like the Wolf Who Never Sleeps, and slammed home a ball.

Lestrade blinked. He hadn't seen play like this since he'd arrested George 'The Tweezers' Weidenfeld in The Nichol. And that was a long, long time ago.

'Now then,' said the dapper little Lieutenant General, steely eyes glinting for a second shot, 'Fitzgibbon. I don't really know what I can tell you, Superintendent. He was my ADC for less than two months, you see. Dicky Haldane asked me up here to set up the Northumbrian Terriers and suggested young Fitzgibbon as my errand boy.'

'You formed no opinion?' Lestrade shouted over the staccato rattle of Baden-Powell's whizzing balls.

'None really,' He of the Big Hat said.

'There was some talk in the Durham Light Infantry . . .'

'There's always talk in the Durham Light Infantry,' Baden-Powell said. 'That's Infantry for you. Wouldn't happen in the Cavalry, of course. And anyway, it was a female goat, you know.'

Yes, Lestrade knew.

'I hunted tiger with his old man, you see.' The Lieutenant General, a perfect model if ever there was one, snooked a curling shot which kissed the cush before driving relentlessly into the bottom pocket. 'With the Fifth in India. Damned fine body of men, the Fifth.' Baden-Powell leaned on his cue to reminisce for a moment. 'Not like these blasted Territorials. I shouldn't say it, Lestrade, but really! Butchers, bakers, candlestick-makers.' He shook his head. 'Let's hope there isn't another war, eh? I promise you, it'll go hardly for us.'

'Yes, sir,' Lestrade nodded ruefully. 'Would you know if Lieutenant Fitzgibbon had any enemies?'

'Enemies? God knows. But then, what man has not? There are a few Boers wouldn't mind my bandoliers around their neks, I can tell you.'

'Quite, quite.' Lestrade waited patiently with his cue. 'Would you say he was the suicidal type?' he asked.

'Suicide?' Baden-Powell paused in mid-crouch. 'Old Bolsover wouldn't let him, surely?' and he downed the last ball. 'I say, Lestrade, I'm sorry. I seem to have cleared the field and you haven't played a shot. Ah well, beginner's luck. Set 'em up again?'

Lestrade replaced his cue in the rack and reached for his bowler. 'I must be going, sir,' he said.

'I have to say, Lestrade,' Baden-Powell reached into the pockets for his balls, 'Fitzgibbon wasn't much of a soldier. The papers said he was shot with a duelling pistol.'

'That is correct,' Lestrade told him.

'But he never had any interest in guns. I remember his old man telling me he couldn't get the boy to go shooting with him at all.'

'But the guns were in his room,' Lestrade said, frowning.

'Well, I've got a sampler in mine,' guffawed Baden-Powell, 'but I didn't embroider the bally thing. Why should a man kill himself with something he didn't know from his elbow?'

'How would you have done it, sir?' Lestrade asked.

'*I* wouldn't.' Baden-Powell brushed past him to the cue rack, selecting an altogether longer stick. 'And I don't think young Fitzgibbon did either. Go back to the old man, Lestrade. I know Bolsover. There's something he isn't telling you. Can you find your way out?' He lunged into his pocket. 'I have a ball of twine here that might help.' He lunged into another pocket. 'Or a compass, perhaps.'

'Thank you, sir.' Lestrade tipped his bowler. 'I'll just walk through the door, thanks.'

And, careful to open it first, he did.

Lestrade never liked leaving London. And even in the stifling heat of mid-afternoon, he was grateful to return to those familiar streets, meaner somehow in the dust and the sharp shadows of summer. As he turned the corner into the Yard a guttural honk on a passing police launch told him that Mungo Hyde was going off duty. He wondered if anybody would notice. All the way down on the train the problem had been taxing him. Anstruther Fitzgibbon was not the suicidal type. Everyone said that. Yet he had a past awash with murkiness. Ever since Mr Labouchere's bill, people of Fitzgibbon's sexual inclinations walked in the valley of the shadow. And the law was no respecter of persons. Look at Oscar Wilde . . . but none too closely, God rest him. There again, there was no suicide note. Not compulsory, of course, but in Lestrade's experience there usually was one. Something along the lines of 'Can't go on. Stop. Must end it all. Stop. No point in living. Stop. Cost of living. Stop. End of world is nigh. Stop. Liberal Government. Stop.' And there was nothing. No note. No explanation. Then there was the gun. An antique heirloom, difficult to operate, awkward to stick in your ear. And supposedly fired by a man to whom guns were a mystery. Mystery indeed. There again, bearing in mind Fitzgibbon's inclinations, plenty of room to make enemies. Twisted, frightened men who would kill rather than let the world know their secret. Bland had searched Fitzgibbon's house in Berkeley Square. No hint of blackmail. No whiff of scandal. All tracks were very carefully covered.

Perhaps, thought Lestrade as he acknowledged the salute of the desk man, he could find a use for Baden-Powell's ball of twine after all. But above all, and he kept coming back to this time and time again as he kicked the Yard lift into motion, above all there was that damned locked room. That said it all really. Bland had been right. There was no way into the room at all other than by the door. And the door had been bolted on the inside. For a fleeting moment, he wondered how the late, great Sherlock Holmes would have coped with this one. He'd probably have smoked a few pipes of shag and scratched on that fiddle of his. Lestrade shook himself. It must be the heat. That and his age.

'There was a bloke to see you, Super,' Constable Hollingsworth informed him.

'Really?' Lestrade grabbed the chipped cup and the day's paper simultaneously, before slumping heavily into his chair.

'Yeah. Some Kraut. Newshound, he was. From Berlin.'

'What did he want?' Lestrade scanned the inner recesses of *The Times*. There it was. MARQUESS' SON SLAIN BY OWN HAND. Well, that was all right then. If *The Times* said it, it must be right. If he'd read it in the *Mail*, he might not have been so sure.

31

'Dunno. I told him you was away. He just asked you to contact him at this address. Oh, and he said two words.'

'Oh?' Lestrade gulped the contents of his cup. Hollingsworth may not have been the world's best detective, but his Rosie Lee was without peer.

' "Nana Sahib".'

Lestrade blinked. He'd missed the German for Detectives lecture. 'Which means?'

'Buggered if I know, begging your pardon, Super. He probably wanted some angle on police coverage of these here Games.'

Lestrade looked at the address. 36 Freedom Street, Battersea.

'This is where he's staying?' Lestrade asked.

'I s'pose so, Super. Shall I go and see him?'

'Detectives of Scotland Yard have better things to do with their time, Hollingsworth. Like, for example, pouring me another cup of your excellent bevvy.'

'Delighted, Super.' Hollingsworth bowed.

'Nana Sahib,' Lestrade repeated absent-mindedly. 'Sounds more Indian really. Oh, Hollingsworth?'

'Sir?'

'When you've poured that, you can cut along to the Strand. You'll find young Bourne in one of the dress shops. Tell him he's had long enough and I want him back here at the double. Where's Mr Dew?'

'He's been called to the White City, sir. They wanted somebody official to supervise the pouring in of the Tod Slaughter.'

'The . . . er . . .?'

'Water, sir. Into the swimming pool they've put up. Must take a lot of bloody buckets, wouldn't you say?'

'Yes,' sighed Lestrade, whose thoughts rested infrequently on cubic capacity, 'I suppose it must.'

The door crashed back, sending papers flying in all directions.

'Ah!' Lestrade looked up. 'Sergeant Valentine. Still a young man in a hurry, I see.'

The detective sergeant removed his boater and removed the breath from his fist. 'Sorry, sir,' he gasped. 'There's a high-level conference going on in the lift. I had to take the stairs.'

'Yes, well, it's all right. Constable Hollingsworth is making a fresh pot.'

'I'm sure, sir, but I haven't time.'

'Ah.' Lestrade was at his most wistful in the middle of a hot afternoon. '"Time, you old gippo, will you not stay?"'

'Superintendent McDowell's compliments, sir. He's got a little problem.'

Lestrade chuckled. 'Yes, I know, but he's past all help from me.'

'He's got a body, sir. In Battersea.'

Lestrade's smile faded. 'Address?' he asked.

'Freedom Street, sir. Number 36.'

Lestrade shot to his feet, snatching up his bowler. 'Did you hear that, Hollingsworth? Freedom Street. Step on it.'

And Superintendent and sergeant exited at the double.

'One lump or two, Sarge?' Hollingsworth emerged from the ante-room. He dropped both cups as though he'd been pig-stuck. 'Gor blimey, Freedom Street,' and he leapt over the mess on the floor, careful not to step on it.

The body of Hans-Rudiger Hesse lay slumped over a desk in an upstairs room. He was a man in his fifties, sandy-haired, clean-shaven, with the unmistakable fingers of a journalist. Lestrade lifted the right hand and peered at the middle finger.

'Writer's ridge,' he muttered.

McDowell had gone but the message he had left at the front door was clear enough. The victim was a foreigner. The Franco-British Exhibition was at its height. McDowell had the misfortune to be able to speak French and he and the other two coppers of the Metropolitan Police Force who could, had been drafted into Shepherd's Bush to help with the communications problem. Particularly from Frenchmen who had not yet come to terms with Waterloo and who shouted loudly in French at shop assistants. McDowell had no time for murder. Especially of a German.

Lestrade took in the room. Comfortable. Middle-class. The rent was probably quite high. He glanced out of the window where the lace nets wafted in the cool evening breeze. Below, in the middle of Freedom Street, a cordon of blue helmets held back a crowd of middle-class noses. He went into the bedroom. 'Anything been touched in here?' he asked Valentine.

'Not that I know of, sir. Shall I do it?'

33

'Tell me, Valentine.' Lestrade placed his bowler on the bed. 'How did you become a sergeant in the CID?'

'Sir?' Valentine looked confused.

'Did no one ever tell you not to volunteer for anything?'

'No, sir.'

'So how did you become sergeant?' Lestrade repeated.

'I volunteered for it, sir,' he and Valentine chorused.

'Who found the body?' Lestrade asked.

Valentine had no need to consult his notepad. 'A Mr Chesterton, sir. Lives down the hall.'

'Anyone spoken to him yet?'

'No, sir.'

'All right. Get a photographer over here. And a fingerprint man. Better get Inspector Collins from the Yard for that. I don't mind who you get for the photographs, as long as it's no one from C Division.'

'Very good, sir.'

'And Valentine,' Lestrade called him back softly, 'take your time. This bloke's not going anywhere.'

'Very good, sir.' Valentine rushed out slowly.

'Constable,' Lestrade called to the uniformed man in the passage.

'Sir?'

'No one at all in here for the next ten minutes. Understand?'

'No one at all, sir. Very good, sir,' and he closed the door.

There were four rooms. A living-room, in which Lestrade stood now, a bedroom, a kitchen and a usual office. Not palatial, but solid and respectable and good enough for a brief let for a man with a mission, as he supposed the late Hesse to have been. He flicked through the drawers, using his finger-nails where possible so as not to make life too difficult for Stockley Collins when he arrived. One or two newspapers, heavy with the Medieval German script; personal letters in the same characters. He'd need to get that lot to the Yard's cypher room, that mysterious green door beyond which he had never ventured. He wasn't even sure which way up the pages went.

An ornate paper-knife was embedded in the back of the man from Berlin. It was of silver, and a knight in prayer formed its chiselled hilt. The evening sun caught it as the nets shivered aside. Hesse had been writing something when the blow had been struck. His pen lay at an odd angle in a corner of the rolltop desk, a trail of ink spattering the paper. The dead man's knuckles on his left hand were formed into a fist. There were the first signs of rigor. He had been dead since the morning. Already the face was turning a nasty grey and the flies which followed Lestrade everywhere buzzed and gathered in anticipation.

Stabbed from behind. Lestrade circled the body, crouching to get the angle. All the furniture was in place. No rucking of the carpet. No sign of a struggle. The end must have been sudden and without warning. Hesse had been writing his letter, his back to his caller – if caller he was. If 'he' it was. But the paper-knife? That would probably have been on the desk itself, to Hesse's left or right. Lestrade did not want to disturb the weapon until the man with the camera had arrived, but the blade was probably blunt. It would have taken a fair amount of strength to force the tip through jacket, shirt and perhaps singlet. Not a woman's hand, surely? There again, some women he knew could crack walnuts with their thighs. Difficult to stab a man, of course, with your thighs. Better keep an open mind at this stage. The aim was good, though – that surely ruled out a woman. One clean, straight thrust below the shoulder blade and into the heart. Was it, he wondered as he paced the carpet in front of the fender, a professional killing? An assassination? Perhaps this one had something to do with professional jealousy? A rival newspaper, perhaps? He wouldn't put anything past Alfred Harmsworth.

Lestrade opened the door and checked with the constable on his way out. Mr Chesterton lived at the furthest recesses of the dark corridor. The Superintendent knocked on the door and a pretty, dark lady opened it.

'Superintendent Lestrade, madam, Scotland Yard,' he introduced himself.

'Ah, yes. You'll want to see my husband. He's in the theatre.'

'How nice,' said Lestrade, always a little wary of actors.

She led him through a much larger configuration of rooms into an empty space. The windows here were hung with black and Mrs Chesterton smiled and excused herself, *en route* to provide some tea.

Lestrade appeared to be alone, but ahead of him, in the gloom, he could make out a raised platform, like a stage.

'Is anyone there?' he asked.

'Ho, ho!' a voice cackled and black curtains on the stage slid back to reveal a wooden puppet dangling from strings. The figure bounced around at the puppeteer's command. It wore a clerical collar and a flat hat. 'Hello,' the puppet crowed. 'I am making enquiries of a most serious nature.'

'So am I,' said Lestrade.

There was a squawk and a crash and the puppet flopped forwards, its heels collapsing over its head. A clatter of feet on wooden steps followed and a large, bespectacled man emerged from the blackness of the corner.

'Good God!' he said, in a voice Lestrade was gratified to hear was totally unlike that of the little wooden priest. 'I'm terribly sorry, my dear fellow. I assumed you were my wife. What can you think of me?'

A number of phrases sprang to Lestrade's mind. Like short-sighted. Cloth-eared. Stupid. Deranged. He kept them all to himself.

'I am Gilbert Chesterton,' the fat man said, tugging on ropes which threw back curtains and allowed the light to flood in. 'You must excuse my little theatre. It's a hobby. I make all the figures myself, you know.'

'Really?' Lestrade found himself wondering why.

'Yes. This one is Father Brown.' The fat man lifted up the collapsed cleric. 'I'm actually a writer. Well, journalist, in fact. But one day I'm going to write a novel about this little fellow here.'

'Ah, a children's book.' Lestrade thought it best to humour him.

'Oh, dear me, no. A "whodunit", I believe they call them these days.'

'Well, that's rather why I called,' said Lestrade.

'Yes, of course, Mr . . .'

'Lestrade. Superintendent Lestrade.'

'Ah, yes. Poor Mr Hesse. What an unfortunate business. I'm just glad that it was I who found him, and not my good lady wife. Oh, do be careful of the . . .'

But it was all too late. Lestrade fell headlong over a pile of cardboard flats, badly grazing his shin.

'My dear Superintendent, are you all right?' Chesterton helped him up.

'Thank you, it's my good leg,' Lestrade explained.

'Please, come into the parlour. Frances will have made some tea.'

'Francis is your man?' Lestrade liked to leave no stone unturned.

'My woman,' Chesterton told him. Lestrade raised an eyebrow. All the same, these actor/journalist/writer chappies. 'My good lady wife,' said Chesterton by way of explanation.

'Ah.'

Lestrade sat where he was told, on a pile of papers.

'Ah, there's my *Orthodoxy*,' said Chesterton. 'Thank you, Mr Lestrade, I'd been looking for those notes.'

'Tea, Mr Lestrade?' Mrs Chesterton swept in with a tray.

Lestrade tried to rise but the physical effort was too much and he merely succeeded in disarranging Chapter Three of Chesterton's *Orthodoxy* once again.

'Thank you,' he said. 'Now, distasteful as it must be . . .'

'I've never had complaints before.' Frances Chesterton was a little hurt.

'No, madam,' Lestrade smiled, 'I am sure the tea will be delightful. I was referring to your late neighbour, Mr Hesse. How long had you known him?'

'Well,' said Chesterton, fitting his pince-nez a little more securely, 'it was that Monday Hilaire came down, my dear, wasn't it?'

'No, dear.' She poured the tea. 'That was Thursday. And it wasn't Hilaire. It was some other man.'

'Hmm,' Chesterton mused. 'Who was the man on Thursday? That sounds a little familiar. Can't imagine why.'

'So was it Monday or Thursday?' After all these years, Lestrade thought he may have to resort to a notebook for clarity's sake.

'What?' asked Chesterton.

'When you met Mr Hesse.' Lestrade kept to the straight and narrow.

'Ah, no, that was Wednesday,' Chesterton told him. 'Perceval introduced us in the lobby.'

'Perceval?'

'The landlord. Literary gent like myself. Only lets to tenants with pretensions,' he chuckled.

Lestrade gulped the tea gratefully. It was a very fine brew, for Battersea on a Friday evening.

'What do you know about him?' he asked.

'Perceval?'

'Hesse.'

'Well, not a lot, really. He worked for the *Berliner Tageblatt*. A man of enormous reputation in the newspaper business. He was over here to cover the Games, of course.'

'So he'd been in England . . .?'

'Oh, many times,' said Chesterton.

'No, I mean how long had he been in the country this time?'

'Oh, it must be – what, Frances? A week or so? I believe he was staying at the Grand before that.'

Lestrade was impressed. 'They pay their journalists well in Germany, then?'

'Oh, it's all down to expenses, dear boy. The whole world runs on expenses.'

Lestrade sucked his teeth. 'Not in my profession, Mr Chesterton,' he assured him. 'Tell me, did Mr Hesse have any visitors?'

'Now you've asked me,' Chesterton realized. 'Frances, dear?'

'It's difficult to say, Mr Lestrade.' Mrs Chesterton joined the Superintendent on the sofa. 'We are in the process of moving, you see – hence all this clutter – G. K. and I are out rather a lot at the moment, making arrangements.'

'Ah,' said Lestrade. 'Where are you moving to?'

'Er . . . where is it, dearest?' Chesterton asked.

'Beaconsfield, dear.' She smiled at him. 'In Buckinghamshire.'

'That's right.' Chesterton clicked his fingers. 'I knew it had something to do with Disraeli. We just don't have the room here, Mr Lestrade.'

Looking at Chesterton's girth, Lestrade could believe it.

'. . . what with the children and all.'

Now Lestrade knew that children made excellent witnesses. Their clarity of vision and simplicity of approach to life made them sharp as buttons – not that he'd ever encountered any sharp buttons in his life.

'How many children do you have?' he asked.

Chesterton patted his wife's hand. 'None, I fear,' he said, 'but the house is invariably full of nephews, nieces, godchildren and friends. I'm just glad that this wretched business, if it had to happen, happened at a rather quiet time in terms of visiting.'

'So you wouldn't know if Mr Hesse had a visitor, say this morning, around ten or eleven?'

The Chestertons looked at each other. 'Well, I was out at that place. What's it called again, dear?'

'Fleet Street, dear.'

'Yes, that's the place. And you . . . er . . .'

'Shopping in the High Street,' Frances recalled. 'I had luncheon at the Pink Provender with Mrs Lewis.'

'Ah, yes,' Chesterton beamed. 'How is dear little C. S.?'

'Oh, very well, he's . . .'

The Chestertons caught the frosty look on the face of the Superintendent on the warm evening and they both giggled.

'But', said Chesterton, 'to more pressing matters. What is your surmise, Superintendent?'

'It's very difficult to say, sir.' Lestrade shrugged. 'Until I know rather more about the late Mr Hesse. Does anyone else live on this floor?'

'No,' the Chestertons chorused. 'Only us and the suite of rooms taken by Mr Hesse,' she continued alone.

'You will inform Reuters, of course,' Chesterton said.

'Who's he, sir?' Lestrade asked.

'The news agency,' Chesterton explained. 'After all, Hesse was a foreign national. And a journalist. Won't there be a bit of a stink about this, Mr Lestrade?'

Mr Lestrade had been thinking that ever since he entered Hesse's study. 'Perhaps,' he said.

' "German Journalist Done To Death In London",' Chesterton was reading the banner headlines of tomorrow. 'And on the eve of the Games, too.'

'Indeed.' Lestrade rose to go. 'There is still much to be done,' he said. 'I fear there will be policemen clumping about for most of the night. We'll try to keep the noise to a minimum. Thank you for the tea, Mrs Chesterton. Oh, by the way, you mentioned someone named Hilaire as having visited recently. May I have his or her surname?'

'Belloc,' Chesterton told him.

Lestrade sighed. 'Well, of course, you aren't bound to tell me,' and he limped towards the door. 'Please let Sergeant Valentine know your new address if your move is imminent,' he said. 'You will know which one he is. He's got "eager" written across his forehead. Good evening.'

'I'll see you out, Mr Lestrade.' Chesterton waddled to the

front door. 'Nasty business, this. Do you think it has anything to do with the Games?'

Lestrade stopped and looked at the man. 'In what way, sir?'

'Oh, I don't know,' Chesterton shrugged. 'I'll make no bones about it, Superintendent, I'm a Little Englander by inclination. I don't like notions of Empire. It smacks of arbitrary government. On the other hand, I'm not all that partial to foreigners, especially the Greeks. Well, they *are* their Games, you see. A friend of mine visited Mount Olympus recently. Could quite understand why the Greeks should be miffed that every Tom, Dick and Harry is muscling in on their idea, as it were. Worst sort of plagiarism, really.'

'And did he enjoy his Olympus trip, your friend?'

'Enormously. But if you'll take my advice, for what it's worth, you'll investigate the Greek connection. I was writing to dear old Reverend Baring Gould the other day. Beware Greeks, Baring Gould, I said to him.'

'Quite, sir. And thank your good lady wife again for the tea. Good evening.'

At the end of the corridor, Lestrade collided with a lathered Constable Hollingsworth. 'Strike a light, guv. I didn't see you in the dark there.'

'That's the mark of a good detective,' Lestrade told him between sobs as his ribs settled back into position. 'The ability to see in the dark. I wish I had it. Where have you been?'

'Well, Super, I missed the station wagon 'cos I was still making the Rosie for Sergeant Valentine. I had to catch the Underground in the end.'

'Well, now you're here, stand there. There'll be a bobby with a camera arriving shortly. And Inspector Collins from the Yard. The room you want is there, on the left. I'm off for some supper and I'll be back. Oh, and Hollingsworth . . .'

'Super?'

'There's a lady in there who makes better tea than you do. So watch it. Your days are numbered.'

It was the edition of the *Daily Mail* the next morning that interested Lestrade. It carried a large obituary on the late Hans-Rudiger by someone who seemed extremely informed. Perhaps that someone could fill in the missing details on the dead journalist; give Lestrade some tangible reason for the man's murder. Above all, the Superintendent would have to move quickly and quietly. The police of the Metropolis were stretched to breaking point. Even with an unusual degree of co-operation from their colleagues in the City Force, their resources were being seriously tested. The new Rotherhithe Tunnel exercised them night and day, with Mungo Hyde's men darting out from their floating headquarters at Wapping to peer into the murky Thames waters for any bubbles that might indicate a leak. A massive rally was rumoured any day in Hyde Park or Regent's – you could never be sure – when an army of Amazons demanding the vote would stretch the thin blue line still further. And most important of all, sixteen big blokes from both London forces spent their days hauling heavy hemp in preparation for the Olympic tug of War. This was 1908. There were priorities.

The bowels of the *Mail* offices in dry, dusty, congested Fleet Street made Lestrade's own accommodation seem palatial. Men in green eyeshades ran everywhere, smoking frenetically. Errand boys in cloth caps dodged this way and that. Typesetters with black fingers fidgeted with clicking machinery. And over the scratching of pencils and the rattle of the typewriters, the mad ringing of the telephone and the throbbing hum of the great presses.

'Mr Grant?'

The man looked up at Lestrade's entrance and tilted back the green shade. 'Yes.'

'Superintendent Lestrade, Scotland Yard. May I have a word?'

'Mr Lestrade.' Grant shook his hand heartily. 'This is an honour, sir. An honour. Didn't we do a story on you last year?'

'After a fashion,' Lestrade said. He found publicity a little disconcerting. It was not his style.

'Yes. Yes. It was the Otterbury incident, wasn't it?' Grant offered him a chair. 'Is it true you solved that one in ten minutes?'

Lestrade chuckled. 'An exaggeration, Mr Grant. But it was a brief case, certainly.'

'Coffee, Superintendent?'

'Thank you.'

Grant called through the open door to a passing boy. 'Two

coffees, Murdoch. At the double. Slug of gin in mine. Mr Lestrade?'

'Just milk and sugar, please.'

'And then there was the Justin case. First class, that one.'

'Ah, I had a lot of help there,' Lestrade confessed.

'From Abberline?' Grant scoffed. 'You're among friends here, Mr Lestrade. We know who the *real* heroes of the Yard are. But how may I help you? Are you on a case?'

'I fear so. Hans-Rudiger Hesse.'

'Ah, yes.' Grant leaned back in his chair and tore off the eyeshade, running his journalist's fingers through his sandy, tousled, journalist's hair. 'What a loss to the profession.'

'You wrote his obituary this morning, I understand.'

'Yes. Well, actually, I wrote it last night. Don't tell me you've found a split infinitive?'

'Sub Inspector Ganymede is in charge of Lost Property,' Lestrade explained. 'I am investigating a murder.'

'Quite so.' Grant looked at him oddly. 'How can I help?'

'You seem to have known Hesse quite well.'

'Ah,' smiled Grant, 'the panache of the journalist deceives the eye. I had actually only met him once – two weeks ago when he first arrived. A group of us from the Street played host to the foreign newsmen who had come over to cover the Exhibition and the Games.'

'You gained a lot of information from one meeting.' Lestrade tapped the screwed-up edition on the desk between them.

'Actually, I pinched it.'

'Oh?'

There was a knock on the door and the coffee boy arrived.

'Ah, coffee, Superintendent.'

'Thank you.'

'Thank you, Murdoch. Euggh!' Grant scowled as the brown liquid hit his lips. 'There's virtually no gin at all in this, lad. You'll get nowhere in the newspaper business if you can't make coffee properly. Never mind. I'm a resourceful chappie,' and he pulled out a hip flask from a drawer and dropped some of its contents into the cup. 'Get out. Now, as I was saying, I pinched it from another journalist.'

'Is that ethical?' Lestrade was benefiting from the ten minutes each day he allowed himself with Chambers Dictionary. The question remained however whether he would ever get beyond 'E'.

'Ethical?' Grant was astounded. 'Mr Lestrade, this is the newspaper business. More than that, this is the *Daily Mail*. All's fair in love and Fleet Street, you know. Besides, she didn't mind.'

'She?'

'Marylou Adams of the *Washington Post*.'

'Is that a newspaper?'

'No, not really. But it's the nearest thing the United States can manage. That and the *New York Times*.'

'I see. So is this Miss Adams a newspaperman?'

'Bizarre, isn't it? Actually, she's a damned good one. Whatever this paper's policy is on the Suffragettes, I have to concede privately that there *are* some jobs women do well. Would you like to meet her?'

'Yes,' said Lestrade, putting down his cup in the conviction that the coffee was made from printers' ink.

'Nothing simpler. I'm meeting her for luncheon at the new club in half an hour. Fancy a stroll?'

They strolled, the newsman and the policeman, along the grimy length of Fleet Street, the great grey dome of St Paul's rising above the smoke and bustle of the City. Was it all those years ago that Constable Lestrade had taken off his City helmet and walked through Temple Bar into the Metropolitan District? His feet may have gone, but he left something of his heart there.

And his heart leapt again in the foyer of the Wig and Pen Club, the new dive for hacks and lawyers across the road from the Temple.

'Superintendent Lestrade,' Grant did the honours, 'I'd like you to meet Miss Marylou Adams.'

'Ma'am.' Lestrade was mildly surprised when the petite lady shook his hand vigorously. She had clear, bright eyes and a captivating smile. What was she? Twenty-seven? Twenty-eight? Her hair was in a short bob and her velvet jacket tight round a figure that made all heads turn.

'I'm very sorry sir,' a pompous man interrupted the trio, 'but ladies are not allowed.'

Grant looked appalled and whisked the pompous man away, whispering animatedly in his ear. In a moment, while Lestrade and Miss Adams stood looking at each other in an awkward silence, he came back.

'I'm terribly sorry, Marylou. I thought with you being a journalist on your side of the Atlantic, and with this club being new, there might be a new spirit abroad. Obviously, it is abroad and not here.'

'Don't worry, Richard,' she smiled. 'And I'm not so sure about a new spirit. Do you know, in New York they've just passed a law forbidding women to smoke in public?'

'Tsk, tsk. Well, that's the colonies for you,' smirked Grant. 'I even told the old duffer that you were the niece of McKern of the Bailey, but it cut no ice, I'm afraid. We'll have to go to Luigi's after all.'

They were leaving the dark little building when the coffee boy from the *Mail* hurtled into Lestrade, knocking him with a bang into the plate glass of Lipton's. The bowler brim crumpled like paper and a purple bruise began to spread across the Superintendent's forehead.

'You idiot, Murdoch.' Grant cuffed the boy round the ear. 'Would you like to press charges for assault, Superintendent? I'll gladly swear this buffoon's life away.'

'No, no.' Lestrade's vision swam in the noonday heat. 'I'll be all right in a minute.'

'Well, what's the matter, you unspeakable urchin?'

'It's Lord Northcliffe, sir,' the boy blurted to Grant. 'He's 'ere.'

'Well, well,' said Grant. 'His Master's Voice. Marylou, Mr Lestrade, I'm sorry. The Old Boy wasn't due until later in the day. Top-level conference on the Games. I fear I shall have to go back into my cage.'

'That's all right, Richard,' Marylou said. 'I understand.'

'*A bientôt* then,' and he kissed her hand, before booting Murdoch along the pavement.

Lestrade was now a little lost. He didn't know Luigi's. And he would never take a lady to the Coal Hole in the Strand. On the other hand, he wasn't sure that Edward Henry would wear the Palace as a legitimate expense. As though she read his mind, Marylou said, 'Actually, I'm not very hungry, Mr Lestrade. But I would love to see the Temple Church. I once wrote a thesis on crusaders.'

'I'd be delighted.' Lestrade offered his arm, if that wasn't an

44

unjournalistic thing to do, and led the way through the dark little alley into the sunlit court. They found the door in the circular tower and wandered through the cool stone archway into the darkness. Shafts of light probed the flagstones, flinging streams of red and gold across the floor of centuries.

They stood, bareheaded under the hammer beams, and wondered. At the far end of the nave, in carved stone polished by a million curious fingers, lay the tombs of the Knights Templars, their legs crossed, their hands in prayer.

Marylou looked down at them and said,

> 'Passive in their broken shells, the Masters of the World
> A great and god-like race of kings with beards trimmed and curled.
> Power rides at their scabbard sides and War is on their swords,
> The rulers of the mystic East acknowledged them their lords.'

'Shakespeare?' said Lestrade, ever conscious of the heritage of English literature.

She smiled, then chuckled, a sound like bells in that hallowed place. 'Marylou Adams,' she said. 'I was seventeen when I wrote that. Awful, isn't it?'

'I liked it,' said Lestrade.

She ran her fingers over the marble mail and the cold folds of the surcoat. At the face she stopped, gazing for a moment into the blind eyes. Lestrade looked too. The Templar's nose had lost its tip, rather like his own. There, the resemblance ended. Lestrade wouldn't be seen dead in a hat like that.

'Lord de Ros,' she said. 'I wonder what he was like? If only the dead could talk, eh, Superintendent?'

He looked at her, but she was still looking at the crusader.

'That's rather why I wanted to talk to you,' he said.

She looked at him, puzzled. 'I thought you were a friend of Richard's,' she said.

'We've only just met,' Lestrade told her. 'I understand you knew the late Hans-Rudiger Hesse?'

She walked away from the tomb, nodding sadly. 'He was a fine man. We shall miss him.'

45

'Mr Grant's obituary,' he walked with her, whispering, 'I gather was your work.'

'Essentially,' she said. 'Richard thought he deserved a piece, and knew that I had known him perhaps better than any English journalist.'

'I'd like to know more,' said Lestrade, 'but perhaps this is not the place . . .' He was aware of black-robed vergers flitting like bats around the columns.

'I think this is very much the place,' she said. 'Rudi . . . Hans-Rudiger taught me all I know about newspapers. My stepfather took me to Berlin as a child. It's the only career I ever wanted. And Rudi made it all possible. I think this is a fine place for us to talk.' She leaned back against a stone niche. 'Who would want to see a man like that dead?' she asked.

'Enemies?' Lestrade suggested.

'All newsmen have enemies, Superintendent. It goes with the job. But Rudi was the most respected journalist I know. A newspaperman's newspaperman.'

'Grant's article said he wrote mostly about politics. Why should he bother himself with sport?' Lestrade asked.

'This was a holiday for him,' she said. 'It was to be his last assignment before he retired. He intended to write a series on the politics behind the sport, as it were. I can't believe he's dead.' She turned away quickly before Lestrade could see her face.

'When did you see him last?' He gave her a moment.

'I hadn't for some months,' she said. 'I've only been in England for five days. We wrote regularly, of course. It's funny. I was going to look him up . . .' Her voice tailed away again and she turned to the wall. Then she stamped her foot and turned back to face him, forcing the tears back. 'Tell me, Mr Lestrade, do you carry a gun?'

'A gun?' Lestrade was surprised by her question. 'No, why do you ask?'

'In Washington the police carry guns,' she told him. 'Do you have any weapon at all?'

He hesitated for a moment, then pulled his hand from the pocket of his jacket. His knuckles gleamed with brass. She raised an eyebrow in surprise. It lifted still further as Lestrade flicked a switch and a short blade flashed silver in the sunlight.

46

There was a gasp from a passing verger who stood nearby, his mouth hanging open like a gargoyle.

'Use it,' she said flatly. 'On whoever killed Rudi. I'll help you all I can.'

'So, what have we got, Walter?' Lestrade absent-mindedly stirred his tea. Beyond the window, the breeze from the river drifted in from time to time. The arc lights along the Embankment twinkled like so many stars on the hot summer night. The rattle of the last motor bus died away along Whitehall. Starry, starry night.

'Hans-Rudiger Hesse,' Walter Dew began, unlacing his boots. 'Do you mind, guv'nor? I've been on my feet all day.'

Lestrade nodded his assent. As other people's sweaty feet went, he was most at home with Chief Inspector Dew's.

'Much respected and well-loved newspaperman. Over here to cover the Games. Been in England for a couple of weeks. Spoke English like a native – is that sort of pigeon, sir?'

'Never mind the pigeon, Walter. What else do we know?'

'Hesse was knocking on. Due to retire in a few months. He'd worked on various German newspapers in Berlin and Munich. Did some freelancing. Been in the business thirty years and more. Nobody has a bad word to say for him . . .'

'According to Miss Adams.'

'. . . According to Miss Adams. What do you make of her, sir?'

Lestrade looked at the Chief Inspector. For a moment he thought he saw the light from the lamp catch a grey hair, but it must have been his eyes. And the fact that it was nearly midnight. 'I don't know, Dew. She's very young. I get the impression she's caught up in a man's world and finds some of it a bit tough going. On the other hand . . .'

'Sir?'

'On the other hand, she seemed very keen to bring Hesse's murderer to book.' He remembered the incident with the switchblade. 'Quite happy for me to kill him, whoever he is.'

'Get on!' Dew looked up, shocked. 'Funny lot, the Americans.' He shook his head. 'That Roosevelt bloke now. Fancy having a cowboy for President!'

47

'Ours not to reason why, Walter,' Lestrade reminded him. 'What did you get from Hawkins's Division?'

Dew consulted the book again. 'Apart from the Chestertons who you talked to, the only other occupant of the house in Freedom Street is a Mrs N. Thrawl. Refused to give Sergeant Valentine her Christian name, though he reckoned it was Nutty. Or her age. But he assumed eighty if she was a day.'

'Did she know Hesse?'

'No. She'd heard him moving about above her apparently, but it says here "deaf as a horsetrough" so I don't know how much credibility we can give her.'

'Eighty?' mused Lestrade. 'Too frail then to pin a full-grown man to his desk with a letter opener?'

'Valentine says shaky on her pins. Takes all her time getting to and from the privy.'

'No maid?' asked Lestrade.

'Daily woman.'

'That's what I could do with,' a cheery voice called as it passed the door. ''Night, guv'nors.'

''Night, Hollingsworth,' Lestrade answered.

'I'll swing for that constable,' muttered Dew. 'No respect at all. It's the Education Act, of course, that's what's done it. Putting schools in the hands of County Councils. It only produces people like him.'

'There, there, Walter,' Lestrade patronized. 'Somewhere underneath that cheeky exterior there lurks a good copper. Indulge him. You'll find it.'

'Maybe,' sighed Dew, 'maybe. What did you make of the Chestertons, sir?'

'Eccentric, Walter. What should I make of them?'

Dew shifted uneasily. Lestrade recognized all the signs. Any minute, he'd get up and stroke his moustache. Then he'd pace the floor. Then he'd start counting on his fingers.

'Well, guv'nor.' Dew stood up. 'As you know, I have a few literal pretensions myself.'

'Ah, yes, Walter.' Lestrade kept his face poker straight. 'Your Great Work.'

'Yes, sir.' The fingers smoothed down the clipped moustache. 'My magnum opium. Well, I know a bit about these writer blokes – how their minds work.'

'Go on.'

48

Dew began to prowl the carpet, like a tiger at Regent's Park. 'Chesterton is a writer. I checked on him myself. Wrote *The Napoleon of Notting Hill*.

Lestrade was unimpressed. 'Doesn't know much about history, then?'

'And all sorts of articles and reviews. The point is, guv'nor, he's an ambitious bloke who's going places.'

'So?'

'So,' Dew's left thumb came into play, the first of many digits to appear. 'Chesterton invites Hesse to that flat. He knows of his reputation already and resents it.'

'And?'

The index finger pointed skyward to join the thumb. 'He waits until his old lady is out of the house . . . where was she?'

'Shopping in Battersea High Street.'

'Right.' Dew's middle finger flicked upwards. 'Chesterton calls on Hesse in the middle of the morning, engages him in conversation. Hesse lets him in. He knows the only other person in the house is old Mrs Thrawl in the flat below. And she's as deaf as a floorboard.'

'So?'

Dew's ring finger stood to attention. The finger that bound the good Chief Inspector body and soul to Mrs Dew, mother of all the little Dews.

'So Chesterton chats to him, biding his time, waits till his back's turned, then sticks him with the letter opener.' The little finger had joined the rest.

'Is that it?' asked Lestrade after a pause.

'I've run out of fingers, guv'nor,' Dew admitted.

'Indeed, Walter. But I'm afraid there are five things wrong with your theory.'

'Oh?' Dew was crestfallen. 'As few as that?' He knew when to play the underdog. All the time.

'First,' Lestrade lifted Dew's thumb. 'Chesterton didn't invite Hesse to the flat. The landlord did – a bloke called Perceval. I've checked him and he's clean.'

'Oh.'

'Second, I checked on Chesterton too. He doesn't remotely write the same sort of stuff as Hesse.' He peeled back Dew's index finger. 'And he writes it in English. In other words, there's no need for any professional jealousy. It's a bit like Mr

Edward Henry and Chief Superintendent Abberline. One's a real copper. The other's an idiot. Chalk and cheese.'

He prised up Dew's middle finger. 'Third, Mr Chesterton has an alibi. He said he was at Fleet Street on the morning of the murder and he was. I checked when I was there this morning. He arrived at The Printer's Devil at nine sharp and went from there to The Wayzgoose at just after eleven. He didn't leave until midday.'

'Blimey,' said Dew. 'What'll he do when this new licensing bill comes in?'

'Same as the rest of us, Walter,' sighed Lestrade. 'Jump on the wagon. Fourth, Stockley Collins came up with the finger-prints from the flat. No dabs at all except Hesse's, Perceval's, a set that turned out to be a cleaning lady's – oh, and six sets belonging to various constables from Hawkins's Division – remind me to have a word with him about that.'

'Chesterton could have worn gloves, sir.' Dew tried to curl his fingers down.

'And fifth,' Lestrade bent back Dew's pinkie. 'I've been a copper man and boy for more years than I care to remember. Chesterton is not the murdering type. Trust me.'

'I do, sir,' Dew said, reluctantly, staring at his upright fingers. 'Shall I put these away now?'

'Yes, Walter,' sighed Lestrade. 'Even so, you were right about one thing.'

Dew's face lit up. 'What's that, sir?'

'The murderer wore gloves.'

'So?'

'So, Walter.' Lestrade took the unprecedented step of crossing the room to pour his own cup of tea. 'That is the mark of a careful man. An informed man.'

'Informed, sir?'

'Fingerprints,' said Lestrade.

'But we've been doing those now for . . . ooh . . . seven years.'

'Yes, except that Hawkins's Division doesn't seem to know that. And remember, there's still only one case on record where the sole evidence was dabs.'

'The Stratton Brothers, three years back.' Dew's knowledge was fast becoming encyclopaedic.

'The Stratton Brothers,' nodded Lestrade. 'Which brings me to another point.'

'What's that, sir?'

Lestrade stared out of the window at his own reflection lit by the lamps. 'Hesse was killed with his own paper-knife. It had "Made in Germany" written on it.'

'That's right,' Dew remembered. 'It said, "A present from Münchengladbach".'

'Which indicates', Lestrade was talking to himself, 'a spur of the moment thing. Otherwise, the murderer would have brought his own weapon. Unless . . .'

'Unless?'

'But a man who kills another on the spur of the moment, by snatching up a paper-knife, perhaps in the middle of an argument . . .'

'Yes?' Dew was on the edge of his seat.

'Does such a man wear gloves, Walter? Does such a man come and go like a ghost with no one to see or hear him?'

'So where does that leave us, sir?' Dew asked.

'Lost,' admitted Lestrade, turning from the window. 'And I can't help wondering why Hesse came to see me. And what did he mean by that message – "Nana Sahib"? Walter!'

'Sir?'

'If you want to know the time, what do you do?'

'Er . . . you ask a policeman,' Dew answered.

'Precisely,' said Lestrade. 'Get me Sergeant Jones or Sergeant Dickens. They're both walking bloody encyclopaedias. And I want some answers.'

3

Three Men in a Boat

The Games began that summer at the White City, that most magical of buildings, at once like the Taj Mahal and the Kremlin with just a hint of the Brighton Pavilion; its domes and turrets, its minarets and ogees reflected in the waters of Shepherd's Bush, pumped there by mile on labyrinthine mile of best British plumbing.

It seemed that everyone in Europe stood on the sweep of the terraces, boaters and bonnets nodding with plumed hats in the summer sun. The top hats of the Olympic Committee shone like black beetles among the magnolias of their ladies and none more gracious than the Queen herself – God Bless Her – radiantly limping around the podium beside the magnificent figure of the King, resplendent in thirty yards of navy blue, beribboned and laced as an Admiral of the Fleet. To the fluttering of Union Jacks and the deafening cheers of an adoring crowd, he gave a speech, first in English then in French.

Lestrade stood flanked by Dew, Valentine and Constables Bourne and Hollingsworth at the far end of the terrace. A slightly nervous little man with eyes darting in all directions stood a little behind the King to his right, his hand thrust into his inside pocket with all the nonchalance his neurotic character could muster. It was Superintendent Quinn of the Special Branch, guarding His Majesty on this auspicious occasion.

'Who's that up there with Superintendent Quinn?' Lestrade muttered.

Bourne was rather taken aback. He was wearing a natty little number in green velvet. 'That's His Majesty, Superintendent,' he explained. 'The King.'

All eyes looked at him.

'Manpower may be stretched to the limit,' said Lestrade, 'but I'm not exactly cock-a-hoop over your breeches, Bourne. Like many other things they went out with Oscar Wilde. Go home and change.'

'Very good, sir.' Bourne bridled and the band struck up 'God Save the King'.

'God save us all,' muttered Dew and glanced at Hollingsworth, who winked at him.

'What are we hoping to achieve, sir?' Valentine asked Lestrade.

'Damned if I know,' the Superintendent told him, 'apart from a stiff neck and aching plates. At least you can tell your grandchildren you saw the Games at first hand.'

'And Twenty-One Events,' said Dew. 'Nothing like it seen before.'

'Do you mind if I mingle, sir?' Valentine asked Lestrade. 'I get bored standing still.'

'Feel free,' Lestrade told him, glad that Constable Bourne had gone before hearing that particular order. 'Gentlemen, I suggest we do the same. Something. Anything. Remember, someone wanted Hans-Rudiger Hesse dead. Perhaps it was someone here,' and he moved off.

'Well,' said Hollingsworth, tilting back his regulation boater, 'it won't take us long to ask these seventy thousand a few questions, will it?'

Other anthems struck up, one by one, as the athletes beneath their straining flags paraded round the track. First, as the host country, the British with the Union Jack on their vests. There was a huge feminist cheer from the distaff end of the stadium when the Ladies' Team walked by. Then the Germans and the Austrians in their navy blue with eagles akimbo, the Swedes in their white flannel and the French, whose Exhibition was next door, in their red, white and blue. Superintendent Quinn at least breathed a sigh of relief: no green, white and purple in sight. Mrs Pankhurst and her Suffragettes were having the day off.

A terrible cacophony burst from the band. The only one on the podium still smiling was the Queen.

'What is it, dear?' she asked His Majesty.

'I was wondering that myself. Quinn, what's that noise?'

Superintendent Quinn had made a special study of these

things. It went with the job. 'It's the American National Anthem, sir,' he said.

His Majesty nodded and turned to the Queen. 'He says it's a terrible row, dear.'

She looked at the athletes with the stars and bars on their chests. 'They may be Americans, Bertie,' she scolded him, 'but I don't think they're any rowdier than anybody else. You must remember, they are still a very new country. Oh, just look at those young Turks,' she cried as their crescent banner rounded the track. 'What grace. What movement.'

And the band played on.

Detective Sergeant Dickens of the Metropolitan Police was the only policeman, apart from McDowell and Sergeant Henri La Touque of Hainault, who spoke French. So it was that he had been drafted into the wilds of Shepherd's Bush to cope with the Exhibition. The equally well-read Detective Sergeant Jones had been drafted unaccountably to the Mounted Division at Imber Court, where he was neither use nor ornament, but spent his days checking the animals for glanders and farcy and reporting to Inspector Edgar-Smith, who was polishing his truncheon and champing at the bit to ride against the Suffragettes. So it was Dickens whom Lestrade found, surrounded by cases of French wine and up to his whistle in French cheese of a particularly noisome variety, as the crowds milled to watch the opening events.

'*Stadium, stadium, stadium, stadii, stadio, stadio,*' Dickens declined as he reclined for the benefit of a passing public schoolboy. 'Ah, morning, Superintendent. Come to rescue me?'

'Go on, Dickens, you're loving every minute of it.' Lestrade flopped beside him on a wicker chair under the shade of a marquee – a French one, of course.

'I'd rather be out solving crimes, guv, than playing nursemaid to these Frogs.'

'Well, that's why I'm here, Dickens. Any of this wine drinkable?'

'No, sir.'

'Right. What do you know about Nana Sahib? Is it German?'

Dickens looked puzzled. 'No, sir. Indian.'

'Go on, then.'

'Nana Sahib. Born about 1821 into the Brahmin caste of the Mahrattas. His name was Dundhu Panth and he was adopted by the last Peshwar, Baji Rao. We wouldn't give him a pension after his father's death in 1853 and on the outbreak of the Sepoy War at Meerut (10th May 1857) he declared himself Peshwar and attacked the British garrison at Cawnpore. Women and children were put to the sword under his orders after he had promised them safe conduct by river. He fled before our relieving forces into the Terai jungles of Nepal where, legend has it, he died. Any help?'

Lestrade closed his mouth. 'You couldn't be more specific, could you, Dickens?' he asked.

'No help then?'

Lestrade shook his head. 'Damned if I know,' he said. 'What do you suppose that has to do with a murdered German journalist?'

'Ah, Hans-Rudiger Hesse. I thought you'd be on that one. The *Mail* said it was Hawkins's case.'

'Well, they would, wouldn't they? There isn't *another* Nana Sahib, is there?'

'Not that I know of, sir. I'd have to look it up.'

'Do that, sergeant.' Lestrade got to his feet. 'I must mingle. What is it they say? "Women must weep and policemen must mingle." Is that it?'

'Something like that, sir. *Bonne chance*, as they say.'

'Do they?' Lestrade wandered away, fanning himself with his bowler. 'Do they?'

Fair stood the wind for France that Tuesday. The *Sorais* dipped and butted in the white caps of the Solent to the enthusiastic cheering of the crowd. She was crowding all canvas and her decks were awash, but still the *Cobweb* held her off. The boom was sounded to mark the end of the race and Blair Cochrane stood on the *Cobweb*'s bows, wet but happy. On the *Sorais* the Duchess of Westminster did not assume that position. Watchers from the piers noted that she crouched on the deck with the men in her crew. Only one was not crouching. He was lying motionless among ropes and rigging, his crew mates hammering in vain at his chest. The eight-metre class race, like his life, was over.

They brought him ashore, carried him across the sands at Ryde, through the crowd whose cheering and flag-waving turned to silence. Her Grace the Duchess was at his side the whole time, ashen-faced, tense. No one watched the *Cobweb*'s lap of honour on the sparkling Solent. No one listened to the official times shouted over the loud-hailers. They drifted away from the sands, numbed by the irony of it all. An Olympic Silver Medal after three successive days of sailing. A triumph for British skill and intrepidity. But a man was dead. Home was the sailor, home from the sea, and Inspector Hunter of the Hampshire and Isle of Wight Constabulary sent a telegram to Scotland Yard.

It should have been Abberline's case, but Abberline was unaccountably held up by prolonged surveillance work at Penge. The only officer of sufficient rank who could be spared was Sholto Lestrade. Yes, Henry knew he had the Fitzgibbon case dangling over him – as Lestrade said, with his vast classical background, 'like the sword of Demosthenes' – yes, Henry knew the Hans-Rudiger thing might blow up any day into an International Incident of ugly proportions. Even so, Henry had said, the request came not from an obscure inspector of an obscure force but from the Duchess of Westminster herself. Lestrade must go.

He packed some spare collars, his pea jacket and jaunty sailor's cap and drove south in Elsa, his Lanchester. He scattered a flock of sheep near Guildford and at least one of them was dead as mutton. At the Devil's Punch Bowl he collided with a haywain, and his registration number was taken by eighteen constables to the north of Petersfield alone. By the time the level of Portchester Castle hove into view, the drive had passed into legend. It won him no medals, of course, but he had reached Portsmouth in record time. One of the pedestrians he nearly killed slowly pulled a pencil from his pocket as though deep in thought and began to scribble on a notepad. All in all, Mr Grahame was lucky to be alive.

'Never heard of such a thing,' the ferryman growled at Portsmouth. 'You can't take one of them horseless carriages on a steam packet. I don't care if you're the bleedin' Prime Minister. We don't even take horses, let alone them infernal machines.'

And that was it. Lestrade alighted at the pier on foot and for all his fifty-four years and the sweltering heat, slung his goggles around his neck and ran the length of the pier, each groan of the planking reminding him anew that the thing had been built in 1813, in his great grandfather's day. The passers-by in their summer fol-de-rols and parasols who applauded him as he ran had no idea he was running for somebody else's life.

Lestrade had been to the Isle of Wight before, on the case of the Man in the Chine. Then he had stayed at Shanklin and had the dubious pleasure of pounds of cottage pie offered daily by the monotonous culinarist Mrs Bush, wife of the local sergeant. On the way down, while he crashed his gears and cursed the slapping foliage of the English hedgerows, logic and mathematics told him that the sergeant must long ago have retired. So it was with something approaching dismay that Lestrade saw a grey, moustachioed figure standing squarely on Pier Street as he hurtled past the barrier, catching his cheek painfully as he did so. Well, what was another bruise among friends?

'Superintendent Lestrade, sir!' the moustachioed figure said. 'How good to see you, sir, after all these years. We've followed your exploits in the Lunnon newspapers.'

'Sergeant Bush?' Lestrade hoped he was wrong.

'Sub Inspector.' Bush straightened. Sixteen years and he had soared by half a rank.

'Incredible,' said Lestrade.

'You remember my good lady wife.' Bush gestured to the black-coated thing beside him. She bobbed and beamed, still wearing her apron.

'Intimately,' said Lestrade. 'And all the little Bushes? They must be a veritable little copse by now, eh?'

The *bon mot* fell on deaf ears. After all, this was the Isle of Wight. Wit had left it with the passing of Tennyson and repartee a long time before that.

'Inspector Hunter's compliments, sir. He isn't expecting you until tomorrow. I happened to be on pier patrol anyway – well, what with all the Overners about.'

'Overners?'

'Oh, beggin' your pardon, sir. Foreigners. Over here from the mainland, sir. Like yourself.' The Sub Inspector consulted his half-hunter. 'You're a mite late for nammet,' he said, 'but if you'll take a ride in my station wagon, Mrs Bush has some rare shepherd's pie in the oven.'

57

Mrs Bush bobbed and beamed again. Not as rare as all that, Lestrade thought to himself.

'I'd rather view the body,' he said. It was not intended to be an insult. He needn't have worried. It was not taken as such.

'This way, sir. They've got him at the Royal Esplanade. 'Ere,' He grabbed the ear of a passing schoolboy. 'Stop dreamin' about them boats, Uffa Fox, and carry the Superintendent's case.'

While Mrs Bush left, no doubt to busy herself with a work of art in the kitchen, Bush and Lestrade were shown into the cellar. Mine host was a nervous man of dyspeptic disposition, acutely aware of what the presence of corpses did in the way of trade falling off. Even so, he was decorum itself and ceased charging sixpence a time to visitors to view the body while Lestrade was present.

'So what happened, Bush?' Lestrade wandered around the makeshift table between the kegs of Burt's Best Bitter, looking at the body for nothing.

'Carried up dead he was, sir. From the beach.'

'Cause of death?'

There was a silence. Bush was no detective. He wasn't much of a policeman. And it was not Hollingsworth-type insolence that made him murmur, 'Shortness of breath, sir.' It was simply the best he could manage.

Lestrade noted the yellow canvas life jacket still strapped under the arms, the sou'wester lying beside him, the heavy sea boots on the floor. 'A sailor then?'

Bush was stunned. 'My eyes, Mr Lestrade. You Lunnon 'tecs know a thing or two. Off the *Psoriasis*, Lady Westminster's yacht.'

'Ah, yes,' said Lestrade. 'Her Grace the Duchess. Who was he?'

Bush had to resort to his notebook. 'Mr Hemingway,' he said, 'of Portman Square, London and Windsor.'

'Professional sailor?' Lestrade asked.

'No, sir. All the yachtsmen in these Games are amateurs, sir.'

Rather like some policemen, Lestrade thought, but held himself in check. He looked at the earthly remains of the late Mr Hemingway. He was a man of thirty or so, with a pronounced centre parting and a clipped military moustache. He looked peaceful enough, his eyes closed, his hands clasped across his chest. Laid out for the undertaker. Well worth sixpence a time. It was the bright green stains down his life jacket that interested Lestrade.

'What do you think, Mr Lestrade?' Bush enquired. 'Heart?'

'Possibly,' murmured Lestrade. 'Do you have a list of his fellow crew members?'

'I do, sir.'

'Where would I find them now?'

Bush consulted his watch again. 'Ooh, they'd be up at the castle by now, sir. Big garden party going on there, there is.'

'How do I get there?'

'I'll take you in my station wagon, sir.'

'Oh, good.'

They rattled through the summer dust along what passed in the Isle of Wight for roads until they took the steep hill that led to Carisbrooke Castle. At the ivy-covered barbican of the noble pile, Bush applied the brake. It had little effect and it took him several hundred yards of hauling on the reins until the constabulary animals obeyed his snarling commands.

'You'd better wait here,' Lestrade said, hurriedly unpacking his pea jacket. 'We don't want your uniform frightening the ladies.'

'Very good, sir. I'll hold my horses.'

The strains of a string quartet reched Lestrade's ears as he walked through the medieval archway into the courtyard. On the bowling green to his right a large gathering of guests made small talk on the afternoon air, to the chink of fine porcelain and the drone of dull speeches made by Princess Beatrice as Governor of the island. Lestrade realized at once that his choice of natty naval attire had not been a good one. Everyone else was gorgeously dressed in frock coats and top hats. He chatted to a flunkey who pointed out an attractive lady in a broad-brimmed, flowered hat.

'Your Grace?' he approached her, surrounded as she was by men. 'I am Superintendent Lestrade of Scotland Yard. I wonder if I may have a word?'

'Of course,' the Duchess of Westminster said. 'Gentlemen, would you excuse us?'

'Is there somewhere we could go?' Lestrade asked.

'The battlements?' she suggested and led the way.

The view from the wall was breathtaking. Miles of country-side, dumb in the summer heat, and the rooftops of the little town below.

'It was from that window that the late King Charles sought his escape from the castle,' the Duchess was saying.

'And did he make it, Your Grace?' Lestrade had never been particularly at one with English history.

She looked at him oddly. 'Thank you for coming so promptly,' she said.

'Why did you send for me?' They stopped, overlooking the great cannons and the outer earthworks of Elizabeth's day.

'You will know that one of my crewmen on the *Sorais*, William Hemingway, is dead.'

'Yes,' Lestrade told her. 'I have just left him at the Esplanade Hotel.'

'I see.' She swept along the mellow stone, her fan superfluous in the breeze from the ramparts. 'He was a healthy, robust fellow, Superintendent. I cannot believe his death was natural. That is why I sent for you. Can you help?'

'How many crew on your ship, ma'am?' he asked.

'Four altogether,' she said. 'Three men and myself.'

'That would be – Mr Hemingway, Mr Hunloke and Mr Crichton?' He remembered Bush's list.

'That is correct.'

'Are these gentlemen here now?'

She looked down at the dots of figures below them on the lawn. 'Philip Hunloke is not here. He had some urgent repairs to carry out in harbour.'

Lestrade looked at her.

'At Mr Ratsey's yard at Cowes,' she explained.

The quartet struck up anew below them and the indescribable notes of a soprano threatened to shatter the glass for miles around.

'Oh, no,' muttered the Duchess, 'Miss Lambert's off again. Shall we take the steps to the keep, Mr Lestrade? Can you manage that?'

'Perfectly, thank you, ma'am.' Lestrade was a little stung by the rebuke, but by the time he reached the top he was gasping more than a little. Her Grace however was ahead of him, staring down a deep hole in one of the chambers, ruined and open to the sky.

'They say this well is three hundred feet deep, Mr Lestrade,' she said. 'And a serving girl threw herself down it in the seventeenth century.'

'Ah, well,' sighed Lestrade, 'that's often the way with serving girls.'

At least in the lee of the great stones, they were relatively safe from the verbal assaults of Miss Lambert. Lestrade perched himself on what had been the medieval privy in the angle of the room and began.

'Perhaps you could tell me what happened?' he said.

The Duchess leaned against the far wall. 'Certainly. My crew and I set sail from Ryde Pier three days ago, returning to that point each day. The eight-metre class race was over sixteen miles.'

'Who else was in the race?'

'Let me see – the French, the Belgians, the Swedes and the Norwegians, besides ourselves of course.'

'And who won?'

'Dear old Blair. Blair Cochrane on the *Cobweb*.'

'Second?'

'Myself on the *Sorais*.'

'And third?'

'The *Fram* from Norway.'

'Who selected your crew?'

'Mrs Allen and I.'

'Mrs Allen?'

'The owner of the yacht,' the Duchess explained.

'Tell me about the dead man.'

'Willie? He was a fine man. Oh, something of an eccentric, I suppose. He believed in daily exercise and keeping fit. Nothing for him to run five miles before breakfast.'

'And he was an accomplished sailor?'

'The best,' she said, 'next to Philip Hunloke, the best man I could have chosen.'

'You'd sailed with him before?'

'Yes,' she told him, 'many times.'

'What happened this time?'

'At first,' she began to pace the worn old stones, 'all was well. The wind was fair. We were all in high spirits. We'd given an interview to the Press and had our photographs taken. Then, all hands on deck.'

'And then?'

'Towards the end of the first day – the Monday – Willie complained of sickness. He had pains, he said, in his stomach. George – Mr Crichton – said it was the champagne. Willie laughed it off. But as we went ashore that evening I noticed how grey he looked. However, we were leading at that stage and we all had high hopes for the Tuesday.'

'And on the Tuesday?'

'Willie was visibly weaker. Most of the day, he clung to the rail, smiling when he noticed one of us looking at him. But he simply couldn't manage the yacht at all. Philip and George carried him, as it were, but it wasn't easy. I tended him as best I could, but the wind had changed north-easterly and we all had our hands full. By the end of Tuesday, we still had a slight lead, but the *Cobweb* was catching us fast and the *Fram* was threatening. We held a council of war on the Victoria Pier and told Willie that he wasn't to sail on the Wednesday. He wouldn't have it. Didn't want to let the side down, as it were.'

'And on the Wednesday?'

'He seemed odd as we set sail. Stupefied almost. He barely had the strength to eat his prunes. As we rounded the buoy for the finish . . .' Her voice trailed away for a moment, then she regained herself. 'As we rounded the buoy, Willie collapsed. His pulse was very rapid. His eyes were glazed and the pupils dilated. He was being very, very sick. He was a good sailor, Mr Lestrade,' she said suddenly, 'and I'll swear there was nothing wrong with his heart. I don't understand any of this.' She broke away to where the steps, worn and uneven, tumbled down the grassy motte to the bailey. 'Oh, it's so wretched. There's to be a ball tonight at the Yacht Club in Ryde. I am to be the guest of honour. The belle of the ball. But I don't feel particularly bellish at the moment.'

He looked at the strong, aristocratic face, the eyes big with tears. Rather like Marylou Adams had looked a few days ago. And he reflected again, as he had a thousand times, what a cold bedfellow is sudden death. No heart. No mercy. Just emptiness.

'Your Grace,' he said, 'I am catapulted into this situation. I'll confess I'm a long way from Whitehall, but I have to place my trust in someone and I feel that someone must be you.'

'Thank you, Mr Lestrade,' she said, afraid of what was to come.

He looked at the dots of Edwardian elegance mingling and being nice to each other on the lawn. There was no singing now. Obviously someone had made a request to Miss Lambert.

'Tell me,' he said. 'You mentioned prunes.'

'Did I?' she asked him.

'You said Mr Hemingway barely had the strength to eat his prunes . . .'

'Oh, yes,' she remembered. 'It was all part of his fitness mania, his eccentricity if you will. He ate prunes each day to keep himself regular.'

'Who knew of this?' Lestrade asked.

'Almost everyone,' she said. 'In yachting circles at least. There was a standing joke about them. He said he used to win races because the prunes moved him on.'

'Did anyone else in your crew eat these prunes?'

She pulled a face. 'Good Heavens, no. As I told you, Willie was eccentric.'

'Clearly.'

'What is the significance of the prunes, Mr Lestrade? Were they bad?'

'Very, ma'am,' he said grimly. 'I am guessing, of course, but as I said, I must trust someone.'

'Your guess then?' she harried him. 'Mr Lestrade, Willie Hemingway was a very dear friend. He died on board my ship. As friend and captain I have a right to know what happened to him.'

'Very well,' said Lestrade, breaking away from the wall to face her. 'Brace yourself, madam. William Hemingway was poisoned.'

'By accident?' She felt her heart stop.

'No, ma'am. By design. The symptoms you describe – the weakness, the sickness, the dilated pupils, the collapse. Above all, the vomit – grass-green, wasn't it?'

She nodded silently.

He nodded too. 'Digitalis,' he said. 'The purple foxglove.'

She gasped.

'One ounce of the tincture – and it's not difficult to get, even with the new Poisons Act – or thirty-six grains of the leaf. Death takes . . . about three days.'

She swayed for a moment against the archway.

'Are you all right, Your Grace?' He caught her arm.

'Yes,' she whispered. She looked at him hard. 'You are telling me that Willie was murdered?'

'Yes,' he nodded. 'Who gave him the prunes?'

She frowned, then gathered up her skirts. 'Mr Lestrade, I must be going.'

But Lestrade put his arm across the archway and prevented that. 'Who gave him the prunes?' he repeated. Prunes had that effect on people.

He saw the lip quiver for a second only. 'Philip Hunloke,' she said.

The ball was at its height on that still and tropic night. Lestrade had had no luck at Mr Ratsey's yard. Philip Hunloke had been there, certainly, but he had gone. It didn't matter. Lestrade caught up with him at last in the ornate conveniences with the swivel washbasins at the home of the Royal Victoria Yacht Club. He had no element of surprise for he came upon Hunloke in the act of washing his hands and the said Hunloke had seen his adversary in the mirror – an odd-looking ferret of a man in a ridiculous jaunty cap and pea jacket.

'I am Superintendent Lestrade of Scotland Yard,' he introduced himself. 'Are you Philip Hunloke?'

'Captain Philip Hunloke, yes.' The man was quite prepared to stand on his dignity. 'What can I do for you?'

'You can tell me about the prunes,' Lestrade said.

Hunloke paused in the drying of his hands. 'Prunes?' he repeated blankly.

'The prunes, to be specific, that you gave to William Hemingway at the start of the eight-metre race.'

'What about them?' Hunloke continued to dry.

'You tell me,' Lestrade persisted.

'Don't fence with me, Lestrade,' Hunloke snapped, looking his man up and down. 'I suspect you haven't the intellect for it. A dear friend of mine died yesterday. We're none of us in the mood for this little bash. Now, get to the point.'

'Very well.' Lestrade straightened. 'The point, Captain Hunloke, is that I believe those prunes were the cause of Mr Hemingway's death.'

'What? Stuff and nonsense,' Hunloke blustered. 'Most they

can do is purge a fellow. They may taste fatal, but they can't kill.'

'They can if they're heavily laced with digitalis.'

'What?'

A little old sailor in a goatee came into the Gentlemen's Smoke Room at that moment. He sensed the odd atmosphere and thought it best to leave.

'Digitalis,' Lestrade repeated when he'd gone. 'The essence of the foxglove. A noble, graceful plant with purple spotted flowers . . .'

'Yes, yes.' Hunloke was angry, with himself more than Lestrade. 'Spare me the botany lecture.' He caught sight of his own face in the mirror. It had turned an ashy grey. 'My God,' he said, 'that means . . .'

'Yes?' Lestrade's eyes narrowed as he sniffed the scent.

'Actually,' Hunloke turned to him, 'I didn't give poor Willie those prunes. Or rather, I did, but I was merely passing them on on behalf of someone else.'

'Oh?' Lestrade raised an eyebrow. 'Who?'

'Nordahl överland, the captain of the *Fram*.'

Lestrade frowned. 'That's the Norwegian ship?'

'Yacht,' Hunloke corrected him.

'Why should Captain Overland want to give Hemingway prunes?'

'Willie's predilection for prunes was well known in yachting circles, Superintendent. And it is the done thing for crews to exchange little gifts before the start of a race. I've a wardrobe full of cravats.'

'Why didn't he give him the prunes direct?'

'Willie was late that first morning. The *Fram* was getting under way and I offered to pass them on to him. God, if only I'd known.'

'Don't reproach yourself, Captain. If there's any reproaching to be done, I'll do it. Outside. I take it Captain Overland is here?'

'What?' Hunloke was miles away in his mind, riding the Solent with Willie Hemingway dying in his arms. 'Er . . . yes. Yes, he is.'

'Would you be so kind as to point him out to me?'

'Yes, of course.'

'One thing more.' Lestrade stopped his man at the door. 'These prunes, were they in a tin or a bag?'

'A bag,' said Hunloke.

He led the way into the hall, lit with the myriad sparkle of the chandeliers. The band, specially sent down by Harrods, was in full quadrille and a marked improvement over Miss Lambert and the Rookley Palm Court who had rather dubiously entertained the group that afternoon. The Duchess of Westminster was magnificent in her ball gown studded with orders and decorations, though none worn more proudly than the silver Olympic medal around her white throat.

'There,' muttered Hunloke. 'The chap with the monocle. That's överland.'

Lestrade took in a dapper little fellow rather of his own stamp but with a hauteur born of the fjords and Oslo University. He was surrounded by a group of sailors built like Dreadnoughts, with fiery red hair and bristling beards. He stepped forward into an International Incident, but as he did so, a hand touched his sleeve.

'Miss Adams.' His jaw dropped.

'Mr Lestrade,' she said, 'what are you doing here?'

The American newspaperwoman now looked anything but. Gone was the black velvet jacket and the short bob. Her dark hair cascaded over her shoulder and only the shine in her eyes dazzled more than the glitter of her gown.

'I may well ask the same of you,' he said.

'Ah, but I asked first,' she laughed.

'I am on duty, madam,' he said.

'So I see.' She took in the grotesquely inappropriate suit. 'And so am I. The *Washington Post*, like Time and Tide, waits for no man. I've been here for two days covering the race.'

'So you know about the death of Mr Hemingway?' he asked.

'Yes. Tragic. I . . .' and the brightness left her. 'Is that why you're here?'

He nodded.

'I'm sorry,' she said. 'I thought it was a heart attack.'

'It may have been,' said Lestrade, 'in the end. It's what led to that heart attack that I am interested in.'

'Lestrade.' He felt Hunloke at his elbow. 'I want to see Willie's murderer brought to book. This is no time for chit-chat.'

'Murderer?' Marylou said rather too loudly and the eyebrow

66

of Princess Beatrice lifted a fraction as she quadrilled past her at the gallop.

'Now, we don't know this for a fact.' Lestrade sensed the ground shifting beneath him. 'I'd be grateful, Captain, if you'd let me deal with this. Perhaps you could ask Miss Adams here to dance.'

'Very well,' he said, grim-faced. 'Forgive me, madam, I am not normally so short on chivalry. These are trying times.'

'They are indeed.' She took his hand. 'I too have lost a friend, Captain Hunloke. No less dear to me than Mr Hemingway was to you,' and they vanished into the rush of the dancing.

Lestrade tried to squeeze round a column, but was caught up by a rushing foursome and whirled around the room by a very large lady wearing a lassoo of pearls that beat him around the nose. As he broke free of her, he was battered from behind and emerged with a florid-faced gentleman whose collar was up around his ears and who apologised profusely for his appalling misconduct, assuring Lestrade that he was happily married and had dozens of children. It was several minutes therefore before the Yard man stood before the knot of Norwegians.

'Captain?' he said.

'Yah!' they all chorused.

'Captain . . . Overland?' He narrowed the field down.

'I am överland,' the monocled man said.

'I am Superintendent Lestrade of Scotland Yard.'

One of the other captains whispered in överland's ear. 'Ah, police,' överland said.

'Yes,' Lestrade said. 'I would like to ask you a few questions concerning the death of Mr William Hemingway.'

'Vat?' The Norwegians crowded round, shielding their captain. 'Vat do you mean?'

'I have reason to believe that Mr Hemingway was poisoned.'

It was one of those unfortunate moments in life when the music had to stop. The polite applause died away and Lestrade's sentence hung like lead on the evening.

'Is zere a problem?' A French sailor hove into view with his own crew at his back.

'Ve can take care off ourselves,' said överland.

'Of course,' said the French captain. 'Capitaine Bompard.' He bowed to Lestrade. 'But you are such a new country. I merely thought . . .'

'Pah!' roared one of the Norwegians. 'Frenchmen never think.'

'I beg your pardon,' another Frenchman intervened. 'I must beg to differ.'

'Please.' Lestrade held up his hand, aware of the silent crowd at his back. 'This matter does not concern the French.'

'French!' the Frenchman spluttered. 'Begging *your* pardon zis time, monsieur. I am Emile Geraud and I am Belgian. How dare you accuse me of being French.'

'What is wrong with being French?' Bompard rounded on his man.

'Gentlemen,' Lestrade shouted, 'I would like to talk to you alone, Captain överland,' and he gestured towards the Gentlemen's Smoke Room.

'Impossible,' the Norwegian said. 'Anything you wish to say to me you can say through de correct diplomatic channels.'

'Having trouble, överland?' Another captain arrived in the colours of the Swedish Navy. He clicked his heels to Lestrade. 'Olef Waldemar,' he said. 'At your service.'

'Vat do you know about service?' överland snapped.

'Gentlemen,' Princess Beatrice, sufficiently cosmopolitan to control matters such as these, stepped forward, only to be sent reeling by an accidental right hook from one of the Norwegian crew. Bompard levelled the man with a single blow and Waldemar's boot crunched into the Frenchman's back. Before Lestrade had a chance to move out of the way, he was poleaxed by a huge Norwegian who began roaring defiance like a Berserker. The whole room was in uproar. Princess Beatrice, nursing a thick lip, began ushering the ladies out, despite efforts by the Duchess and the newspaperlady to remain. The band struck up the Gay Gordons for want of any requests and did the best they could. Harrods, even on a Saturday, was never like this.

One chandelier crashed to the ground. Bodies rolled and tumbled this way and that. Fists flew and teeth cracked, while the air was riven with the most appalling language in at least five different tongues. Passers-by on the road outside tutted and nodded together as the windows went. What rowdy people these sailors were. And worse was to come. Next week they'd all move up the road to Cowes.

In the end, it was good old Sub Inspector Bush who saved

the night. His blue-coated bobbies hustled into the hall in a body, to add to the many bodies threshing this way and that.

And the 'Now come along there sirs' were interspersed with the thud of truncheons and the click of handcuffs as the room was restored to order.

Lestrade had missed most of the fun. He had been hauled out unconscious from under a table, his pea jacket liberally spread with one of the more delicious dips by courtesy of Mr H. G. Nutt of the Pier Hotel, and the bandmaster's baton had been carefully removed from his right nostril. Apart from that and the mild concussion manifested by the purple lump on his forehead, he was fine. Finer anyway for coming to under the gentle ministrations of Marylou Adams.

'Aaarggh!' He sat bolt upright, dislodging the ice pack from his head.

'Steady, Mr Lestrade,' she said, plumping his pillows.

It was something of a cliché but Lestrade said it anyway. 'Where am I?'

'Room Thirteen, Yelf's Hotel, Ryde. I hope you're not superstitious, Mr Lestrade?' She smiled at him.

'Of course not,' and his fingers strayed to the wood of the bedside table. 'How long have I been here?'

'A few hours,' she said. 'Do you feel able to stand the light? I'll open the drapes.'

'Just the curtains, please,' he said.

She let the light flood in. 'You had us all worried.'

He suddenly froze and peered downwards. He was sitting there in his pink combinations, lightweight, summer, for the use of.

'Don't concern yourself,' she laughed. 'Mine host got you into bed with the help of Sub Inspector Bush. And the best news,' she sat by him on the coverlet, 'is that Mrs Bush is sending over a plate of her delicious shepherd's pie all the way from Shanklin.'

'Oh good,' Lestrade grimaced, but the effort was too much and he fell back. 'I don't want to sound an Old English stick-in-the-mud,' he said, 'but aren't you worried about your reputation, being alone in a man's room?'

'In a *policeman's* room,' she scolded him. 'But no. Despite the rather cranky little smoking laws in New York, I am an emancipated woman. Or shouldn't I mention that phrase to an Englishman?'

He smiled. 'I'm very glad you're here,' he said.

'So am I.' Her smile faded. 'Because you need help,' and she crossed to a bedside cabinet. 'Brandy?'

'What time is it?' he asked.

She looked out of the window at the clock opposite. 'It's nearly half-past ten.'

'Ah, off duty,' he sighed. 'Yes please.'

'Tell me, Mr Lestrade.' She poured him a stiff one. 'Have you ever tried bourbon?'

'I thought that was a town in South Africa,' he confessed.

She laughed that merry, tinkling sound he liked.

'Well.' She sipped her own glass and sat beside him again. 'What have we got?'

'We?' She sounded for all the world like Walter Dew. He looked at her bright, laughing eyes, the little freckles across her upturned nose, the petite figure and the firm breasts under her pelisse. Not at all like Walter Dew really. Walter never wore pelisses; they did nothing for him.

'Mr Lestrade.' She spoke seriously, a hard, almost ruthless edge to her voice. 'Let's understand one another. I am, first and foremost, a newspaperman. I may, to quote your own late, dear Queen – God Bless Her – have the body of a weak and feeble woman, but under here,' she tapped the folds of her bodice, 'is pure newspaper.'

Lestrade nodded. That must have been the rustling sound he heard.

'A man very dear to me was murdered recently. As you know, I want his murderer found. And my whole training – the training I received from Hans-Rudiger – has led me to pursue matters to their logical conclusion. Whatever the danger. Whatever the cost. You are the law here in England and I'd prefer to work with you. But if I cannot, then rest assured, I will work alone.'

'I see,' he said. 'But I am not at liberty to . . .'

'But Hans-Rudiger's killer is at liberty, Mr Lestrade. And that is a situation which is intolerable. Now, do we work together or separately?'

Lestrade looked at the frail-looking girl in front of him, the eyes burning fiercely, the lips and jaw set firm. All *his* training, from the knee of Adolphus Williamson through Howard Vincent, Monro and McNaghten, had told him to work alone. Trust no one. Never, never divulge, least of all to the Pressman.

'Together, then,' he said.

For a moment, there was stillness between them. Silence captured in a look.

'Together,' she said. 'First of all, about last night . . .'

He felt his head throb anew. 'Don't remind me. One little point we've both overlooked is that once news of that reaches Mr Edward Henry at the Yard, I may be out of a job anyway.'

'Nonsense,' she said. 'No one is pressing any charges against anybody. The Duchess of Westminster has offered to pay for all the damages and the Olympic officials have managed to get all parties to shake hands. Except for Captain Bompard, of the French team, whose hands are broken . . .'

'Both of them?' Lestrade asked, sensing carelessness when he heard it.

'It's all right,' she said. 'The surgeons at the County Hospital say he will be able to play the piano again.'

'Oh, good.'

'But the most interesting news,' she poured him another brandy, 'is that Captain överland was *given* those prunes by somebody else.'

He sat upright. 'How do you know that?' he asked.

'I am a newspaperman, remember?' she told him. 'It's my business to know. The information about the prunes I got from Captain Hunloke. He feels dreadful about his part in the wretched business. As for Captain överland, before I came here, I spent a rather unpleasant hour bobbing about on his yacht in Cowes Harbour. He feels equally dreadful – though his broken collarbone didn't help. He says that although he made the gesture of the prunes, he actually got them from someone else.'

'Who?' Lestrade asked.

'That's just it,' she sighed. 'He can't remember. There were so many people at the start of the race, newsmen, photographers, tourists, all crowding round, back-slapping and so on. It could have been anybody. It doesn't help, does it?'

'Well, at least I don't have to risk a war with Norway by

arresting him,' Lestrade observed. 'If what he tells you is true, of course.'

'I've met some pretty accomplished liars in my time,' she said. 'If överland is one of them, he's very good.'

'If he *is* very good,' Lestrade gingerly removed the ice pack, 'if he doctored the prunes himself, what would be his motive?'

'Professional jealousy,' she said. 'Perhaps Hemingway was a better sailor than he was.'

'Perhaps so,' said Lestrade. 'But why Hemingway only? After all, the *Fram* came third in the race. Which means that Overland was beaten by *two* British ships.'

'Yachts,' she corrected him.

'Why not kill Blair Cochrane, who won? Or the Duchess, who came second?'

'They didn't like prunes?' she suggested.

'There are other ways,' he said. 'No, it doesn't make sense. Unless there is some other link between Hemingway and Overland that we don't know about.'

'I can check that,' she told him. 'But I have to get back to Fleet Street. I'm sure Richard Grant of the *Mail* would help.'

'I can check it too, as you say,' he told her. 'But I'd have to get back to the Yard. I'm equally sure Superintendent Quinn of the Special Branch wouldn't help. But that's neither here nor there.'

'But what if överland's telling the truth?'

Lestrade sucked his teeth, suddenly aware that his nose was painful and swollen. 'Then we've lost our man,' he said. 'He was milling in that crowd on the pier at the start of the race and we've lost him. Were you here then?'

'No. I told you. I've only been here three days. I missed the first day entirely. I was with the British Ladies' Team at the White City. There is, of course, another possibility that we haven't discussed.'

'Oh?'

'That we're not looking for the murderer of one man, but of two.'

'Two?'

'That the same man who killed William Hemingway also killed Hans-Rudiger Hesse.'

Lestrade shook his head. 'Not possible,' he said.

'Why?'

'Well, for one thing, the murder weapon. In my experience, murderers usually use the same weapon – a knife or an axe. Hemingway was poisoned. Hesse was stabbed. Take my word for it, we're looking for two different men. My problem is that with resources so stretched at the Yard, I'm saddled with both.'

'I see,' she said, standing up. She whirled to her handbag on the cabinet and snatched out something from inside. Lestrade could hardly believe his eyes. He was staring, as she held her arm at full length, into the muzzle of a little pistol.

'This is a Derringer,' she said. 'Very handy for killing Presidents of the United States . . . or Superintendents of Scotland Yard. I'm not likely to miss from this distance. And if I do, there's a second shot.'

She laughed and clicked the hammer on to empty barrels. 'If, of course, it's loaded. Actually, you're lucky. It usually is.'

'Do you have a licence to carry that?' he asked her, gulping down the brandy.

'Why, Superintendent dahlin',' she suddenly drawled in her best Southern Belle, 'Ah really don't believe Ah need one, y'all. Anyway,' the voice had become hard again, 'none of this matters, because there'd be no point in killing you with a pistol when I've already poisoned your brandy.'

For a brief instant, his pulse leapt. He stared at the glass, sniffed it. Was his tongue tingling? The muscles of his gut tensing? 'Relax.' She sat down again, patting his hand. 'The point I'm trying to make is that if I wanted to murder you – or anyone – I'd have a back-up, just in case.'

'In case?' he said, his heart slowly descending from his mouth.

'In case something went wrong.' She shrugged. 'You know the deck of an eight-metre yacht is a pretty public place to die. How else was the murderer supposed to despatch Hemingway? If he'd clubbed him with an oar or fired a salvo from a passing warship, it'd be a tad obvious, wouldn't it?'

'As you say,' said Lestrade, catching her drift. 'A tad.'

'Whereas with Rudi, he was alone. And he took the weapon that came to hand. The paper-knife.'

'How did you know it was a paper-knife?' he asked her.

'Tsk, tsk,' she scolded. 'You're a suspicious old sourdough and no mistake. It was in all the papers. Don't you read those?'

'Not if I can help it,' he said. 'But what is the link between Hesse and Hemingway?'

'That's what I intend to find out.' She snatched up her handbag. 'And for that I need the resources of Fleet Street. Can you manage by yourself? I think you'll find the Duchess has paid your hotel cheque.'

She stopped at the door and smiled. 'Will I see you in London?' she asked.

'Knowing you as I do, Miss Adams, I have no doubt of it.'

And she blew him a kiss, as emancipated women will.

4

The Four Hundred Metres;
Fifty seconds dead

Admiral Crichton was of less use as far as information was concerned than Philip Hunloke. Yes, he knew of Hemingway's absorption with prunes. Yes, he knew that Captain Överland had presented him with some. No, he had no idea where they came from. So while the Olympic Committee sent a telegram from Baron de Coubertin himself expressing sorrow to Hemingway's nearest and dearest, and arrangements were made for the post-mortem and the funeral, Lestrade took his leave from the young men and the sea and crossed by the steam packet to Portsmouth. But he had been gone for four days and the little lad he had employed to look after his Lanchester had been called away on urgent business and the Superintendent's cherished motor car, itself a Mark of Esteem from the Highest in the Land, was standing off the roadway on four blocks of bricks, its silver-spoked wheels gone. Lestrade arranged for it to be refitted, complete with spare, and to have it driven back to the Yard by a constable. He himself took the train, much to the relief of other road-users in the vicinity.

He returned to the windy corners of Scotland Yard and a little after luncheon to find a man built like an elephant waiting for him.

''Ello, guv.' Constable Hollingsworth seemed relieved to see him. 'Oh dear, been doin' a bit of shadow boxin'?' He nodded at the Superintendent's swollen forehead.

'Something like that,' said Lestrade, 'only the shadow punched back. Who are you?'

The elephantine man clicked his heels together and bowed stiffly. 'I am Inspektor Aloïs Vogelweide,' he said, 'of de Berlin Politzei.'

He shoved his papers to Lestrade who read, as though with a practised eye, the heavy Germanic script.

'These seem to be in order,' he said.

'Ah zo,' Volgelweide beamed. 'You read Deutsch?'

'I thought you said you were German.' Lestrade was confused.

So was Vogelweide, but he swept on with the ruthless efficiency for which Prussians are famous. 'I am coming ahead of the Kaiser,' he explained, 'who will be beating your Köenig Edward's boat at Cowes next week.'

'I see,' said Lestrade, clicking his fingers in Hollingsworth's direction. 'Do you drink tea in Berlin?'

'In Berlin, *ja*, but not over here. Turkish coffee, *bitte*.'

'You heard the Inspektor, Hollingsworth,' Lestrade said. 'Bitter Turkish coffee.'

'Strike a light, guv, I'll have to send out to Abdul Pasha's in the Strand for that.'

'Then do it, man,' Lestrade told him. 'We're always glad to help our friends from over the water.'

The constable exited, muttering.

'I am here to look into de matter of Hans-Rudiger Hesse,' Vogelweide explained. 'Your Englischer newspapers zay zat he vas murdered.'

'I'm afraid so,' said Lestrade, carefully lifting the bowler off his bandage.

'Vat are you doing about zis?' the Inspektor asked.

'Everything we can,' Lestrade told him. 'Perhaps in the meantime you would be able to tell me why anyone would want him dead.'

Vogelweide paused for a moment, as though to translate Lestrade's words in his head. 'He vas a very distinguished journalist,' he said. 'Fearless and vizout de corruption. Such men make enemies, *ja*?'

'Perhaps?' said Lestrade.

'Zo vat is it zat you are zinking?' Vogelweide pumped him.

'Perhaps,' said Lestrade again, 'that the killing of Mr Hesse on English soil was merely a coincidence. That someone followed him here from Berlin.'

'Zo?'

'So.' Lestrade crossed to the door and opened it. 'Perhaps your best bet would be to make your enquiries at home – in Berlin.'

'*Nein*,' Vogelweide smiled. 'I have three zergeants vorking full time on zat. In ze meantime, I vill arrange for ze body to be zent home so zat zere can be a funeral in Berlin.'

'Very well,' Lestrade said.

The huge Inspektor clicked his heels. 'Ven I have done zis, I vill look in on you again, old shap, and ve vill vork togezzer, *ja*?'

'No,' said Lestrade. 'I cannot really help. Turkish coffee is one thing, but co-operation? I suspect that our methods would be totally different.'

'Nonzenze,' chuckled the big man. 'Ve are both detectives. Ve are both after the zame thing – ein murderer. I would like to do zis vith you, but if I cannot, I vill do it vithout. *Gutentäg*. I vill take my coffee later.'

'Goodbye,' said Lestrade, as emphatically as he could. 'And don't do anything I'd do,' and he watched the man click his way down the corridor.

'Good morning,' he heard Inspector Gregory call as he met Vogelweide on the stairs.

'Iz it?' he heard the German answer.

'Constable Bourne?' The Superintendent put his head round the door to the outer office. 'A word in your ear.'

The detective constable minced in. 'Yes, Superintendent,' he said.

'That man who just left.'

'Derek Hollingsworth, sir?'

'No the other one.'

'Oh yes,' smiled Bourne. 'The big one. Looked like a circus strong man.'

'Yes, that's the one. Well, he's a policeman, rather like you are supposed to be. But for all his smiles and heel-clicking he's a foreigner. And for all he has no jurisdiction over here, I can't help feeling he's going to get in our way.'

'Yes, sir.'

'Your job, Bourne, whether you decide to accept it or not, is to shadow him. Everywhere he goes, you go. Got it?'

Bourne's eyes lit up. 'Everywhere, sir?'

Lestrade's eyebrows arched a little. 'Use your discretion, constable,' he said.

'I take it with me everywhere, sir,' and he left.

*

The gun shattered the stillness of the morning. From the puff of smoke the watches ticked. Straw boaters and feathered hats craned forward to catch the moment as the five men got into their stride.

Kent Icke of the *Daily Graphic* took up the commentary on his loud-hailer:

'And it's J. C. Carpenter; J. C. Carpenter of the United States on the inside with that unmistakable action. Just look at those nether limbs going, ladies and gentlemen. Behind him is W. C. Robbins, also of the United States – he's looking strong, not pushing the pace. And in the third position – they're not using strings today – it's a cracking pace out there; our own, our very own Wyndham Halswelle, neck and neck with his running mate of Worplesdon Harriers, Martin Holman. And beginning to trail at the moment, the Negro J. P. Taylor on the outside. He's widely tipped as the favourite, but things are looking rather black for him at the moment. Robbins, Robbins now moving up – just look at that swing. It looks as though a good time will be had by all. Taylor making ground . . . And what's happening? Robbins, Robbins has cut across Halswelle – oh dear, oh dear. He's crossed Halswelle and the London Scot's had to manoeuvre. Oh, what a calamity! Robbins is with Carpenter on the inside. I don't know what the track judges will make of that. They're on the long home straight now. On the straight. And it's still anybody's race. Except Holman's. He seems to be losing it. He's falling back. Here's Halswelle. Halswelle's challenging Carpenter. Oh dear. Carpenter . . . This is astonishing. Quite astonishing. Carpenter's running diagonally for the tape. Halswelle's having to go for the outside. The crowd are on their feet – aren't you, ladies and gentlemen? I've never seen such a thing in my years as a sports loud-hailer. Well, well. Carpenter gets the gold, Halswelle the silver . . . But wait a minute. The tape's gone down. The track judges have dropped the tape. One of them's waving to me. At least, I think he's waving. Carpenter thinks he's got it. He's starting on a lap of honour. There's a track official talking to him now. Oh dear, Carpenter seems to have knocked him over. I can't quite hear what he's shouting . . . it sounded like "You cannot be serious". Well, well. I always knew Americans were appalling sports, but this takes the biscuit. And it's over to Dorian O'Hehir at the long jump pit.'

Amid the furore at the tape, the shouting and recriminations, no one noticed Martin Holman collapse by the trackside. He looked pale and his chest was heaving. It was some minutes before officials with white armbands bundled him on to a stretcher and carried him from the field. By evening he was dead.

They put the body into the mortuary at the White City. Curious they should build one, really, unless they expected their athletes to die. It was his heart, of course. He was unfit. He hadn't trained enough. Worplesdon Harriers weren't what they had been. The doctor who happened to be in the crowd signed the death certificate and he was still there when Lestrade arrived.

'Dr Harris,' he said, taking off the boater the sweltering heat of the day had forced him to adopt, 'how are things in Camberwell?'

The greying, moustachioed medico looked up. 'Lestrade,' he said, 'what brings you here?'

'The nose of one of my sergeants, doctor,' Lestrade told him.

'Not Dew!' Harris sneered.

'Walter Dew is Chief Inspector now, doctor. Ever since the Hallowed House case.'

'Oh yes,' muttered Harris, 'I'd forgotten. Did you like old Watson's "Six Napoleons", by the way? Well, his and Conan Doyle's?'

'I always thought there were only three,' Lestrade told him with the hauteur of a man who attended French History Classes for Policemen. Harris looked at him oddly. It was a common enough reflex. 'No, actually, it was Sergeant Dickens. He's on duty at the Exhibition and found all this rather odd.'

'Odd?' Harris repeated. 'The Games are afoot, Lestrade. This poor fellow merely fell martyr to the heat. It could kill us all, you know. When Watson was in Afghanistan . . .'

'Yes,' Lestrade interrupted. 'Tell Inspector Gregory some time.' He looked at the corpse. 'Heat?' he asked Harris.

'Heart, actually. I'd guess and say his right vena cava wasn't as superior as all that.'

Lestrade lifted the lids. 'How long has he been dead?'

'Three hours or so,' Harris said. 'Had a veritable army of medical chappies here for most of the day. Poor blighter.'

Lestrade eased aside the long shorts. 'What's this?' he asked.

Harris was astounded anew at Lestrade's innocence. 'It's a leg, Lestrade,' he said.

'These blotches,' the Superintendent clarified the situation.

'Lividity.' Harris poked the dead athlete's quadriceps femoris with his bodger. Not surprisingly, he didn't react at all. 'In layman's terms, the blood, once it has ceased to pump, drops to the part of the body nearest the ground. It answers the call of gravity.'

'Thank you, doctor.' Lestrade was patient. 'But these pin-pricks on the *top* of the leg.' He poked the sartorius with his pencil.

'Ah.' Harris had to think on his feet, never his most comfortable position. 'Obviously he's been turned over.'

'Obviously. How long did you say he's been dead?'

'About three hours. I'd been called away in the meantime. Why?'

'He's quite limp,' Lestrade said.

'Well, of course. He's dead,' Harris explained.

'What about rigor mortis?' Lestrade asked. 'He should be stiff as a board by now.'

'Oh, it varies, Lestrade.' Harris dismissed the matter with his years of experience.

'It does. Unless the deceased has been involved in physical exertion – Holman ran most of the four hundred metre race. Unless he'd had convulsions – a track official told me he'd had several and really shouldn't have run. In which case, rigor sets in very rapidly.'

'You're quite good at this sort of thing, aren't you?' Harris said grudgingly. 'So what do you surmise?'

Lestrade flicked the knife with the brass knuckles from his pocket. He placed the point carefully against the dead man's forearm and nicked the skin with it. A drop of blood oozed out and trickled down on to the slab.

'What are you doing, man?' Harris was amazed. Had Lestrade turned surgeon now? Or was it vampire?

'Running blood,' said Lestrade. 'I never believed stories of bleeding corpses until I became a detective sergeant. At that point, I saw the light.'

'Which is?' asked Harris, still very much in the dark.

'Which is that in certain cases of poisoning, rigor mortis comes and goes. It's my guess he's been stiff already and he'll be stiff again in a couple of hours – and the blood remains, as you medical men would say, fluid.'

'Good God.'

'Can you perform a post-mortem, doctor?' Lestrade asked.

'Er . . . well.' Harris brushed his moustaches, covering fluster with bluster. 'You want cause of death, I suppose.'

'I know that already.' Lestrade wiped his knife tip on his jacket and clicked back the blade into the knuckles, 'Holman was poisoned. What I want is a look at his stomach contents.'

'I haven't brought my saw,' Harris explained.

'Borrow one,' suggested Lestrade. 'Doctor, I need answers. Strictly between you and me, Holman is the second athlete to die by poisoning in the space of a week.'

'Really? Lord, yes. I read it in *The Times*. That sailor chappie in the Solent. Good God, Lestrade. What does this mean?'

The Superintendent shrugged. 'I shall have to ask a lot more questions before I can answer that one, doctor,' he said. 'And at least one of them concerns prunes.'

While Mr Edward Henry held a Press Conference to assure the gentlemen of the Press and therefore the public that there was no cause for alarm, that everything possible was being done and that London was still the safest capital in the world, Lestrade travelled to Worplesdon. He left his Lanchester at home, having no wish to have his wheels stolen again, and went instead by train. There was not a single case on record of anyone stealing the wheels of a locomotive.

He arrived at the track mid-afternoon and the lone figure trotting round the small arena was pointed out to him as Lieutenant Wyndham Halswelle. He was conventionally handsome, with a rather long nose and centre parting; aerodynamically perfect, although Lestrade didn't know it, for covering middle distances at speed.

'Jock,' said Halswelle, shaking Lestrade's hand. 'The inevitable handle, I'm afraid, for an officer of the London Scottish. Care to jog with me?'

'Jog?' repeated Lestrade.

'Run slowly,' Halswelle repeated.

'Well, I'm hardly dressed . . .'

'Take your jacket off.' Halswelle helped the Yard man to disrobe. 'And your hat. I can't stay still, you see. In training.'

'Yes, I've got a sergeant like you. You have another race to run?' Lestrade felt his lungs tightening already. Combine Worplesdon in July with too many years and too many cigars and you have the explanation for the wreck that was stumbling along beside Halswelle in the deserted stadium.

'They're restaging the four hundred metres,' the Scotsman said.

'Because of Holman?' Lestrade wheezed.

'Because of Carpenter,' Halswelle explained. 'He cut me up twice and they disqualified him. I'm not altogether happy about it. It's not using strings to run in that causes it. There's bound to be some argie-bargie.'

'What can you tell us', gasped Lestrade, 'about Martin Holman?'

'Good man,' said Halswelle earnestly, barely, on his eighth lap, breaking into a sweat. 'I'll miss him.'

'Can you think of anyone who would want him dead?'

Lestrade had been looking for a line to stop Halswelle running. Evidently, he had found it. The London Scot looked at him. 'What are you saying?' he asked.

Lestrade longed for something to lean against. Other than Halswelle, there was nothing. And it would have been too undignified to collapse, even for a moment, on the man's shoulder.

'Don't you read the papers?' Lestrade rasped, his chest heaving with the effort of his forty yards or so. 'The morning editions?'

'Only the sports columns,' Halswelle explained. 'Kent Icke, Bill Waring, Alan McLaren.'

'Is there anywhere we can talk privately?' Lestrade asked, at last feeling the iron ball which was his throat relaxing a little.

Halswelle surveyed the little stadium, the sweep of silent seats. He and Lestrade were the only ones there. 'I don't think you can get anywhere much more private than this, do you?'

He suddenly dropped to the ground, lay on his back and thrust his legs in the air, sawing the sky with them as though inverted on an invisible bicycle. Lestrade stepped back just in time to avoid a running shoe up his moustache.

'Martin Holman was murdered,' he said. 'By person or persons unknown.'

For a moment, Halswelle lost his stride, then recovered it. 'How?' he asked.

Lestrade was grateful to sit down beside him. 'He was poisoned.'

'How?' Halswelle repeated.

Lestrade looked at the strong features, a little crimson now with the rush of blood to the head. He said again, 'He was poisoned.'

Halswelle's feet crashed down and, as they did so, his body came up like a mole trap. 'Poisoned by what? How was it done?' he asked.

'An acquaintance of mine in the medical profession spent all last night examining his stomach contents.'

'What did he find?'

'Well, eventually, he found the stomach. And in it a quantity of poisonous toadstools.'

'*Boletus luridus*,' Halswelle said.

'I beg your pardon?' Lestrade's Latin had never got beyond the first declension and sometimes not even to there.

'*Boletus luridus*, Superintendent. It's a fungus.'

'Poisonous?'

Halswelle shook his head. 'Suspicious,' he said. 'It depends on the alkaloids present as to how powerful these poisons are. *Muscaria* can certainly be fatal to some people.'

'You seem very knowledgeable about poisons, Lieutenant,' Lestrade could not help observing.

'Not poisons,' said Halswelle. 'Fungi.'

'How do you know which one Holman ate?'

'I don't,' shrugged Halswelle. 'But I know which ones I picked for him.'

'You picked?'

'Yes. In Worplesdon Wood a few days ago. I was out running and I was staggered to see them so early in the season.'

'Why did you pick them?'

The Lieutenant leaned toards him. 'Because, Mr Lestrade, Martin was an artist. Oh, amateur of course, like his athletics. But he was quite well known in London circles for his still life. He wanted a quantity of fungi with a certain texture for a work he was completing. Naturally, he asked me.'

'Because of your knowledge of them, naturally?'

Halswelle nodded. '*Luridus* has the colour he wanted. My God, I didn't expect him to eat them, merely paint them.'

'Did you warn him not to eat them?'

'No, of course not. I didn't think it necessary. The British are a fungiphobic lot, Superintendent. If they don't buy it at the grocer's, they don't usually eat it. Oh, this is awful.'

'May I ask how you know so much about toadstools?'

'A lifelong interest,' Halswelle said. 'Some men fish. Others ride. I pick fungi.'

Lestrade struggled to his feet, wondering if he could manage the walk back for his jacket and boater.

'There's one more thing.' Halswelle was up beside him. 'Something you should know about Martin Holman.'

'Oh?'

'I believe he was being blackmailed.'

It was one of those rare moments when Sergeant Valentine was sitting still. The day had been oppressive in its heat and he and the Superintendent stood on the roof walk of Scotland Yard, high above the limes and the sparkling brown of the river. Feet below, tiny people milled around the Embankment; theatre-goers going to the theatre, drinkers dying for a drink, characters in search of an author. But if Lestrade had a moment to observe to himself that all human life was there, Valentine did not. It was nearly dusk. He had places to go.

'Your best guess, then, from the search of Holman's rooms?' Lestrade asked, watching his cigar smoke float away across the rooftops.

'The letters are interesting, sir,' Valentine said, 'but it's the diary that says it all.'

'Does it?'

'Well, nearly all.' Valentine whipped a small notebook from his pocket. 'Look at this. March the fourteenth: "M getting difficult. Wants more." And this for April the third: "She's bleeding me dry. Can't reason with her. We must have it out." And for June the twenty-second: "M putting the squeeze on. Must see G and confess all."'

'M?' Lestrade repeated. 'G?'

Valentine shrugged. It was his most relaxed gesture.

'What did Bourne and Hollingsworth come up with about him?'

'Do you really want to know, sir? All right. Bourne said that he quite approved of Holman's curtains, but the chintz of the settee just didn't go . . .'

'Yes, I'm not sure his ulterior design sense was what I had in mind. I'll swear Bourne was a woman in a previous incantation. What school did he go to?'

'Holman?'

'Bourne.'

'Haberdashers' Aske's – for a term.'

'I knew it!' Lestrade clapped his hands and a group of pigeons moved along there. 'What about Hollingsworth?'

'Ah, well, this is better. He spent the morning at Messrs Glanville and Fritillary, Purveyors to His Late Majesty King Richard III.'

'What do they do?'

'Supply brawn and other parts of pigs to the gentry. You know when the nobs have their luncheon baskets from Fortnum's?'

'No.'

'Well, apparently, there's usually a Glanville and Fritillary jar of Something or Other in Jelly packed in those.'

'And Holman worked for them?'

'Yes. He was highly thought of. Had a promising future.'

'So he was the brains behind the brawn?'

'You might say that, sir.'

'Who did Hollingsworth talk to?'

'Er . . . the manager, sir. A Mr Glanville.'

'"G",' muttered Lestrade.

'Well, it's not really all that amazing, sir, bearing in mind the family name and all.'

'No, I mean "G" – the letter G. You said Holman's diary said "Must see G and confess all."'

'Oh, yes.'

'Had Hollingsworth seen this diary?'

'No, sir. Detective Constable Bourne did the rooms. I popped in for a short while.'

'Yes, of course you did. What time is it?'

Valentine tore out his half-hunter. 'Half-past eight, sir. I must dash . . .'

'Yes, you must. Get me a cab and have it waiting at the side stairs. I think Mr Glanville and I must have a teensy chat.'

In the corner of a quiet little restaurant off Ludgate Hill, two newspapermen sat over a candlelit supper, enjoying the warmth of each other's company, the wine and the glow of a summer's evening.

'It's very kind of you, Richard, to let me have the run of the *Mail* offices.'

He clicked his glass against hers. 'My pleasure, Marylou. Just don't let old Harmsworth find out.'

'I thought he represented all that was new and pioneering in journalism,' she said. 'In the States we think highly of him.'

'Maybe, but for all his bravado – and his undoubted genius as a newspaperman – I'm not sure he'd like an American snooping around the office.'

'Will he get *The Times*, do you think?'

'Bound to,' Grant grinned. 'He's working his way through Fleet Street systematically – up one side and down the other. What he really wants, of course, is the Law Courts at the bottom – or is it the top?'

'Richard.' She tapped him with her napkin. 'That's unworthy.'

'I know,' he laughed, 'but if you can't be bitchy about your boss, who can you be bitchy about?'

'What about Lestrade?' She changed the subject.

'Yes,' he reflected, 'I could probably be bitchy about him.'

'That's not what I meant and you know it,' she said. 'Seriously, Hans-Rudiger was a good friend. All I know about journalism I learned from him. Is Lestrade up to snuff, as you British say?'

'Funnily enough, I've been doing a bit of spade work on the dear old Superintendent. Last year he solved the Otterbury case in record time – a bank job, Farrow's in Cheapside. City Force didn't have a clue.'

'How is he on murder?'

'Ah, well. He handled the Hallowed House case a few years ago. Some say, of course, he's a numbskull.'

'Really? Who?'

'Well, Arthur Conan Doyle for one. He and John Watson

have been pillorying the man for years. I'm amazed he stands for it.'

'Oh, that's the Sherlock Holmes stories?'

'That's right. No, it's very difficult to gauge a man like Lestrade. The Yard's come on no end of course now that Edward Henry's Commissioner. Tell me, Marylou, what are your thoughts on Hans-Rudiger?'

She was silent for a moment. 'It's not as simple as Hans-Rudiger,' she said. 'I believe that whoever killed him also killed Captain William Hemingway in the Solent.'

'What's the connection?' he asked.

'That's just it. I can't find one.'

'And Martin Holman?'

'Who?' She frowned.

'Ah, Marylou,' he scolded her, 'the fatal trap. The problem in going back over old stories – even last week's – is that you can miss the new ones. Martin Holman collapsed and died after the four hundred metres two days ago.'

'Is there a connection?'

Grant nodded grimly. 'I believe there is. He was poisoned, as was Hemingway.'

'You covered this?'

'No, my junior, Chaim Gestetner. Used to work on the *Daily Star of David*. He talked to the doctor who carried out a post-mortem on Holman. It was fungicide.'

'What?'

'Death by eating toadstools.'

'My God. Do the police have any clues?'

Grant laughed. 'They don't usually,' he said.

'Is Lestrade on it?' she asked.

'Yes.' He closed to her. 'Marylou, I think we're on to something big here. Two athletes and one newspaperman covering athletics are dead and all in the space of a fortnight.'

'A what?'

'Er . . . sorry . . . two weeks. London is swarming with Europeans, as well as some of your exalted countrymen. I don't have to tell you the tensions that tax our world, Marylou. Greeks versus Turks; Turks versus themselves; Frenchmen versus Germans; Englishmen versus Frenchmen. This whole French Exhibition thing is merely a front to cover God knows what hostility. Remember Fashoda . . .'

She nodded. 'I was at school at the time.' She smiled wistfully.

'Bitch,' he grinned. 'Take it, then, from a slightly older and slightly wiser generation. We are staring down the muzzle of international terror. And what a heaven-sent opportunity the Games are. But this time the sniping is not only verbal. It's real.'

'What can we do?'

Grant leaned back, tapping the side of his wine glass. 'How close can you get to Lestrade?'

'I don't know,' she said. 'Do you think it's important?'

He nodded. 'Yes. If we're to get this story – you for the *Post* and me for the *Mail* – we've got to know the moves. You must find out exactly what the police are doing.'

'But how will we know what the murderers are doing?'

'Quite,' he sighed. 'If we knew that, we'd have the biggest story of the decade.'

'I'll drink to that,' she said. 'The biggest story of the decade,' and their glasses met and their eyes flashed in the flame.

It was a worried Mr Glanville who spoke to Lestrade that night. There was no need to summon him untimely from his bed for Mr Glanville was already at his offices, armpit-deep in dusty ledgers in an office which looked as though it still belonged to Mr Scrooge.

'You people move damned fast,' he said. 'I didn't discover a problem until this afternoon. Who called you?'

'No one, sir,' said Lestrade. 'I am here on an entirely different matter, though I suggest they will turn out to be one and the same – your matter and mine. Let me guess – your books don't balance.'

'Correct,' said Glanville, wiping his forehead profusely. 'Like a stork with no legs. I've got the auditors in next week. Where's it all gone?'

Lestrade placed his boater on the topmost ledger. 'Some of it into the pockets of the late Mr Holman. The rest into the pockets of a lady whose name begins with M.'

After he had lifted his lower jaw from the desk, Glanville turned quite pale. 'I can't believe it,' he mumbled.

'The lady whose name begins with M?'

'Martin Holman,' he said. 'He's been with us for years. A stalwart of the firm. No, no. It must be a clerical error.'

'Check your figures again, Mr Glanville – especially those initialled by Mr Holman. I think it's there you will find a certain creativity in the accounting.'

Glanville sucked his pen, scratched his head, ran a troubled finger up and down the rows of double entry book keeping like a schizophrenic librarian. He leaned back in his chair, exhausted, defeated. 'My God, my God. Who can you trust these days?'

'Who indeed? You didn't know?'

Glanville shook his head. 'Not a clue.' He stood up. 'You'd better come out, Miss Fendyke.'

There was a gasp and a rustling sound, then a filing cabinet door slid back and a rather elegant lady stood there, in stays and drawers. Her face was bright crimson.

'There's no point in hiding anything now, Madeleine,' Glanville said.

Miss Fendyke clearly disagreed in that she hauled the linen cover off the nearest typewriter and attempted to cover what was left of her modesty.

'Madeleine,' said Lestrade, 'did you know that Mr Holman had his fingers in the till?'

She looked apprehensively at Glanville. 'Yes,' she said at last.

'Madeleine!' he roared. 'How could you?'

'You old skinflint!' She turned on him. 'Yes, I was blackmailing him. Yes, he was stealing from you. Only you were so besotted with me, you dirty old lecher, that you didn't notice. If only you'd paid us all better, none of this would have happened. Martin wouldn't have needed to help himself and I wouldn't have to sit on your revolting lap.'

Both Glanville and Lestrade looked at the lap in question. As corporate laps of providers of brawn to the gentry went, it seemed quite respectable.

'But Madeleine, we had something . . .'

'You've probably got something,' she snapped. 'I just hope you haven't given it to me.'

'Mr Lestrade,' Glanville sobbed, 'I had no idea. No idea of any of this.'

'Miss Fendyke, do you have a dress?'

'In my locker,' she said.

'Could you put it on? I'm afraid I must ask you to accompany me to Bow Street Police Station.'

She stood upright, jutting a pretty impressive chest in Lestrade's direction. 'Am I under arrest?' she asked.

'We'll work out the formalities later,' he told her. 'For the moment you are not obliged to say anything. Anything you do say will be taken down and may be used in evidence. Do you understand?'

She nodded, flashing fire at the quivering Glanville and flounced off to her locker.

'Er . . . Superintendent,' said Glanville, 'my wife . . . she doesn't understand me, you see. Madeleine and I . . . well, it won't have to come out, will it? About the whips, I mean? And the manacles?'

'I don't see why it should, Mr Glanville,' said Lestrade.

'And the chains . . .'

Lestrade's face turned sourer. 'I am concerned with the death of the late Mr Holman,' he said. 'Anything else is by the way . . . at the moment.'

He led Miss Fendyke towards the stairs.

'And the mastiff wasn't my idea,' Glanville called after him. 'Not really.'

In the station wagon, Miss Fendyke was very forthcoming. She also told Lestrade quite a lot he wanted to know. And some that he didn't. It was as well that Walter Dew wasn't with him. A married man with certain sensibilities would have found Miss Fendyke's frankness rather alarming. Martin Holman had worked for Messrs Glanville and Fritillary for nearly fourteen years. He had an excellent record, but Messrs Glanville and Fritillary were the sort of employers who expected total loyalty and believed that working for them was reward in itself. Whereas any employee was entitled to countless jars of Things in Jelly, actual cash was in short supply. Miss Fendyke had found her own salvation in this context. First, as third secretary to old Mr Fritillary, she had wormed her way into his confidence. Yes, he did a lot of dictating after hours. Yes, he had died with a smile on his face. Second, she had become first secretary to the present Mr Glanville – and Lestrade had gathered something of their relationship. Mrs Glanville had all the warmth of an ice cap and the bolster that lay between her husband and herself in bed was rumoured to be made of barbed wire. Although there again, probably not, because Mr Glanville would have enjoyed the challenge of that. Third, Miss Fendyke had discovered the ends of Holman's fingers firmly embedded in the firm's till and had put the screws on so to speak to the tune of nearly five hundred pounds over a two-year period. Miss Fendyke was almost socially secure when the idiot had run out of breath on the White City track. Yes, he had pretensions to being an artist, but although critics made favourable noises about his still life, nobody actually bought anything. Holman used to say it didn't matter. One day he would come into money and then Messrs Glanville and Fritillary could jump into one of their own vats and he would buy his own gallery and studio et cetera, et cetera. Miss Fendyke was sure it was all a pipe dream.

By the time Constable Hollingsworth had taken this statement with the aid of Lestrade, who helped him with the spelling, it was nearly dawn. Sergeant Valentine flew in, without taking his coat off, to inform his superior that trouble was brewing at the Oval.

'Surrey going to lose again?' Lestrade yawned.

'No, sir. Suffragettes, sir. They're going to take over the ground.'

Lestrade frowned at Miss Fendyke, in whose mouth butter would not melt. 'Women!' he said.

Inspector Edgar-Smith sat his roan at the edge of the pitch, his seventy mounted policemen behind him. The early-morning sun fell on the ground mist that lent an eerie stillness to the scene. Bemused gentlemen carrying cricket pads and wearing tasselled caps walked the gauntlet, one or two of them whistling in an attempt to lighten the moment. At the far end of the ground a steadily growing army was mustering, fanning out from the van to form wings to right and left. Slowly, their banners rose in the dawn, elaborate gold letters on fields of green, purple and white. Edgar-Smith lowered the rim of his helmet to read their legends – 'Brixton Matchbox Makers', 'Golders Green Confirmation Wreath Makers', 'Pimlico Vamp Beaders'. Determined eyes under broad-brimmed hats met the steady stare of the police. Flags rose and fell, fluttering on the breeze. Only the crowd spoke, mostly men, confused, uncomfortable, stumbling along the tiers of wooden seats to take their places, colliding with each other, craning their necks to scan the monstrous regiment of women. None of them had known the fair sex so silent. It was designed to unnerve and it did.

By the time Lestrade, Valentine and Hollingsworth arrived, the sun was up and the mist had gone. A thin blue line of policemen stood with arms folded in front of the horses. There was no sound except the occasional snort and pawing of the ground. The animals were silent.

Lestrade lifted his boater to see the opposition.

'Cunning bitches,' murmured Edgar-Smith. 'They've positioned themselves to the east, y'see. Got the sun behind them.'

'Why are your men here?' Lestrade looked up at the man, an ox in the saddle.

'We got a tip-off there'd be trouble. I've sent for reinforcements from Hyde Park. I can have another hundred men here by ten. If only they'll hold off till then.'

'And a baby Howitzer, I suppose,' Lestrade asked.

'No.' Edgar-Smith missed the point. 'We don't need the army. I can handle things.'

Lestrade scanned his own lines. 'I believe I hold the senior rank,' he said.

'Of plain-clothes, yes.' Edgar-Smith did not take his eyes off the banners.

'Of *all* ranks,' Lestrade reminded him.

'Except the Mounted Division.' Edgar-Smith was adamant. He was also right. A Superintendent of Scotland Yard had no jurisdiction over the Mounted Branch. And clearly Edgar-Smith was determined to get his man. Or, in this case, his woman. 'They'll attack from the flanks,' he said. 'First right, then left. They're weakest over there, by the popcorn stand. That's where the whole thing will start.'

Lestrade went as close as he dared to the man's stirrup. He had never been at home in the saddle or even close to one. 'You sound as if there's going to be a battle,' he murmured.

Edgar-Smith glanced at him for the first time. 'Of course there is,' he said. 'And Mrs Pankhurst and I are the opposing generals. You can do what you like with the Infantry, Lestrade. My boys are ready. One twitch of that line and we'll charge.'

'Charge?' Lestrade took off his boater. 'Are you mad? They're unarmed women.'

'Unarmed women?' Edgar-Smith spat his contempt on the carefully rolled grass. 'Look for yourself,' he said. 'Look at those forearms, those fists. You don't see many clinging vines there, do you, Lestrade? What are they carrying in their handbags, do you suppose? Hankies? Smelling salts? No, Superintendent: bricks. And if they catch you with two of those, you'll know all about it.'

Lestrade felt his flesh crawl.

'And that's not the worst of it. See those hats?'

Lestrade did. Row upon row of them.

'Well, they're held on with the deadliest fashion accessory known to man – hatpins. They can take a man's eye out at forty paces.'

'I can't believe I'm hearing this.' Lestrade was bewildered.

'With respect, Superintendent, you've had it cushy in plain-clothes. Here at the chalkface we're used to dealing with the real world. Look at it – the unacceptable face of womankind.'

Lestrade glanced behind him, then back to Edgar-Smith. 'Give me a minute to talk to them,' he said. 'Has anybody tried so far?'

Edgar-Smith reached forward, patting the pommel of his truncheon lovingly. 'This does my talking for me,' he said.

'Yes, very eloquent,' commented Lestrade. He hauled out his half-hunter. 'It's eight thirty,' he said. 'Give me five minutes. Your word you won't start anything until then?'

Edgar-Smith flicked out his watch. 'Five minutes,' he said, 'then we make some arrests.'

Lestrade nodded. He took off his jacket and gave it to Hollingsworth. He motioned Valentine to him. 'I'm going across to talk to them,' he said.

'Bloody 'ell, guv'nor,' mumbled Hollingsworth, who knew raw courage when he saw it. 'Watch out for your cashews out there.'

'Bless you,' said Lestrade. 'If anything goes wrong, if you see Edgar-Smith go for his truncheon, then stop him. I don't care how you do it. But stop him. If he's unleashed on those ladies, it'll make Bloody Sunday look like a Sydenham Park picnic.'

'We'll stop him, sir,' Valentine assured him and Lestrade turned to face his enemy. Perhaps to meet his Maker.

'Which one is Mrs Pankhurst?' he asked without turning.

'In the centre,' Edgar-Smith told him. 'The square-faced old boot under the WSPU banner.'

Lestrade strolled out from the line of blue. A murmur rose from the crowd to his left and right. Knuckles whitened on flagpoles; boots stiffened in stirrups. Valentine whispered to the nearest copper to block the way in front of the horses in the event of trouble.

An umpire, already swathed from head to foot in other people's sweaters, ran across to the bare-headed, shirt-sleeved Superintendent. Valentine looked on. Was this the end of the umpire?

'Excuse me,' the umpire said, 'the chaps are wondering when we can start play.'

Lestrade kept his eyes fixed on the knot of ladies in the centre. 'We'll let you know,' he said. 'In the meantime, keep them back. We can't be held responsible.'

The umpire melted away, shrugging to the pavilion as he went. Lestrade came to within a dozen or so yards of the ladies' line when three huge women crossed his path.

'We are the Forlorn Hope,' one of them said. 'To reach our leader, you must pass through us.'

'Mrs Pankhurst?' Lestrade shouted. The name rang around the Oval, echoing and re-echoing in the morning. The women took up the chant, 'Pankhurst! Pankhurst!'

The crowd started to boo and hiss. Edgar-Smith's men drew their truncheons and carried them at the slope, against their shoulders. In a moment of indecision, the bobbies shifted feet, leaving gaps for their horsed colleagues to ride through.

There was movement behind the Forlorn Hope and the chanting subsided. A small woman in the colours of her order squeezed through powerful biceps to confront Lestrade.

'Superintendent Lestrade, madam,' he said, 'Scotland Yard.'

'Pig!' an elderly voice screamed from the ranks.

There was laughter.

'We've met, Superintendent. Though I believe you were an Inspector then.'

'Indeed we have, madam. The Hallowed House case. You were a lady then.'

It was the wrong thing to say. A stone hurtled from nowhere to ping painfully off Lestrade's nose. He felt his eyes fill with tears and the blood trickle over his moustache. But he didn't flinch. He knew that if he crouched now or changed position in any way, Edgar-Smith would have a field day.

'Please, Mr Lestrade,' Mrs Pankhurst said. 'We don't want to hurt anyone,' but the glint in the eyes of the Forlorn Hope told him otherwise. 'We merely intend to disrupt this gentlemen's game. Women have been playing cricket since the eighteenth century, you know.'

Lestrade didn't know. 'You are free to continue playing, madam.' He said as distinctly as possible with a mouthful of blood.

'But that's just what we can't do,' she told him. 'Not here. Not at Lord's. Not at any of the county grounds. There is no Ladies' Taverners. No phrase such as Ladies and Players. There are no groundswomen. And why is the last batter not known as twelfth woman? Look behind you, Mr Lestrade.' The little grey woman pointed to the line of mounted police, the horses tossing their heads and flicking their tails. 'They smell blood,' she said. 'That is the unacceptable face of Asquith's Britain.'

Silence fell. Lestrade closed – one step, two. He felt his nose beginning to spread across his cheeks. The Forlorn Hope flanked their general, hatpins gleaming in their hands.

'They will ride you down, Mrs Pankhurst,' Lestrade whispered. 'The man at their head is an animal. His sole regret in life is that his men's truncheons aren't longer. Tell your men – er . . . your ladies – to go home. There's nothing to be achieved here.'

She moved closer to him. One step. Two. They were almost nose to nose. 'I wish I could, Mr Lestrade,' she said.

There was silence again. Then a voice to Lestrade's right shattered the morning. 'Oh, bugger this!' All eyes turned to see a little man from the crowd hop over the white fence and scurry across the hallowed turf towards the left wing of Mrs Pankhurst's army. 'Ethel, you're coming home this minute, my girl. If I'd a known you'd be here, I'd have fetched a carpet beater to you!'

It was the red rag Lestrade had feared. The left wing recoiled for a moment, then fell back, leaving Ethel alone in the path of her advancing spouse.

'I'm the only carpet beater in our house!' Ethel suddenly shouted and without warning swung her handbag across her husband's head. 'That's for sixteen years of hell, George Witherspoon.'

George Witherspoon swayed for an instant as the blood trickled down through his hair. Then his eyes crossed in disbelief and he went down. Sure enough, as Edgar-Smith had predicted, the left flank surged forward, toppling the fragile popcorn stand as it went. Out of the collapsing hut tumbled an equally fragile popcorn seller, before they ripped his striped apron off and impaled it as a trophy of war on one of their banners.

'Pimlico Vamp Beaders!' Mrs Pankhurst shrieked, waving her arm. There was a ghastly falsetto roar as the purple cohorts of that calling tore along the perimeter fence, punching, kicking, lashing out at the men in the front rows who buckled like a house of cards and fell back, their pride not the only thing hurt.

Lestrade whirled to see Edgar-Smith's truncheon high in the air and his horsemen break forward with the running bobbies. Hollingsworth in a crucial moment of decision tried to see if it was possible to trip up a horse. It wasn't and he rolled to the ground, clutching his ankle in agony. Valentine, eager, resourceful, a young detective in a hurry, mindful of his guv'nor's words and vaguely aware of the actions of the 92nd Foot at Waterloo, grabbed stirrup leathers to right and left and lifted his feet off the ground. That too failed and he landed painfully on his face amid the droppings of Edgar-Smith's horses.

Now the right wing, stronger, more determined, snatched their handbags and dashed forward at Mrs Pankhurst's command. The Confirmation Wreath Makers were a doughty lot, piercing the blue sky with their staves, shrieking like banshees. Lestrade lunged for the general and briefly, in the dust of the Oval, he and Mrs Pankhurst danced what was almost a polka before he was beaten to the ground by all three of the Forlorn Hope.

'The main body will advance,' he heard the general shout. 'We are Emancipated Women. We cannot fail.'

On the steps of the pavilion the Surrey XI and the Middlesex XI forgot their enmity born of leather and willow. The umpire pointed in appalled and silent disbelief before the strangled cry burst from his lips. 'They're going for the square. The stumps. My God, the stumps.'

A thousand heels bit deep into the hallowed turf. As the Vamp Beaders crossed to the centre, they were hit in the flank by twenty-two white-clad cricketers, their blood up, trying to snatch the wickets from the jaws of death itself. In the event, it was Edgar-Smith's horsemen who did more damage, cantering across the Silly Mid On and into the Slips. Wickets, balls, batsmen, bowlers and ladies by the dozen tumbled to them and the Oval became a battlefield that day in July, the Year of Our Lord 1908.

As the blue helmets of reinforcements rushed across the pitch, as cricketers sat with their bloodied pads and broken stumps, crying into their tasselled caps, ladies sheathed their hatpins and quickly dropped piles of masonry from their handbags. The banners came down, the lathered horses wheeled into line again.

A battered Superintendent Lestrade, his nose black and red, his waistcoat brown with the sacred soil of Surrey, stumbled back to his own lines. Valentine and Hollingsworth were there, looking worse than he did.

'Sorry, sir,' gasped Valentine. 'We did what we could.'

Lestrade nodded. He noticed a placard lying in the dust that read 'Hang Winston Churchill'. He picked it up. 'Evidence,' he smiled at a red-faced bobby, 'Inspector Edgar-Smith.'

The Inspector saluted with his truncheon and wheeled his roan to the head of his troops.

'For all you've done today,' wheezed Lestrade, returning the salute with the placard. Suddenly, he twisted it, whirling it up in both hands, and brought it cracking down on the man's helmet. The truncheon fell from his grasp, the reins hung slack and an insensible Inspector of the Mounted Division rolled quietly over his crupper and lay still.

There was a deafening cheer from the ladies and, had they been able to break the police cordon, they would have carried Lestrade from the field, shoulder high.

5

Death in the Fives Court

On the day that the Americans pulled out of the four hundred metres re-run, the day that 'Jock' Halsewelle ran it alone in fifty seconds dead, the day that Richard Grant earned the Headline of the Year award with HALSEWELLE THAT ENDS WELL, Sholto Lestrade was on the carpet (again) in the office of the Assistant Commissioner of the Police of the Metropolis.

Edward Henry was the Policeman's Policeman. He had a reputation second to none, this diminutive copper who had tamed a sub-continent and brought the word 'dabs' to the civilized world. He had read the reports, he had seen the Stop Press in the dailies. He couldn't wait for the evening editions.

'Lestrade.' He looked squarely at his Superintendent, the boater tucked in the crook of his elbow, the new white bandage across his face. 'I don't know whether to suspend you or shoot you. Good God, man. How could you? A fractured skull, the hospital report says. They're not sure he'll survive.'

'Edgar-Smith, sir?'

'Edgar-Smith be buggered,' snapped Henry, though the prospect was unlikely. 'I'm talking about this fellow George Witherspoon. What were you doing?'

'Attempting to talk Mrs Pankhurst out of it, sir.'

'And you failed, Lestrade,' the Assistant Commissioner reminded him, 'failed signally.' He crossed behind his man, turning with a snarl. 'And as for your treatment of Edgar-Smith! Beneath contempt!'

'He is, sir,' Lestrade agreed.

'Privately, Lestrade,' Henry fumed, 'I happen to agree with you. The man is a perfect pig with all the finesse of a Dreadnought. That's why I've transferred him to the curatorship of the police museum. But publicly, he's resting. I can't have my officers brawling in public. Can you imagine the field day the gentlemen of the Press will have with this? I understand that the ladies of the WSPU have made you an honorary woman?'

Lestrade blushed under the bruising. 'Well, I'm flattered of course,' he said, 'but I couldn't accept such an honour.'

Henry picked up a paperweight, speechless in his fury. But he was a man of decorum, a martyr to restraint, and he put it back again. 'You'd better sit down,' he said. 'If I shot you I'd be arrested and if I suspended you I'd be even more short-staffed than I am now. Apes like Edgar-Smith don't grow on trees, you know.'

Lestrade collapsed gratefully into a chair. 'Indeed not, sir.'

'Bolsover,' said Henry.

'Sir?'

'The Marquess of Bolsover. What news of his son's death?'

Lestrade slapped his forehead and instantly regretted it as the room swam in his vision.

Henry's face relaxed into a look of utter incomprehension. 'You'd forgotten all about it, hadn't you?'

'In a busy life,' he said, 'it's the one thing that had to go.'

'Luckily for you, he's had a stroke.'

'The old man?'

'Yes. He's not expected to recover. In a coma.'

'They buried the boy.' Lestrade at least knew that.

Henry nodded. 'They say it was the post-mortem that sent Bolsover over the edge. That and the shame of suicide of course.'

'But it wasn't suicide, sir,' Lestrade told him.

'Not?' Henry frowned. 'But I read Bland's report. The locked room.'

'I know,' nodded Lestrade. 'But I have a nose for these things sir.' He patted the bandage. 'At least, I did have. It doesn't smell right.'

'Well, it's all that lint, Lestrade,' Henry reasoned. 'Are we talking about murder?'

Lestrade nodded. 'And it's just possible,' he said, 'that it was the first of several.'

'Go on,' Henry cut himself a cigar.

'Anstruther Fitzgibbon, hurdler, is found shot dead in his

99

bedroom in Berkeley Square. William Hemingway, sailor, dies of poisoning aboard an eight-metre boat in the Solent.'

'Yacht,' Henry corrected him.

'No, I'm sure it was the Solent, sir.' Lestrade was adamant. 'Martin Holman, runner, collapses on the track at the White City and dies of poisoning.'

'The connection?'

'Obvious,' Lestrade shrugged. 'All athletes.'

'And Hans-Rudiger Hesse?'

'Ah.'

'You see, I read your reports closer than you do, Lestrade. You said there was some connection.'

'I believe there is,' he nodded, though his report had omitted to say that it was Marylou Adams who had put the idea into his mind. 'But he doesn't fit the pattern. First, he was stabbed. Second, he was no athlete.'

'So he's nothing to do with the others?'

'Well, he was over here to cover the Games,' Lestrade said, 'and he did come to see me for some reason.'

'Nana Sahib.' When it came to memorizing reports, Edward Henry had a great affinity with the elephants.

'Nana Sahib,' echoed Lestrade.

'Four men dead,' mused Henry. 'Two by the same means. How far have you got on Holman?'

'I'm continuing the hunt, sir. He was being blackmailed. The lady in question is currently having her vitals measured on her way to Holloway.'

'Did she do it?'

'I don't think so. Although Holman was about to go to his boss and confess his embezzlement, I don't think Miss Fendyke has it in her. Besides, she doesn't know a fungus from her elbow.'

'So where does that leave us?'

'I have men at the White City night and day, sir.'

'Who do you suspect?'

'Everyone – and no one.' Lestrade thought it best to play safe.

'We can't put a man into every team, Lestrade,' Henry said. 'They'd smell a rat.'

'What about the Press, sir?' the Superintendent asked.

'Are you mad? Give those people an inch and they'll take a mile.'

'I know, sir, but they can also be useful. They can snoop without raising suspicions. They also offer money where we offer handcuffs.'

'Do you have anyone in mind?'

'Two people,' Lestrade said. 'Miss . . .'

Henry held up his hand. 'I don't want to know,' he said. 'If it gets out that we're making enquiries via Fleet Street, we'll all be curating the police museum.'

'I also have a friend who's about to take part in the Olympic fencing,' Lestrade said. 'He's not the brightest chap in the world, but I think he'd be useful.'

Henry nodded. 'Very well, but all this is strictly hush-hush, Lestrade. This conversation has never taken place.'

'What conversation is that, sir?'

Henry actually smiled. Then the telephone rang. 'Yes?' It squawked and clicked in response to his voice. 'Where?' He was suddenly stern. 'When? How?'

He put down the receiver. 'There's been another one, Lestrade.' He looked ashen-faced at the Superintendent. 'A member of the Ladies' Olympic Team.' He scribbled something on a pad. 'This is the address. It's becoming a bloodbath, Lestrade. I want it stopped.'

In those days, the manor of Touchen End could be reached only by road. Old Sir Theobald Touchen had been at Cuidad Rodrigo with Wellington and at the port with everybody else. The one thing guaranteed to get up the old soldier's flaring nostrils was the groan and clank of rolling stock and the snort and growl of locomotives. Legend had it he'd shot one surveyor of the London and Windsor Railway Company and hanged another in his own chains. The accession of the young Victoria had mellowed him to the extent that he allowed a spur to reach to within eight miles. Any closer than that and he'd set the mastiffs on them.

So it was, with Theobald Touchen a-mouldering in his grave, but tradition dying hard, that Superintendent Lestrade alighted at Windsor, and hired a cab the rest of the way. The Fives Court had been the elephant house, a bizarre building full of odd arches and angles, originally the gift of a grateful nation to the crusty old general who, before he stood in the breaches of Badajoz, had been very at home on a howdah. Lestrade fancied that the aroma of the great beasts still lingered in the paddock as he and Constable Hollingsworth entered by a side gate.

A statuesque lady in a figure-hugging sporting costume met them.

'Superintendent Lestrade,' he introduced himself. 'This is Detective Constable Hollingsworth.'

'Frizzie Dalrymple,' she said in an accent bred of Roedean and Girton. Hollingsworth was mesmerized by the size of the lady's frontage, the nipples straining against the linen like organ stops.

'Look at the long-taileds on that,' he whispered from the corner of his mouth.

Unaware of his inferior's surprising grasp of ornithology, the Superintendent swept on. 'Good morning, madam. I understand the local police have been?'

'And gone,' said Miss Dalrymple, 'save for one solitary idiot they've left guarding poor Effie. This is so undignified, Superintendent. Can't we at least carry her indoors?'

'Not at the moment, madam,' Lestrade told her. 'Perhaps you could wait up at the house? My colleague and I will join you later. Could you assemble the occupants?'

'It was a man, of course,' Miss Dalrymple snorted.

'What was, darlin'?' Hollingsworth asked.

She turned on him as though aware of a vague smell. 'I am not your darling, you contemptible little man.'

'Nor anyone else's, I shouldn't think,' Hollingsworth muttered, but he caught the red-eyed gaze of the Super and let it go.

'I am referring to the murder of poor, dear Effie,' she said, returning to Lestrade. 'It was a man.'

'I'm sure it was, madam,' Lestrade agreed. 'Perhaps we could discuss it later?'

She spun on a finely tuned heel and sprinted across the paddock. Hollingsworth felt his eyes water. 'Know what she needs, Super?' he asked. But Lestrade had gone, making a beeline for the Berkshire constable who lolled on the gate.

'Lestrade, Scotland Yard,' he said. 'Who are you?'

'Constable Morse, sir.'

'Who's your guv'nor?'

'Chief Inspector Challoner, sir.'

Lestrade raised an eyebrow. 'Never heard of him. Where's the deceased?'

Morse fumbled with a series of keys on the end of a long chain. He stuffed one into the keyhole of an old wooden door which reached his chin. Even Lestrade had to stoop just a little. Inside was a square court, bounded on four sides by walls of brick and stone. Jutting from the opposite angle was a buttress, newer than the rest, across which hung a white tarpaulin.

'It's under 'ere, sir,' Morse said and peeled back the sheet.

Dear Effie lay on her back over the ridge of tiles. A beautiful girl, pale, deathly pale beneath the short-cropped black hair. She wore the same sporting garment as Frizzie Dalrymple, reaching to just above a pair of dimpled knees. Hollingsworth walked around the body, chewing the tobacco he'd been saving since the station, and stopped short at the upper end of the torso. The same astonishing frontage met his gaze, although by virture of the girl's position, flanking her ears. The difference here was that the singlet was slashed brown with blood, in a double curve that crossed the ribs and trickled down over the breasts.

Gingerly, Hollingsworth tapped the rigid nipples. They hurt his knuckles.

'Super,' he frowned.

'Hmm?' Lestrade was still looking at the well-turned calves and the nailed shoes.

'Does rigor mortis start in your extremities?'

'I think it already has in mine,' Lestrade grunted, squatting with as much grace as possible in a man who had faced a Gorgon not four hours before.

'Have a look at this, guv,' Hollingsworth suggested.

Lestrade came around the buttress and gazed on the pale face. He shook his head. 'Tragic,' he said. 'What? Eighteen? Nineteen?'

'More like forty-two,' Hollingsworth observed and nudged Effie's upper portions with his toe.

'Good God,' Lestrade said. 'Morse, has anybody examined this body?'

'I don't believe so, sir.'

'Who found her?'

103

'Er . . .' The constable consulted the back of his hand. 'Lost my notebook, sir,' he mumbled, by way of explanation. 'Mr H. Bandicoot.'

Lestrade stood up sharply. 'H. Bandicoot?' he repeated. 'Tall bloke? Blond, curly hair? Good-looking in a fairly simple kind of way?'

'Yeah, that's 'im, sir,' Morse replied.

'Do you know 'im then, guv?' Hollingsworth asked.

'Never heard of him,' Lestrade said. 'Are you a married man, Morse?'

'Yes, sir. After a fashion.'

'You, Hollingsworth?'

"Fraid so, guv,' he grunted. 'We've been together now for fourteen years and it don't seem a day too much.'

'Quite. Right then, gentlemen, you won't be too shocked by . . .' and he grabbed the singlet in both hands, tearing it apart in one fluid movement. 'My God!'

All three policemen stared. Above the angry gashes across the diaphragm rested a contraption known to few women and even fewer men.

'Your best guess, then?' Lestrade it was who first had the presence of mind to speak.

'They're colanders,' said Morse. 'My wife strains cabbage in them.'

'She'd strain a lot more than that,' Hollingsworth commented. 'This pair has killed this one.'

He was right. The blood lay congealed and brown on the curled rim below each breast. It was crusted too on the buckles at each side. Hollingsworth moved to run his fingers over the colanders with their aerated nipples the size of golf balls.

'Don't.' Lestrade tapped his hand away.

'You're right, guv.' Hollingswowth looked shame-faced for the first time in his life. 'Not decent somehow, is it?'

'Decency be buggered,' Lestrade said. 'Look at that face.'

Hollingsworth did.

'Now the hands.'

Hollingsworth did. Lestrade held them up to reveal ulcers along the fingers and palms.

'Got a handkerchief, Morse?' the Superintendent asked.

'Yes, thank you, sir. Oh, I see,' and the constable whipped it out.

Lestrade wiped away the brown blood from the chest wound. More ulcers came to light. 'Thank you, Morse.'

The constable could not bring himself to return it to his pocket and stood with it dangling rather stupidly.

'Chrome sores,' said Lestrade. 'Bichromate of potassium. What do we know about this lady, Morse? Did she work in the dyeing trade?'

'You only do that once, sir,' Hollingsworth grinned, but the attempt at levity fell on deaf ears.

'I don't believe she worked at all, sir.'

Lestrade checked the hands again. Beneath the sores, the skin was soft and gentle.

'Right, gentlemen. I want the body taken to the mortuary at Windsor. Is there a telephone in the house, Morse?'

'Yes, sir. I believe so.'

'Right. Hollingsworth, make the arrangements. And before you and the lady part company, I want you to unbuckle that halter thing she's wearing. And when you do, wear gloves. Unless you want to end up like her.'

Lestrade questioned the servants first. He knew the lore of country houses. The master paid the bills and rode the grounds, but those really in the know lived below stairs and they had a propensity for wearing starched white and tugging their fore-locks. It was a dreary day, however, until he interviewed the head-groom-turned-chauffeur, crisp in his plastron-fronted tunic and peaked cap.

'Now, I'm not one to talk,' he assured Lestrade.

'Of course not . . . er . . .?'

'Mansell, sir. His Lordship's driver.'

'His Lordship?' Lestrade had neglected to ask the most obvious question.

'Lord Bolsover. 'Course, 'e's on 'is way out now.'

'The Marquess of Bolsover owns Touchen End?'

''As for years,' Mansell told him. ''Is dad bought it off of old General Touchen before 'Aldane was in the militia. Owns most of Berkshire, 'e do.'

''Aldane?'

'Bolsover.'

'So who was the host for these few days?' Lestrade began a new tack.

'That stuck-up cow Miss Fizzie, I suppose. But they're takin' it in turns while these games is on. Few days Touchen, few days Tranby Croft.'

'Who? The athletes?'

Mansell nodded. 'Athletes, my arse,' he growled. 'They're only down 'ere for the bubbly and the 'ow's yer father in the woods.'

'How's your father?' Lestrade repeated.

'Dead these donkey's years,' Mansell told him. 'That Miss Effie, she was a one. Not that I'm one to talk, mind yer.'

Lestrade loosened his collar and stretched his legs. He offered one of his best Havanas to the man. It must have been the warmth of the library and the glass of port with his luncheon.

'A one, was she, Miss Effie?' He blew careless rings to the Inigo Jones ceiling.

'One? Two at a bloody time more like. Went like a Silver Ghost.'

'Quiet runner, was she?' Lestrade turned his back on the chauffeur and flicked open the locked tantalus with his switchblade. 'Brandy?'

'Well, I'm not a drinking man,' muttered Mansell, 'but seein' as it's Wednesday . . .'

'It's Thursday.' Lestrade thought it best to set the record straight.

'Seein' as it's Wednesday I don't drink, I'll 'ave a small one.'

'Was there anyone in particular in Miss Effie's life?' Lestrade partook of the amber nectar himself.

''Ow about the Second Battalion the Gordon 'Ighlanders?' Mansell sniggered, quaffed the glass, cleared his throat and held his arm out for more. Lestrade obliged. 'No, straight up. I seen 'er in the woods only yesterday.'

'Go on.'

Mansell looked around to make sure the oak panelling could keep a secret; to check that the books were mum.

'I'm not one to talk, you understand.'

Lestrade tutted and shook his head in support.

'It were a man.'

Lestrade collapsed back in the library chair. 'No,' he said.

'They were well away. Didn't notice me, of course.'

'You were alone?'

'No, old Smithers the gamekeeper were wi' me, but 'e's blind as a goat and deaf as a ferret, so 'e didn't twig what was goin' on.'

'What *was* going on?' Lestrade leaned forward.

''E 'ad her fol-de-rols off.' Beads of sweat formed along Mansell's upper lip.

'Did he?' Lestrade whispered. 'Who?'

'Miss Effie.' Mansell began to doubt the basic intelligence of the Yard man.

'No, I mean who was removing the fol-de-rols?'

'Dunno. Couldn't see 'im. It's dark in the woods of an evening'. Nights be drawin' in.'

'Could you hear any conversation?'

'Few "oohs". Some "aahs". One or two "ugghs" unless I'm mistaken.'

'They weren't ones to talk either, then?' Lestrade commented, refilling the chauffeur's glass for the third time. 'Would you say that the man was one of the guests here, at the house?'

'Now you've asked me,' Mansell stroked his chin, 'I knew Miss Effie by 'er whatsits.' He held his hand in front of him. 'I'd never seen 'is thingummies afore.'

'Did you make a habit of looking at Miss Effie's whatsits?'

Mansell was sharp for all his three brandies and he perhaps sensed charges in the wind. 'She left 'em out all over the place,' he complained. 'Full-blooded bloke like me can't 'elp but notice.'

'And Mrs Mansell?' Lestrade arched an eyebrow.

'She ain't got none to speak of. Leastwise I ain't seen 'em since 1879.'

'So she had her blouse off, in the wood the other night?'

'And her corsets.'

'Was she trying something on?' Lestrade asked.

''E was the one tryin' something on,' Mansell told him.

'If you had to plump for one of the guests,' Lestrade tried to pin his man down, 'who would it be; the man with Miss Effie?'

'Now you've asked me,' Mansell realized again, 'probly that big blond bugger, that Bandicoot. 'E looks as if 'e puts it about a bit.'

*

'Put it about a bit, do you, Harry Bandicoot?' Lestrade strolled on the verandah.

'What?' the big blond bugger puffed on his cigar.

'Let's walk by the river. I'd like to see the Fives Court again.'

They left the verandah to the moths of the July evening, dancing and fluttering in their blind quest for the light. The plaster shone white on the nose of the straw-hatted man in his grey serge, so that the watchers from the house thought it was a will-o'-the-wisp against the trees.

'I'm sorry, Harry, I've had to leave you to the end.'

'That's all right, Sholto. Beastly business, this. Nice young thing, Effie Jennings.'

'Was she?'

'Oh yes. Charming. Simply charming. She was voted the Girl Most Likely To in 1906.'

'Yes, I heard something along those lines. How's Letitia?'

'Very well. Coming up to the White City in a few days for my bouts.'

'Aren't you well?'

'At the moment I am,' laughed Bandicoot. 'I'm not sure I will be when I've crossed swords with the Hungarians.'

'Oh, the fencing. Of course. Emma told me all about it.'

'You never write to her, Sholto.' The big man was suddenly serious.

'I know.' Lestrade kept on walking, gazing out on the trout rings that plopped in the evening gold.

'She is your daughter, Sholto. How long has it been since you saw her?'

'Nearly a year,' he said. 'She must be quite a lady by now.'

He rested his arm against the trunk of a gnarled old birch that jutted out over the water.

'She is. Fourteen going on thirty, Letitia says. She misses you, you know.'

Lestrade turned quickly away. 'Look at that, Harry,' he said. 'What do you see?'

Bandicoot scanned the dark line of trees. 'Trees,' he said. 'And there's a heron flying home.'

Lestrade watched the silhouette rise above the elms, its wings huge against the sunset. Then it sank again, silent as it had risen. He nodded slowly. 'I see blood, Harry,' he said softly, 'and mean streets. The cold dark eyes of the people of the abyss. Look at this.' He pointed to his nose.

'I didn't like to ask about the bandage,' he said.

'Not the bandage. The tip of my nose.'

Bandicoot peered. 'I can't see it, Sholto.'

'That's because it isn't there, Harry.' Lestrade was patience personified. 'I lost that to a sabre in Highgate Cemetery.'

'I know,' Bandicoot said. 'I was there.'

'So you were,' smiled Lestrade. 'Faithful old Harry. You saved my life at Hengler's Circus and now you're bringing up my daughter for me.'

'Letitia and I are proud to do it, Sholto.' Bandicoot knelt to pick a rose and tucked it into the buttonhole of his jacket. 'We'd – that is Emma – would like to see more of you.'

'I was saying,' he said, 'the nose I lost at Highgate. This,' he pointed to the bandage, 'at the Oval this morning. I'll spare you the inventory of the rest. It's no sort of life for a girl waiting at home to give her old dad his pipe and his slippers. What if her old dad doesn't come home one night? What if he's lying in an alley somewhere, with a blunt instrument where his head used to be? And even apart from all that, Harry, I couldn't even afford one of her dresses on what they pay me, you know that.'

'I know she loves you, Sholto. And she wants to see you. She'll be at the White City with Letitia and the boys. Promise me you'll see her.'

Lestrade looked at the man's honest, pleading face. He looked again at the livid waters of the lake as the last rays of the sun left them cold to the night.

'I promise,' he said.

'Now,' Bandicoot slapped Lestrade's back so the Superintendent wheezed and stumbled. 'What did you want to ask me?'

'Can we get to the elephant house from here?'

'Yes, just cross the bridge.'

'You'd better lead the way. I'm on strange ground. Tell me about these gatherings.'

'Well, there's not much to tell, really. A group of us from various sports who have been chosen for the Games decided to meet at each other's houses since February and practise.'

'And Effie Jennings?'

'Hurdler with the Ladies' Team. She and Frizzie Dalrymple

were stable fellows, though between you and me they didn't get on.'

'Oh?'

'Well – you've interviewed Frizzie?'

'Not yet. She's the last one, after you.'

'Oh dear. She won't like that. Come to think of it, I didn't see her at dinner. A sure sign she's sulking. By the way, have you eaten?'

'I ate in the library,' Lestrade explained, feeling his feet springing on the planking of the bridge. 'I didn't think it wise to eat with the guests. Why won't she be pleased?'

'Two reasons.' Harry was calling back through the gathering gloom. 'First, she's indescribably bossy. Second, she hates men.'

'Ah.' Lestrade felt his old twinges coming back in his nose. The ones he'd been having since shortly after dawn when the stone hit him.

'Which I suspect is why she and Effie were less than enchanted with each other.'

'I see.'

'Well, the whole thing was supposed to be Effie's bash, actually. I mean, she's a protégée of old Bolsover's . . .'

'Is she?'

'Well, she was, poor thing. Of course, he's not exactly chipper at the moment, is he? But in his younger days he was quite an athlete apparently. Once ran a mile while the kettle was boiling.'

Lestrade was unimpressed. In his experience, watched pots never boiled anyway.

'But as it was, Frizzie turned up and began shouting the odds. Had everybody jumping in all directions. Perfectly vile to the servants. I'm just glad she didn't accept my invitation to Bandicoot Hall. She and Letitia would have been a perfectly matched pair in the Greco-Roman.'

'I'd put my money on Letitia any day,' Lestrade chuckled. 'So she doesn't like men?'

'Didn't you notice her field strip this morning? Green, white and purple. The colours of Mrs Pankhurst's movement.'

'I've seen rather a lot of that recently.'

'Sholto, I have to ask. Your nose? I didn't know you played at the Oval. Sticky wicket?'

'Very,' said Lestrade. 'Let's just say it'll be a long time before

110

the Police XI ask for my services again. I thought a bowler was something you wore on your head. Tell me all you can about Effie Jennings.'

'Well, I'm not one to talk of course . . .' Bandicoot ducked under the trees of the orchard.

'There's a lot of you about.'

'What?'

'Nothing. Go on.'

'They say her pitcher hath been too oft to the well.'

'Do they? Who?'

'People who didn't like her, I suppose. She was a pleasant enough sort, Sholto, but I don't really go in for . . . you know . . . there's Letitia.'

'Never been tempted, Harry?' Lestrade cocked an eyebrow at him. 'Did Miss Jennings . . .?'

Bandicoot flashed a glance right and left. 'As a matter of fact, she did.'

'When?'

'Last night.' He led the way into the paddock before the dark silhouette of the elephant house.

'Last night?' Lestrade stood rooted to the spot.

'We were in the library. A group of us. There was a telephone call for her. When I looked up, I realized we were alone. I made my excuses, as she was on the line as it were, but she motioned for me to stay.'

'Who was this call from?'

Bandicoot shrugged. 'I've no idea, but from the way she was flirting with him, it was a man.'

'Do you remember any of the conversation?'

'Er . . . let me see – "You naughty boy . . . er . . . you're boasting again . . . No, I couldn't possibly . . ."'

'Just the gist, Harry,' Lestrade said.

'Well, it seemed she was arranging a . . . oh, my God.'

'What?'

'She was arranging to meet . . . whoever it was . . . for a game of fives this morning. Sholto, I hadn't connected the two. Until now.'

Lestrade patted the man's iron bicep. 'Never mind, Harry,' he said, 'there was nothing you could have done. Did you see Miss Jennings this morning? Before you found her body, I mean?'

'No. After she . . . became friendly, I thought it best to give her a wide berth . . . er . . . I mean . . .'

'You mean you were hiding, Harry.' Lestrade found the words for him.

'Yes.'

'She tried to seduce you in the library.'

'Right under Gibbon's *Decline and Fall*, all fourteen volumes. The Narwhal Edition, of course.'

'Is there any other?' Lestrade quipped.

'I really don't know,' confessed Bandicoot, to whom the Remove at school had been a second home.

'Well,' smiled Lestrade, 'your secret's safe with me.'

'Nothing happened, Sholto,' Bandicoot assured him, somewhat petulantly, 'nothing at all.'

Lestrade smiled again, enigmatic to the end. He opened the court door. 'Let me draw on your expertise again. Tell me about fives.'

'Well.' Bandicoot walked the perimeter. 'This is the Eton game. This', he patted the buttress where the body had been found, 'is the hazard. You have a ball and you bounce it off the wall.'

'Is it a ladies' game?' Lestrade perched on the hazard.

'Not really. It gets a little rough, you see. Some chaps wear gloves. I don't.'

'So that's it. Just a ball and a hand?'

'Most of us have two, Sholto,' Bandicoot thought it best to remind him.

'Then how . . .?'

'What?'

'Harry, I don't usually confide in members of the public, you know that.'

'I do,' he nodded.

'In this case, I have no choice.' Lestrade closed to his man. 'You played the game at Eton?'

'Of course.'

'And since?'

'Occasionally.'

'You said it was a rough game. What kind of injuries are likely?'

'Well . . . er . . . broken wrists, twisted ankles, the odd concussion when a chap hits the brickwork. That sort of thing.'

'Not a gash across the diaphragm?'

'Where?'

'The chest, Harry.' Lestrade resorted to the layman's term.

'A gash? Is that what happened to poor Effie? I didn't like to look too closely.'

Lestrade nodded. 'My guess is she died of blood poisoning. The cuts must have been made by the edge of her underwear.'

'Her underwear?' Bandicoot was puzzled. 'I didn't realize that whalebone was so vicious,' he said.

'Ah, this is special,' Lestrade said. 'She could have hit the wall, or been pushed. Either way, the effect would have been the same – the metal rim would have been rammed into her flesh. The poison would have done the rest.'

'Why, Sholto?' Bandicoot leaned against the wall. 'Why should anyone want to kill Effie?'

Lestrade looked at the great house, with its twinkling summer lights.

'I may have that answer in a few minutes, Harry,' he said. He felt his bandage. 'Then again, I may not,' and they wound their way to the drive.

Harry Bandicoot was right. Frizzie Dalrymple was not at all pleased to be kept waiting all day. Lestrade sat in the library, careful not to sit beneath the Narwhal Edition, and awaited the onslaught.

'I have no intention of answering any of your questions,' Frizzie told him, tossing her wiry fair hair and tilting her nose under the chandelier's sparkle.

'Then how can I discover who killed Miss Jennings?' Lestrade tried the wide-eyed approach.

'That', Frizzie extracted a cigarette from a little wooden box, 'is your problem.'

'I thought she was a friend of yours.' Lestrade chivalrously struck a match for her, but she struck faster and he merely succeeded in burning her fingers.

'She *was*,' she said pointedly. 'Unfortunately, sergeant . . .'

'Superintendent,' he reminded her.

'Unfortunately, she . . . went with men.'

'Anyone in particular?'

'Anyone,' Frizzie answered coldly, blowing smoke down her quivering nostrils like a thoroughbred on Epson Downs.

'You didn't approve?'

'Call me pernickety if you like . . .' She began.

'Let's keep this formal shall we, Miss Dalrymple?'

'What my views are on Effie Jennings – or any other subject – is strictly my concern.'

'And men?'

'Ah, yes, *that* subject I certainly do have views on. And very vocal ones. Why, for example aren't you a woman?'

It was not a question which had taxed Lestrade often. 'I expect God had His reasons,' he said.

'I expect She did,' Frizzie countered, 'though looking at you now, She certainly moves in mysterious ways. Are there *any* female police?'

'No, madam,' he said and decided not to add his usual 'Perish the thought' for the sake of his vulnerable nose.

'A Women's Parliament met in London last February,' she told him. 'Are you aware of that?'

'Vaguely, madam,' he said.

'The day will come when we will rule the earth, constable. The worm shall turn.'

'Maybe, madam, but until then . . .'

'Until then "Harvest your humbled husbands while ye may". The day of reckoning is at hand, Lestrade. The city of London did the only sane thing in its history by giving Florence Nightingale the freedom of its limits.'

'Quite. Now, about Miss Jennings . . .'

But Frizzie was in full cry. 'Yvette Guilbert summed it up brilliantly last week in the *Westminster Gazette*. Did you read it?'

'No, I . . .'

'Can you read?'

'Well, I . . .'

'She was advocating the wearing of a divided skirt and she said, "Ladies, cultivate muscle, for by muscle only will you conquer."'

'About your underwear . . .' Lestrade began, but no sooner were the words from his lips than the cultivated muscle of Miss Dalrymple's right hand smacked him painfully around the

114

moustache, sending the lint flying and bringing tears to his eyes.

'Libertine!' she shrieked and fled from the room.

He couldn't sleep. It wasn't the harvest moon slanting through the nets and lending the room a lurid glow. It wasn't the fact that they'd put him in the topmost attic room so that his head hit the ceiling with every turn. It was that contraption; the one that had caused the death of Effie Jennings. Hollingsworth had gone off holding the killer corset at arm's length and had had some very strange looks from passers-by. But during his brief interview with Frizzie Dalrymple, Lestrade had noticed something heaving beneath her pale green singlet, something firm and domed, and he had said to himself, 'They can't be natural.' Could it be, he pondered as he collided with the wallpaper one more time, could it be that Miss Dalrymple too wore such an appliance? And if so, did she have a hand in lacing her former friend's with bichromate of potassium?

He wrenched back the linen covers. He crouched upright in the angle of the roof. He glanced out over the leads where the great stone beasts stood sentinel in the moonlight. That damned moon wouldn't help. But even so, he had to find out. He had to know. Was it, he wondered, as he rummaged for his stockings, that Effie had outraged her friend's sensibilities by cavorting with men? Men, the arch enemies? Men, those devils inconsulate? Or was it something darker? Was this another in the terrible series that began somehow with Anstruther Fitzgibbon? Another athlete brought down before the tape? What did they have in common, he asked himself for the thousandth time as he peered round the door. Effie Jennings was a girl and a slip of a one at that. At least, all day, he'd been hearing how people slipped her one.

It was the eighth tread that brought his heart into his mouth. It must have wakened everybody. Even Effie Jennings might have stirred on her cold slab in Windsor morgue. But no. If the house dogs heard it, they were deaf or unconcerned or both. He followed the twisting stairs into the darkness. His white shirt betrayed him at the landing as the moonbeams caught it. The grandfather in the hall below solemnly chimed the hour of two and he flattened himself against the flock, regretting it instantly as his battered nose reminded him of the dawn.

He slithered along the carpet, shuffling rather like his king did on similar nocturnal ramblings in great country houses. But Lestrade's quest was different, his purpose nobler. He had to get his hands on Frizzie Dalrymple's corsets. He had made a note earlier of which door was hers – the green baize at the end of the passage. Here he waited, ear pressed to the panel. Silence. Damn. He'd have preferred it had she snored. Still, one couldn't have everything. He placed a sweating hand around the knob. One twist. Two. A click. The hairs on the back of his neck stood on end. Surely, she'd have heard that? He waited for what seemed an eternity, not daring to breathe. What would he say if she woke up? 'There was just one more question, Miss Dalrymple?' or 'I thought I heard a noise?' or 'I didn't thank you for being so frank?' Yes, that was it. Still, hopefully it wouldn't come to that.

A tipless, bandaged nose came round the door, followed by dark eyes, blinking in the dimness of the room. She'd drawn her curtains. Thank God. The moon was no hindrance now. But conversely the darkness was. He let his eyes become acclimatized. He made out the bed, double, opulent, and the sleeping figure sprawled in the centre. He could see no day clothes at all. They'd probably be in the wardrobe, huge in its mahogany darkness in the shadowy corner. He tiptoed across the carpet, careful to edge round the wash-stand. He sucked in his breath as the marble top collided with his legs. Why hadn't he put his trousers on? The situation was far more compromising than it need have been, although the noise was reduced by less material.

There it was. A pair of canvas and metal domes lay like a model of a bactrian – or was it two dromedaries – on the dressing table. He picked them up carefully. They were heavier than he thought. And he just had time to whip them up the front of his shirt before the light snapped on and Frizzie Dalrymple sat there, bolt upright in bed, screaming. Curse these new-fangled gadgets. What possessed old Bolsover to have electric lights upstairs?

'I didn't frank you for being so thank,' he blurted.

'What are you doing here, you beast?' she screamed, hysterical. 'And what's that?'

She pointed in horror at the two bulges showing through Lestrade's clothes.

'Er . . . nothing, madam. I haven't been well. Not since the operation.'

The door crashed back and astonished faces peered in. Two lady athletes sprinted over to Frizzie and protected her with their bodies. Burly servants threw a ring round Lestrade. Only Harry Bandicoot had a good word to say for him. It was 'Libertine'.

Lestrade was getting very used to the carpet in Mr Edward Henry's office. Rows of Victorian policemen looked down on him from sepia photographs, their arms folded disapprovingly. The Policeman's Policeman sat stony-faced, facing the Superintendent.

'First, you brain a fellow officer in full view of the public,' he said. 'Next you are found without your trousers in a female witness's boudoir. She's filing charges, of course.'

'Of course, sir.' Lestrade thought it best to concur, even without stooping.

'Lestrade, I don't usually pry into the private . . . er . . . doings of my officers. You're a widower, aren't you?'

'Yes, sir.'

'And are there any . . . that is, is there a lady in your life?'

'Not as such, sir.'

'And do you make a habit of breaking into ladies' boudoirs?'

'No, sir.' Lestrade was appalled. This was only the fourth or fifth time he'd done it, and always in the line of duty.

'According to the report sent to me by the local constabulary, you were in a state of arousal.'

'Not exactly, sir.'

'Lestrade.' Henry slapped his desk so that his hand stung. 'I am not going to bandy words about relative degrees of tumescence. Did you or did you not have your . . . membrum virile exposed?'

'I didn't even take it with me to Touchen End, sir,' Lestrade assured him.

'Damn it, man, your . . .' and he leaned across to whisper in Lestrade's ear. Mrs Henry would have preferred it that way.

'How dare you, sir?' Lestrade was outraged. 'What the young

lady saw, in her hysterical state, was this.' He triumphantly produced the domed contraption.

'Good God, Lestrade. Is that some sort of marital device?'

'It could be, sir, but actually it's Bhisey's Improved Bust-Improver.'

Henry's jaw fell slack. 'I don't think this helps your case,' he said. 'What did you want it for?'

'On the contrary, sir. It helps my case enormously. Well, a little. Before I came here at your . . . er . . . request, I sent Detective Constable Bourne on a little errand.'

'Bourne? Oh, yes, I know the one you mean. Rather limp-wristed, isn't he?'

'On the surface,' Lestrade said. 'Well, he's been trailing a man for a few days and I thought I'd give him a break.'

'And?'

'And he visited one Shanker Abaji Bhisey of 323 Essex Road.'

'Why?'

'Because the said Mr Bhisey makes these things. The whole Ladies' Team in the Games have apparently been wearing them.'

'What has this to do with the death of this Effie Jennings?'

'Effie Jennings wore a special one. I've got back the one she was wearing from the laboratory. They are made circular or oval or any other suitable shape and you pump them up to the desired size, by pumping this whatsit here.'

Lestrade did and the dome rose to vast proportions, thrusting the perforated nipple towards Henry's nose.

'But presumably, you wouldn't have just one blown up?'

'No, no, I shouldn't think so,' said Lestrade. 'Both, I suppose.'

'Quite.' Henry handled the device. 'Otherwise one would be blown up out of all proportion.'

'And the other is so small, it's hardly there at all,' Lestrade commented.

Henry shook himself free of the technical spell of the thing. 'How do you mean Miss Jennings's was special?'

'It lacked the padding around the lower rim. It had no ventilation channels.'

'Leading to excessive glowing, I suppose,' Henry suggested.

'Leading to murder. With this edge sharp and coated in poison, all you need do is push sharply and the skin is cut. The

118

rest – the poison travelling around the arteries into the tentacles – is merely a matter of time. Remember that Miss Jennings had been playing fives before she died. Her blood was pumping firecely. It would have been very quick.'

'Do we know who bought this special . . . um . . . thing?'

'Bourne got the name. In Bhisey's ledger,' said Lestrade proudly. 'One Victor Ludorum. I've got my man.'

'No, you haven't, Lestrade. Do you have Latin?'

The Superintendent frowned. 'Not often, sir,' he admitted.

'Victor Ludorum means the Winner of the Games. It was the title given by the Romans to their greatest athletes and charioteers. It is a pseudonym, Lestrade. A sobriquet. Did Bhisey describe the man?'

Lestrade shook his head. 'He couldn't remember him at all,' he said. 'Well,' he sighed, 'back to the shoeboxes. With your permission, sir.'

'No.' Henry stopped him. 'I'll have to consider your future, Lestrade. Carry on for the moment. But for God's sake, keep your nose clean. No, I'll keep this.' He fondled the device. 'Mrs Henry might like to see it – as a curiosity, you understand.'

'I understand, sir,' smiled Lestrade. But curiosity of course had killed the cat.

'My card,' the man with shoulders like tallboys said.

Lestrade had had enough that morning already. A furious Inspektor Vogelweide had hauled an embarrassed Constable Bourne into the Superintendent's office demanding to know why this *schwuler* had been following him. At first he thought it was the cut of his lederhosen or that his luck had changed. Then, on flicking Bourne over his wrist and smashing his head against a wall, he frisked his pockets and realized he was a policeman. Why, he wanted to know, had Lestrade given orders to Bourne to follow him? Was this the Yard's idea of co-operation? Was this how a British policeman extended courtesy and help to a *bruder*-officer, by having him followed? In future, Vogelweide would work on his own and he would only trouble Lestrade again when he needed to extradite the murderer of Hans-Rudiger Hesse.

And now this. Lestrade looked at the card – an open eye and the legend 'We Never Sleep.'.

'Maddox,' the huge man said, 'the Pinkerton Detective Agency.'

'How may I help you, Mr Maddox?' Lestrade was almost afraid to ask.

'It's the other way round, brother.' Maddox slumped in a chair and lit himself a cigarette. 'Smoke?' he said.

'Yes, I do,' Lestrade confessed.

'Well, that's something we have in common,' and he put the packet away. 'Now, look, Lootenant . . .'

'Superintendent,' Lestrade said.

'Right. I'm over here to check up on these Limey officials at the Games, see. Been givin' our guys the runaround. Breakin' the tape an' all.'

'Yeah, well your blokes can't run in a straight bleedin' line, that's the problem,' Hollingsworth felt compelled to chime in.

Maddox sat upright, his massive fist clenching and unclenching.

'I'm sorry about him,' Lestrade said. 'He's got a bad ankle.'

'And a bad mouth,' Maddox added.

Sensing Anglo-American relations were not all, at that moment, that they could be, Lestrade dismissed the constable to make a pot of tea.

'Never touch the stuff,' Maddox assured him. 'Coffee. Black and lots of it. You know, I don't know how you guys stick it, drinkin' that stuff all day.' He reached a silver hip flask from his pocket. 'Red eye?'

'Yes,' Lestrade patted his bandage. 'But it's getting better.'

Maddox shrugged and swigged in one fluid movement. 'Effie Jennings,' he gargled.

It was Lestrade's turn to sit upright. 'Who?' he said.

'Don't come that with me, Lootenant. You're investigatin' the dame's death.'

'No, she had no title as far as I am aware.'

'So you *are* investigatin' her?' Maddox grinned triumphantly. United States, one; Great Britain, nil.

'Just what is your interest, Mr Maddox?'

The Pinkerton man puffed on his Old Glory. 'Effie Jennings was the fiancée of J. C. Carpenter, our All-American star athlete. It's bad enough that your guys loused up the four hundred metres for him, but when one of 'em cuts loose on his girl, well, we never sleep.'

'So I've heard.' Lestrade patted the calling card with his finger.

'What have you got?' Maddox asked.

'An awful lot of paperwork,' Lestrade sighed.

'Come on, Lestrade. I gotta right . . .'

'No, Mr Maddox. I'm afraid you have no rights at all. Miss Jennings is a British subject who died on British soil. That makes it *my* concern and not yours. And if I may say so, Mr Carpenter was one of many.'

Maddox nodded slowly. 'Well,' he drawled, 'I kinda figured that. OK, Lootenant, I get the picture. Scotland Yard ain't gonna play ball, huh? Well, that's all right. Just one word of advice, though.' He stood up so that his Homburg touched the ceiling. 'Don't none of you guys get in my way, y'hear?'

Hollingsworth was entering with a cup of tea as Maddox left and the American dropped his Old Glory stub neatly into the cup. Lestrade noted the curling lip and whitening knuckles of his constable. 'He can't help it, Hollingsworth,' he said. 'He's from the colonies.'

The man from the colonies was as resourceful as the rest of his race. Of the same pioneer stock as Dan'l Boone, Jim Bridger and Davy Crockett, Maddox made for the only other source of criminal information besides Scotland Yard – Fleet Street. Here, under the distant grey dome of St Paul's, between brewers' drays and clerks' articles, moved some of the most criminal men in the world. And most of them worked on newspapers.

Marylou Adams was sitting looking out of the window when she stiffened as a pair of enormous shoulders hove into view, jostling costermongers and barristers aside. Her voice tailed off in mid-sentence, causing Richard Grant to look up.

'Don't tell me the Golden Girl of the *Washington Post* is lost for words.' He frowned and crossed to her. 'Marylou.' He took in the parted lips, the tense stare. 'What's the matter?'

'That man down there.' She nodded towards the big American, looking now for the door of the *Mail* offices.

'Who is he?'

'John Maddox, Pinkerton man,' she said.

'Pinkerton? Well, well. Do you know him?'

'Everyone in Washington knows a man like Maddox. He's an animal.'

'Wonder what he's doing here?'

'I'd rather not find out, Richard. Do you mind?' She turned to collect her hat.

'I'll see you out,' he said. 'In the meantime, we ought to liaise with Superintendent Lestrade, what with that murder at Touchen End.'

'Do you think so?'

'Stands to reason. Effie Jennings was an athlete, like nearly all the others. I'm sure he'd value the female angle from you. By the way, did you know there was a German copper named Vogelweide here in London?'

'No, I didn't.'

'What with your Pinkerton man . . .'

'He's not mine, exactly,' she snapped.

'Sorry.' He sensed a raw nerve. 'But soon, there'll be more coppers to the square inch than victims.'

Grant saw Marylou out the back way, then doubled back to meet the Pinkerton man in the street. Maddox and the Englishman went out in the midday sun.

6

Parry of Sixte

They walked well apart, the two Superintendents. Patrick Quinn was the wrong side of forty-six and the wrong side of Sholto Lestrade. The Strand that morning was busy as it always was. Detective Constable Bourne, smarting somewhat from his rough handling from Vogelweide, was on lighter duties, investigating the theft of some singlets from lockers at the White City. He was clearly the best, nay, the only man for the job, with his vast experience of pleat and ruche coupled with months in Lost Property.

'So how are things in the Special Irish Branch?' Lestrade asked, lighting up a well-earned cigar.

'Special Branch,' Quinn corrected him. 'You know perfectly well we dropped the Irish four years ago.'

'Ah, not all of 'em, Paddy me boy,' Lestrade brogued. 'We've still got you.'

Quinn's hand snaked out suddenly to his left and caught the collar of a passing urchin. Without breaking his stride, he turned the protesting child upside down and shook a packet of cigarettes from his pocket. He trod on the offending articles, cuffed the lad round the ear and walked on.

'So what are your views?' Lestrade asked.

Quinn fixed his eyes ahead. 'You know I cannot divulge,' he said.

Lestrade had heard rumours to that effect, but time was of the essence. 'Damn it, Quinn, I don't enjoy trampling your patch any more than you do mine, but when the Policeman's Policeman suggests we liaise, what's the first thing we do?'

'Look it up in a dictionary?' Quinn was trying to be helpful.

'All right, the second thing!' Lestrade clamped the damp butt firmer between his teeth.

'Well.' Quinn sidled nearer to his man so that serge almost brushed serge at the elbow. 'You know it's international, of course?'

'Oh? Why?'

Again, Quinn snatched a passing lad, swung him round against a shop window and frisked him. He crushed the Weights in his fist, smacked the boy's neck and walked on.

'Stands to reason,' he said. 'Four athletes dead, all of them British. One of them dead before the Games started.'

'Fitzgibbon, yes. So who's our money on?'

Quinn edged closer still. 'Frogs,' he said.

'The French? Why?'

'Alsace and Lorraine,' Quinn confided from the corner of his mouth.

'Accomplices?' Lestrade enthused.

'Who?'

'Alsace and Lorraine. Who's Lorraine?'

'Not *who*, Lestrade,' Quinn snapped, '*Where*. Good God, man, have you no knowledge of current affairs at all?'

'Only Abberline's.' Lestrade admitted.

Quinn's left foot suddenly jerked sideways and brought a lad crashing to the pavement. He hauled the dazed youngster's head upright, snatched the Woodbine from behind his ear and crushed it into the ground.

'What's your name, sonny?' he snapped.

'Harold Abrahams, sir.'

'What do you want to be when you grow up?'

'A runner, sir.'

'Not with that nose, laddie!'

In an instant he was off again, dodging pigeons with Lestrade through Trafalgar Square.

'Who's the victim who doesn't fit the pattern?' Quinn asked.

'Hesse,' said Lestrade.

'And why doesn't he fit?'

'He's a journalist.'

'And what else is he?'

'A German.'

'Exactly,' Quinn beamed. 'There's hope for you yet, Lestrade.

I never really believed that nonsense in *The Strand* magazine, you know. By the way, did Sherlock Holmes really exist?'

'No,' said Lestrade. 'I suppose somebody felt they had to invent him. What has Hesse being German got to do with this?'

Quinn sighed. It was a sigh born of frustration. Of years spent poring over the maps of Europe, the ones that hadn't been rolled up for ten years. 'Alsace and Lorraine', he explained as though to the village pump, 'are provinces taken by Herr Bismarck in 1871. Germany has claimed them for her own. France says they are hers.'

Lestrade blinked. 'So?'

'So,' Quinn ripped a Burlington from the lips of a passing errand boy and deftly kicked him off his bike, 'France is just itching for a chance to get Alsace and Lorraine back. What better way to exact a little revenge on the side, while you wait, so to speak, than to knock off a famous German journalist at an international gathering. It's quite a *putsch*.'

Lestrade didn't see the canine connection, but he let it go. 'What about the others?'

'Well, that's the brilliance of it, Lestrade.' Quinn swung left into Whitehall. 'It's a cover-up, you see. Our man wants Hesse dead, to strike a blow for La Patrie, but he wants it to look like a mass murder. So he kills a few others to put us off the scent . . . And in your case, it's worked.'

'But why *British* athletes?' Lestrade persisted.

'I don't know, man. I only deal with the damned foreigners. I can't do it all, you know.'

He leapt across Lestrade's path and dragged a struggling boy down from a brewer's dray.

"Ere!' roared the brewer, hauling on his reins. 'Whaddya do that fer?'

It was a question which had occurred to Lestrade in the last ten minutes.

'I am Superintendent Quinn of Scotland Yard,' the Superintendent said, plunging his hands into the boy's pockets. 'According to the Children's Act of February last, I have the powers to search the clothing of said minors and to confiscate tobacco as and where I find it.'

He duly found it and crumbled it into the nosebags of the snorting animals. As he turned back, another quarry met his gaze and he bent down in one fluid movement and lifted the urchin on to the back of the nearest dray horse. He hadn't noticed in his zeal that this urchin was rather well dressed, in topper and tails. Not until he began frisking him did he see the gold fob, the studded waistcoat. He looked up with the eyes of a basset hound caught peeing in the larder.

'I am Superintendent Quinn,' he began, 'sonny?'

The eyes and wrinkled face of a little old man met him, sparks crackling from the rubbery ears.

'Flattery will get you nowhere,' the midget croaked. 'I am Mervyn Tiny-Teeny, of Mr Barnum's Circus, and I am thirty-seven years old. Clod!' And the next thing Quinn knew was an immaculate leather boot crunching into his nose and he collapsed gracefully into Lestrade's arms. The midget leapt from the horse's back and bounded away along Whitehall in a series of somersaults.

'Is everything all right, sir?' a passing constable saluted and enquired.

'It's Superintendent Quinn,' said Lestrade, throwing the recumbent form to the uniformed man. 'One too many, I'm afraid. See him safely to the Yard will you?'

The horses shifted uneasily, tossing their heads and rattling their chains. Even the Life-guardsmen looked at him oddly under their flashing helmets. The crowds of children and ladies clustered round them, while a man crouching under a black cloth and clutching a tripod called, 'Left a bit, right a bit. Can't you keep that horse still?' while waving an arm in the air.

Lestrade took it all in in a glance. It was nothing he hadn't seen countless times before. Sharp swords carried at the ready under Queen Anne's arches, plumes gusting in the summer breeze. Milling tourists in mutton chop sleeves and parasols. The ladies were nicely dressed too.

But today something was different. He was aware of a man behind him, walking with a steady, sauntering gait. Once or twice he turned and noticed below the carefully macassared hair a slight groove around the forehead. The face was lean and tanned. Perhaps he was a colleague of the circus midget who had laid Superintendent Quinn low moments before. But he was altogether bigger. Lestrade stopped to tie his shoe on a step and caught another fleeting glance. The man turned to admire the Horse Guards as the cavalry went through their paces, boots clattering on the cobbles, orders barking under the canopy. Lestrade noticed that in his hurry to appear normal, his shadow was reading *The Times* upside down. An Australian, perhaps?

'Excuse me,' a voice hailed him and a little man with a northern accent tapped him on the shoulder. 'Could you tell me which side the Admiralty's on?'

Lestrade stood up so that the man's parting reached his tie. 'Ours,' he said, 'I think,' and wandered away.

He continued to saunter until he suddenly turned sharp left into the yard behind the Yard. In the shadows now, he pressed himself up against Norman Shaw's granite, waiting his moment.

'Cabbie demanding his fare?' Inspector Tom Gregory grinned, hurrying across the forecourt at that moment.

Lestrade waved him frantically away and Gregory veered to his left, whistling loudly, with all the subtlety of a stevedore. The tall man walked past and, as he did so, Lestrade's finger jabbed into the small of his back.

'Right, cobber,' he said, 'this is a gentleman's excuse me. I am the gentleman and you're going to have to excuse me.' He grabbed the man by his collar and swung him against the Yard wall, careful to keep his index finger primed and cocked.

'Monsieur Le Strade, would you please remove your finger from my back?'

'You know who I am?' Lestrade frowned, straightening.

'But *mais oui*,' the tall man said. 'May I . . .'ow you say . . . turn round?'

'Be my guest,' said Lestrade. 'Who are you and why are you following me?'

The Frenchman reached inside his jacket, but Lestrade was faster, gripping his arm.

'Please,' said the Frenchman, 'people will talk. I look like Nelson – 'e of the column.'

'Tips of your fingers, then,' Lestrade told him. 'No monkey business.'

'No, no,' the Frenchman said earnestly, 'I assure you, no business of ze monkey.' He produced a card. 'I am Inspecteur Claude Monet of ze Sûreté.'

'The Sûreté?' Lestrade checked the card. It might as well have been in Greek. 'How is old Goron these days?'

'Old,' Monet confirmed. "E 'as retired. 'E sends you 'is regards and suggests it is time you do ze same.'

'Ah, how kind,' Lestrade said. 'Why are you following me?'

'I wanted to know what you know.'

Lestrade chuckled. 'My dear boy, as my dear old dad used to say, you haven't finished shitting yellow yet. Come and see me again in twenty years or so.'

'I very much regret, *monsieur*,' Monet was serious, 'zat I cannot do zat. M. Hugo will be a little 'igh by zen.'

"Ugo? I?' Lestrade found the conversation difficult to follow.

'Besançon Hugo, ze great French coach. 'E is dead.'

And so he was. Chief Inspector Dew sat in the locker room at Prince's, the club founded in Piccadilly in 1853 for tennis enthusiasts; but times were fraught. Space was at a premium. The courts now rang to different strokes. Detective Constable Hollingsworth was at his elbow. Sergeant Valentine had been there momentarily too. The whole place smelt of cold metal and leather polish and sweating humanities. Lestrade did the introductions – the tall French detective with the mark of the kepi around his forehead.

'Newly transferred from ze traffic,' he explained.

'Traffic?' Lestrade and Dew chorused.

'Doesn't look like a hit and run to me, Walter,' Lestrade said. 'What does it look like to you?'

'Murder,' said Dew, looking vacantly at Monet.

And so it did. The great French coach lay neatly on a trestle table, his arms folded across his chest, a lily clasped firmly in his hands. Lestrade's jaw dropped.

'What's this?' he asked.

'It's a flower, guv.' Hollingsworth was proud of his botany.

'*Le fleur de lys*,' said Monet.

'His team did this,' Dew explained. 'They found him earlier this morning and they laid him out.'

'How did you get here?' Lestrade asked. 'You were at the White City, weren't you?'

'Four days and nights, guv, that's enough for any man,' Dew

128

grumbled. 'I was just on my way home, when a constable flagged me down.'

'And you, Mr Monet?' Lestrade said slowly and loudly. 'How did you know about it?'

'I was over 'ere to watch ze Games. It is – 'ow you say – a vacation.'

'That's what you say, mate,' said Hollingsworth. 'We say holidays, know what I mean, Jean?'

'Zis man is insubordinate, Monsieur Le Strade,' Monet observed as a matter of course.

'Yes, I'm sorry,' said Lestrade, 'he's a Londoner, I'm afraid. What have you got, Walter?'

'Monsieur Le Strade,' Monet interrupted, 'I must remind you zat a fellow countryman of mine is dead. I am ze officer in charge 'ere.'

Dew whistled quietly through his teeth and turned away.

'And I must remind you, *monsieur*, that you are a visitor to this country and as such are here on sufferance. You have no jurisdiction whatsoever. As a favour to Monsieur Goron, for whom I have the utmost respect, you may stay. But only on the condition that you stay quiet until I speak to you. Is that understood?'

Monet nodded. 'I will be as silent as ze grave,' he said.

'So, Walter?' Lestrade smiled at his Number Two.

'Gunshot, sir.' He bent the lily aside with his finger. 'Just here.'

'*Mon Dieu!*' Monet gasped as the bloody shirt appeared above the waistbelt.

'As the grave, remember.' Lestrade spun round to him. He placed his straw boater into Hollingsworth's hand. 'How's the ankle?' he murmured.

'Agony, thanks, Super,' the detective told him. 'How's the hooter?'

'Likewise.' He crouched near the wound, unbuttoning the dead man's shirt and peering down. 'Clean bullet hole,' he said. 'Revolver?' He grabbed a towel lying on a table nearby and wiped the stomach. 'No powder burns. Reasonable distance then. What time did his blokes find him, Walter?'

'About eight apparently. I've had the building sealed off, as you saw, but people are beginning to talk. There's a fencing bout here this afternoon. I've had the manager on my back for the last hour.'

'Eight.' Lestrade checked the dead man's pupils. He was fifty, if he was a day, iron grey, but trim and taut. 'At a guess,' he said at last, 'he's been dead for eight or nine hours. That means four or five this morning. Presumably, there have been sports officials and bobbies tramping all over the place out there?'

"Fraid so, sir,' Dew shrugged. 'Not to mention the Press.'

'The Press?'

Hollingsworth had distinctly heard Dew say that he wasn't to mention the Press, but the Super was the Super and you didn't cross him lightly, if at all.

'Well, a lady newshound anyhow.'

'A lady?' Lestrade cocked an eyebrow. 'Who?'

'Dunno, guv,' said Hollingsworth. 'I only got this from one of the blokes on the door.'

Lestrade eyed him coldly. 'This bloke on the door; does he have any stripes on his sleeve?'

'Could be, sir, could be.' Hollingsworth had a soft spot for the uniformed branch. He'd been one of them himself until recently.

'Well, he hasn't now,' growled Lestrade. 'Have you talked to any of these Frog . . . Frenchmen, Dew?'

'No, sir, I'm afraid I don't sprechen the lingo.'

'Clearly,' agreed Lestrade. 'All right, Monet. Start earning your keep. Where are these people, Dew?'

'Upstairs, sir. The whole bloody fencing team.'

'Right. Monet, with me. Dew, I want a photographer here now. And not that Bailey bloke. He's useless. Who else have we got?'

'PC Lichfield, sir.'

'All right, Bailey it is. Hollingsworth, your job is to find a member of the English fencing team, one Harry Bandicoot. He's probably on his way here now. When he arrives, get him to me upstairs. And don't make a production of it. Hush hush. Clear?'

'As a bell, guv,' and he vanished.

Monet certainly had his uses. Had he not been there Lestrade would have grown old examining the fencers witness by witness. As it was, various *sabreurs* had to keep nipping in and out, claiming via Monet that they had been on the *piste*. Judging by the way they lurched, Lestrade felt inclined to agree. As the police cordon thinned in the street below and members of the public were allowed in for the afternoon's entertainment, Lestrade began to piece together the story.

Besançon Hugo had been highly thought of in the Cadre Noir which Lestrade has assumed, when he thought of it at all, was composed of Negroes. Hugo, however, was as white as your chapeau, especially lying on the table in state, so that couldn't be right. Anyway, he was champion swordsman of the army but had resigned his commission, like a good many others, when that revolting little Dreyfus had been reinstated. Since then, he had spent his time breeding bloodstock and teaching fencing. Some of the greatest names in France – Camembert, Brie, Port Salut – had called him friend. It was natural therefore that he should have coached the French Olympic team and natural that he should check the equipment on the night before the opening bouts.

His body had been found slumped against the far wall, and with the aid of a tape, Monet acting brilliantly as the corpse, Lestrade was able to surmise what had happened. Hugo would have entered by the door. There was a light in the hall behind him, but none in the locker room itself until the gas was lit in the centre of the room. No one could remember turning out the light after the body was found so it was likely that the murderer was lying in wait in the dark. Hugo would have made an easy target framed in the doorway with the light behind him and whoever had fired had done so, Lestrade guessed – and he moved PC Bailey aside to probe with his switchblade the congealed wound – by shooting from a kneeling position. Why? Not a good shot perhaps? A midget? For a moment he remembered the deadly feet of Mervyn Tiny-Teeny, but he dismissed it. Hugo had not been kicked to death.

The point was that a stomach wound would not have killed instantly. Hugo had had time to crawl to the door – the blood smears on the floor proved that. There was blood on the doorhandle too. He tried to open it after the murderer had gone, thoughtfully closing it behind him, but his strength had failed him.

'But of course,' Monet had said when the last member of the

team went down to try his luck, 'zere was zat business wiz ze letter J.'

'What business with the letter J?' Lestrade frowned.

'Ah, I am sorry. Ze last one, Monsieur Alibert, 'e saw zis letter written on ze glass panel of ze door. It was written in ze blood.'

'What?' Lestrade straightened in his seat. 'Why didn't you tell me?'

'I 'ave,' shrugged Monet.

Lestrade fumed. So much for international co-operation. 'J,' he mused. 'What does that mean?'

'It is ze letter of ze alphabet between I and K,' Monet explained to him.

'Brilliant!' Lestrade roared. 'Are we to suppose the late Monsieur Hugo was improving his writing skills to while away the moments as the life force left him? What is the significance, man?'

Monet was silent for a while. 'I was brought up at ze knee of ze great Goron,' he said. 'In 'is Cookshop at ze Sûreté, we learned a ting or two.'

'And which ting is this?' Lestrade asked.

'What none of ze team 'as told us in so many words is zat Hugo was – 'ow you say – anti-Semitic. 'E 'ated the Jews. 'Ence 'is resignation over ze *affaire*.'

'The affair?' Lestrade repeated. 'I didn't get anything about an affair. Who with?' The world was passing him by.

'*Non, non, monsieur*. We Frenchmen refer to ze Dreyfus case as ze *affaire*.'

'Ah, I see,' Lestrade nodded. 'So you think J stands for Jew?'

'I know zat J stands for Jew,' beamed Monet confidently. 'Ze point is, which Jew was 'iding among the épées in wait for him?'

'And why do it in London? Who outside France would know that Hugo hated the Jews?'

'No one, I suppose,' Monet shrugged.

'Precisely. So why not kill him in Paris? Why go to all the trouble to follow him to London?'

'Ah,' Monet grinned. 'To put us off ze scent. If 'e is a Frenchman, even a French Jew, 'e will know 'ow wonderful are ze Fench police. In England, 'e only 'as ze English police to worry about.'

'Charmed,' beamed Lestrade icily. He flicked out the half-hunter. 'It doesn't look as though my constable has found Mr Bandicoot. Shall we take in a bit of fencing, Inspector?'

It had been impossible, at such short notice, to cancel the afternoon's events. People had come from all over the world to see the clash of steel at Prince's. There would have been a riot had they been turned away. Similarly, it was impossible to explain the extraordinary police presence and, however careful Messrs Digham and Berryman had been, there was no disguising a seven-foot coffin with a lily sticking out of the top. When the detectives reached the hall, the first bout was under way, but the murmur of conversation in the audience was of the murder. Someone had leaked the death of Besançon Hugo, and every newspaperman in the building had left the *piste* to hover around the changing rooms, badgering constables and plainclothesmen alike.

Lestrade wedged himself between Monet and a lady with an extraordinary outsize hat whose ostrich feathers got right up his nose. The August heat was stifling and even the open windows only let in more August heat from the burning Piccadilly pavements outside. Fans and boaters wafted the heat around, but achieved little else. Lestrade felt his armpits crawl. Ripples of applause announced the end of the first bout and a tall, good-looking old Etonian took his place on the floor.

'Someone called Bandicoot,' the big-hatted lady read from her programme. 'Fenced for Eton.'

'Who's he against?' the gentleman beyond her asked.

'Jeno Fuchs,' she read.

Lestrade turned to glance at her. There was surely no call for that. The man had only asked a civil question. Monet did not stir. Obviously the French had another word for it.

'Who's he?' the gentleman asked.

'A captain in the Hunyadi Hussars.'

'Damned foreigner,' the gentleman muttered.

This time Monet turned to scowl at him. Lestrade looked stolidly ahead. Then he caught a woman waving frantically at him. It was Letitia, Harry's wife, and to her right, all three waving frantically, the boys, Ivo and Rupert, and Lestrade's own daughter, Emma. His eyes misted a little as he realized again, in her grown-up dress and with the afternoon sun shining on her face, how like her mother she was. It was nearly a year since he had seen her. My God, how lovely she'd grown.

Fuchs and Bandicoot saluted each other with their sabres and at the call 'On Guard' slid their blades together. Lestrade couldn't believe the position of the Hungarian's legs, bent akimbo in the dust particles borne on the sun. There was a slow scraping of steel on steel and judges nodded together as thumbs came down on stop watches. The Hungarian moved like lightning, his blade slicing through the air in a wide arc. But Bandicoot was faster. He caught the impact on the sword-guard and turned it in mid-air to thump against the Hussar captain's chest. Whistles blew amid the applause. First blood to Bandicoot, and both men retired.

Perhaps Goron had been right, mused Lestrade. Perhaps he should do the same. At the far end of the *piste* from him, a second bout, with épées, was just beginning.

He didn't catch the names. He just saw the two men in white salute each other with their swords and put on their masks. They crouched as the Hungarian had done. Then a strangled cry of outrage from the woman beside him brought him back to Bandicoot's bout. 'Boundah!' she shrieked.

'Dirty foreigner!' the gentleman next to her called.

Bandicoot was drawing back from a failed lunge and the ripple of Hungarian clapping was drowned by a barrage of British boos. But the boos rose to a scream and all eyes swivelled to the far end of the hall. One of the swordsmen was staggering, blood trickling from his throat under the mask. He dropped the sword and struggled with his headgear before slumping to the floor on his knee and pitching forward on his face. His opponent stood back, his broken blade still at the parry, shaking his head in disbelief. Judges' whistles shrilled through the hubbub. Mothers turned their children's heads away. Fuchs and Bandicoot forgot their quarrel and dashed down the *piste* to the fallen fencer.

'My God,' muttered Lestrade and snatched the programme from the ostrich-hatted lady.

'Beast!' she bellowed in outrage.

He scanned the page without looking at her. 'No, madam, police,' he said.

'Arbuthnot!' She rounded on her companion. 'Did you see what this beast did? He stole my programme.'

Arbuthnot lifted his nose from his own. 'Well, at least he's British, my dear,' he snorted.

But Lestrade had gone. He and Monet in one less than fluid motion somersaulted over the row in front and travelled across the highly polished floor for some yards on their knees, so that the Frenchman looked more like Lautrec than Monet. When they scrabbled upright, they had to fight their way through a substantial crowd.

'Make way there!' Lestrade shouted. 'I am a policeman.' People parted for him at the back as though he were a leper. But those in front were more obstinate.

'*Pardon!*' roared Monet, slashing the air with his boater. '*Je suis un détective.*'

The Frenchmen in the crowd pulled back, but there was still an inner ring of onlookers.

'I am a doctor,' another voice called. 'Let me through, please.'

The more humanitarian of the inner ring made room, until only a hardened core of the ghoulish stood around the crouching knot of swordsmen in the centre.

'Stand aside, please,' another voice demanded, 'I am morbidly curious,' and the last few broke away, allowing Lestrade and Monet through.

The Superintendent wrenched off the dying man's mask. His nose and moustache were awash with blood and the steel point of the blade lay imbedded upright under his chin.

'*Tonnerre!*' whispered Monet and he crossed himself.

'Who is he?' Lestrade asked, suddenly realizing he was elbow to elbow with Harry Bandicoot. 'Mr . . . er . . .?'

Bandicoot blinked. 'It's me, Sholto,' he said.

He noticed Lestrade's flickering left eye and couldn't make sense of it. Perhaps his old guv'nor had become a prey to nervous disorders since they had last met.

'Do I know you, sir?' Lestrade said pointedly.

Bandicoot swept off the mesh and canvas of his mask. 'Of course . . .' and he winced as Lestrade's boot took the skin off his white-stockinged shin, '. . . you don't. Who are you?'

'Superintendent Lestrade,' he said, 'Scotland Yard.'

'This is Hilary Term,' Bandicoot told him, 'the Cambridge Blue.'

The fencer of that name caught Lestrade's sleeve as the Superintendent crouched beside him. He opened his mouth to say something, but the effort was too great and his head fell back into the arms of an official.

'What a tragic accident,' muttered Fuchs in impeccable Budapest English.

'Accident be buggered,' snapped Lestrade in only slightly better Pimlico tones. 'This man has been murdered.'

The cry was taken up by the nearest bystanders. 'Let me through,' shouted the morbidly curious man, now even more curious than before. But the press held him back. And the Press in the other room, still sniffing the scent of the Besançon murder, now came howling back into the main hall, cameramen with their tripods and black curtains floundering in their wake.

'I want this room cleared now!' Lestrade barked and from nowhere, an army of constables began hauling off the newshounds, shepherding the spectators away.

'Harry,' Lestrade whispered in the mêlée, 'you'd better get Letitia and the family out of here. Things could get nasty. But don't go too far away. I'll want to know more about the late Mr Term.'

'You murdering bastard!' All heads swivelled to the Metropolitan sergeant who, as horrified onlookers looked on, was steadying the throat of Term's hapless opponent prior to sticking one on him.

'Sergeant!' Lestrade shouted, but the fist was mightier than the tongue, and the Frenchman went down.

'*Un moment,*' said Monet, tapping the sergeant on the shoulder, and proceeded to spin him round and break his nose. An English official brought his knee up into Monet's groin and, as the detective doubled up, pandemonium broke out at Prince's in Piccadilly.

'Now would be a good time, Harry!' Lestrade called, but the Old Etonian was busy cracking together the skulls of two Frenchmen.

'*Sauve qui peut!*' Lestrade heard Monet shout before an enormous Hungarian fist made the room swim and the lights go out.

*

They stood with their backs to the river, a haunting pink under the evening sky. The boater-hatted detective with the purple cheekbone looked even sorrier for himself than usual. The Homburged Old Etonian, of course, didn't have a scratch, but he did carry himself a little stiffly.

'All right, Harry?' Lestrade asked. 'How are you feeling?'

'Rather silly, Sholto, really,' Bandicoot told him. 'It's one of the properties of sprung steel that if you step on one end of it, the other end whips up and catches you one.'

'I thought you fencers wore martingales or something . . . down there?'

'Not in the British team, Sholto.' Bandicoot was a little upset that his old friend should mention it. 'I believe the Jocks wear straps.'

'Quite.' Lestrade slid his hand past his bruised ribs. 'Cigar?'

'Thanks. Good Lord, how long have you had that tooth missing?'

Lestrade felt the gap with his tongue. 'About six hours,' he said. 'Did Letitia and the children get away all right?'

'Oh, yes.' Bandicoot eased himself down on to an Embankment seat. 'They're safe and sound at the Grand.'

'Good. Now. Mr Hilary Term. You're my eyes and ears among the sportsmen, Harry. I tried to reach you before the fights started – the official ones I mean – to see what, if anything, you'd gleaned from our fencing team. What happened this afternoon? God, we seem to be having this sort of conversation regularly nowadays.'

'Well, of course, I didn't see it,' Bandicoot said. 'Had my hands full with Captain Fuchs. But what appeared to have happened was that – who was the Frenchman?'

'Alphonse Leotard – I checked in the programme.'

'Leotard probably lunged. The impact caused his blade to break and the point shot upwards under Term's jaw.'

'Is that usual – the blade breaking?'

'Extremely rare,' Bandicoot said. 'I've only ever heard of it; never seen it until now. Of course, there's something doubly odd.'

'Oh?'

'Well,' Bandicoot rummaged in his bag. 'Have a look for yourself.'

He produced the Frenchman's broken blade.

'Where did you get that?' Lestrade was astonished.

'From the floor of Prince's, Sholto.' Bandicoot realized that Lestrade was slowing up.

'But it's evidence, man. I thought Monet picked it up.'

'Yes, he did, but in the scuffle . . . Will there be trouble for you over that, by the way?'

'I expect so,' Lestrade sighed. 'You'll note how we're sitting upwind of the Yard at the moment. I'm giving the place a wide berth as the expectant elephant said. Explain this to me. Cutlass drill was a long time ago.'

'This is the end you hold.' It was not usual for Bandicoot to be able to condescend to his former guv'nor. He was rather enjoying himself. 'With the épée, the idea is to hit your man on the torso with the tip.'

'But that's damned dangerous, isn't it?'

'Not normally, because the tip is covered in a rubber cap. And the steel is blunted anyway.'

'I see.'

'Except in this case.'

'What?'

Bandicoot fished about in his pocket. 'This', he said triumphantly, 'is the point of Leotard's blade.'

Lestrade squinted at it in the evening sun. 'It's sharp,' he said.

'As a needle,' Bandicoot agreed.

'So . . .'

'So someone sharpened the tip and replaced the rubber cap, knowing it would be superficially inspected by the judges before the bout and that, within the first few passes, the cap would come off.'

'Would that be inevitable?'

'Yes,' said Bandicoot. 'Parry of quarte or parry of sixte should do it. Then, there'd be nothing between Leotard's point and Term's throat.'

'So the snapping of the blade . . .?'

'Was by the way. The point should have gone through Term's jacket. Either way, of course, it would be fatal.'

'Risky though,' Lestrade mused.

'Suicidally,' agreed Bandicoot. 'What I can't understand, Sholto, is why Leotard should want to kill his man and do it in such a public way.'

'I think you've missed the point, Harry, unlike poor old Term. Leotard is just a prawn in a much greater game.'

Lestrade knew of old the glazed look in the Old Etonian's eyes and he leaned forward to explain. 'It came to me in a flash,' he said, 'as soon as I saw Term go down. The reason I was at Prince's in the first place today was that Besançon Hugo was murdered last night.'

'I surmised that.' Bandicoot was on his dignity. Having bested Lestrade on the épée, he now sensed the ground slipping from under him.

'It's my guess his death was accidental. He caught someone in the act of doctoring one of the swords – to be precise, that one. I understand from the French team that everyone has their own favourite weapon?'

Bandicoot nodded.

'So Mr X broke into Prince's last night and sharpened the point on Leotard's sword, which means he must have been well acquainted with the team. He was in the middle of this when Hugo found him. So Hugo had to die.'

'So that's what you meant when you said it was risky,' Bandicoot nodded triumphantly.

'No,' Lestrade said, 'the risk came in using Leotard's sword. All right, so the rubber cap was bound to be knocked off. But how could Mr X *guarantee* that the sharpened point would kill his man? If it hit him in the hand, the arm, the leg, it would wound, perhaps only scratch. He couldn't know that Leotard's blade would snap and drive it into an unprotected part of the body.'

'Oh.'

'Unless . . .'

'Unless what?'

'Unless what Mr X was going to do when Hugo interrupted him was to smear poison on the tip.'

'Poison?'

Lestrade nodded. 'That would be certain to kill, wherever it landed. As long as Leotard was half-way decent as a fencer, he'd be bound to draw blood, wouldn't he, with a sharpened tip?'

'Almost certainly,' said Bandicoot.

'But when Hugo disturbed him, Mr X lost his nerve and ran.'

'So it's *another* of the French team.' Bandicoot wrestled with the logic of it all – a sport in which he was ill equipped to compete. 'You are actually looking for *Monsieur* X.'

'I don't think so, Harry,' Lestrade sighed, leaning back. 'Think about it for a moment. Hugo is killed – shot from close range. Why?'

'Er . . . because he disturbed Mr X.' Bandicoot breathed a sigh of relief. He hadn't realized Lestrade would be asking questions.

'Precisely, but why go that far? If Mr X was a member of the French fencing team, couldn't he have dreamed up some excuse for being there, in those changing rooms, even in the wee small hours? Checking his kit one last time or something?'

'Er . . . yes, I suppose so.'

'No. Mr X was someone who should definitely *not* have been there, yet perhaps – and this is mere injecture of course – perhaps it was someone he knew and would recognize again. Know what I mean, Harry?'

'Er . . .'

Lestrade nodded grimly. 'Quite. One of the *English* fencing team,' he said. 'Tomorrow, Harry, I'll start working my way through them. Can you spare me ten minutes? I don't want to blow your cover. It's important that you and I remain at arm's length as it were. You're still valuable as my man on the inside.'

The body of Hilary Term, Cambridge Blue, gave Lestrade little he didn't already know. The bruising high on the chest, the jagged wound below the jaw, the severed tongue, it all underlined Bandicoot's injecture as to how Leotard's blade had been fixed. And the details of Hilary Term's life yielded little either. He'd been to Oundle, not yet a hanging offence, and had graduated by rather mysterious means to King's, Cambridge. His undergraduacy had been marked by all things sporting and he had excelled in fencing, being a founder member of a rather esoteric group of handsome, debonair young men who called themselves the Gay Blades. Other than these, he had few friends. There seemed to be no women in his life, but his family were known to be close to General Baden-Powell. On this name in the depositions, Lestrade's purple-ringed eyes rested. The plot was thickening. It was becoming murky, tacky even. And in the midst of it was He of the Big Hat, a little nut-brown man who was the hero of the hour. Lestrade made various enquiries. He of the Big Hat was to be found at that very moment on Brownsea Island with large numbers of rather small boys. He reached for his boater, but as he did so, an urgent telegram reached his gnarled old desk. It was from the Foreign Office. He crept down the back stairs so as not to disturb Mr Edward Henry and hailed a cab in the sunshine.

7

Red for Seven

The ducks quacked at him as he hurried by them. Little children in sailor suits and nannies with perambulators veered out of his path. A middle-aged man in a hurry. Lestrade was no stranger of course to the Foreign Office. They had finished it with an opulent Italianate swagger in the year he'd joined the City Force. It rose like a large public urinal looming over St James's Park.

Its inner recesses he was less familiar with. A pompous flunkey with a smell under his nose showed him up the extraordinary main staircase, the one normally reserved for Ambassadors, Plenipotentiaries and Ministers who had forgotten their Portfolios. He would normally have been whisked in the back way reserved for the men who came to read the gas meter, but that particular corridor of power was blocked by just such a meter-reader and time was of the essence. Gigantic blooms hung in the afternoon stillness and flies droned heavily around the enormous rubber plants. Maids buckled in bombazine, with uniformly steel-grey hair whipped into buns, flitted this way and that, tickling the vast polished greenery with feather dusters.

He was shown into a room with wall-to-wall maps, mahogany desks and indescribable escritoires. On a stiff-backed leather chesterfield sat the stiff-backed leather Secretary of State for the Foreign Office.

'Superintendent Lewgrade, is it?' he said.

'Lestrade, sir,' the Yard man corrected him.

'Quite. Thank you. Hurd, get out.' The flunkey exited. 'You know, of course, of the gravity of the situation?'

'Er . . .'

Sir Edward Grey paced his tiger-skin rug. 'Good God, man, what happened to your face?'

Lestrade looked yellower than normal under the white nose sling and purple eyes. He resembled a rather jaundiced banana split.

'All in the line of duty, sir.'

'Well,' Grey sensed imminent collapse, 'you'd better sit down. I won't disguise the fact from you, Lestrade. The lamps are going out all over Europe.'

Lestrade was unaware of an energy crisis.

'It's all about careful steering, you see, rather than bold strokes. You see that?' He pointed to a machine in the corner of the room. 'Know what it is?'

'Well,' Lestrade was on strange ground, 'it looks like Rintoul's Horse Castrator, sir.'

'Yes, I know.' Grey loosened his collar. 'But actually it's a telegraphy machine of the very latest type. So late in fact that even the Patent Office haven't got one. When anything happens anywhere in the Empire, I am told via that machine instantly – ooh, within three weeks at most.'

'Astonishing, sir!' Lestrade was almost speechless with admiration.

'And it's been telling me some pretty rum things, Lestrade. I don't need to tell you what's going on, of course.'

'Er . . . of course not, sir.'

'First, an Anglo-French Exhibition. Admirable, of course, admirable. I'm a Francophile myself. Up to a point. Yes, I backed them at Algeçiras. That's common knowledge. Wouldn't want my daughter to marry one, of course. Not that any of them would ask her. It's her rat-trap mouth, you see. Got her mother's mouth. Still, there it is . . . Where was I?' He trod heavily on his tiger's head and a solitary glass eye popped out and rolled across the floor.

'The French Exhibition, sir.'

'Yes, of course. Of course. Well, old Henry's kept me informed. Can't get a bally thing out of the Home Office, of course. Helpful as a dose of cholera, they are. But Edward Henry, he's been abroad you see – out . . . there.' He gestured vaguely to all the maps on the wall. 'He understands my position. It's vital to keep absolutely informed, of course. Now, these Games are being sabotaged, aren't they? Who's behind it?'

'I wish I knew,' Lestrade confessed.

'Good God, have I got the wrong man? Henry told me you were on the case.'

'Well, yes, I am.'

'Well, then. The Empire wasn't won by idiots, Lestrade. And it won't be held together by them either. We need results. How many athletes have died?'

'At this morning's count, sir, six.'

'Six. Good God, that's epidemic proportions.' He whirled around several times on the rug, then pirouetted earnestly to alight on the chesterfield by Lestrade. 'You know it's the Turks, don't you?'

'The Turks?'

'This is *absolutely* hush-hush, Lestrade. If a word of what I'm about to tell you leaked – well, I'd have to go back to fly-fishing for a living.'

'Absolutely, sir.'

'The Sultan has been forced to accede to the Young Turks' threats. He's ordered democratic elections throughout the Ottoman Empire.'

'Tut, tut.' Lestrade shook his head.

'You see what's happening, don't you?'

'Er . . .'

'Quite, quite.' Grey patted Lestrade's knee with something approaching patriotic pride. 'Too politic to say so, eh? Good, good. I like circumspection in a man.'

Lestrade glanced down, wondering how Sir Edward's diagnosis could be so wrong, with his hand so far away and all.

'This is the Sultan's way of getting his own back on us in the West. By wreaking havoc in the Games, he hopes to exact some warped revenge. Never trust a man in a fez, Lestrade.'

'Oh, I wouldn't, sir,' Lestrade assured him. 'But I think this particular Turk wears a bowler.'

'Ah, of course. Yes. A disguise. The ingenious little Moslem.'

'No, sir, I mean, I think our murderer is an Englishman.'

Grey sat bolt upright. 'I don't think you've been listening, Superintendent,' he bridled. 'At the very nearest, our man is a Persian.'

'A Persian?'

144

'You know the Shah has been reforming his Parliament, of course?'

'Well, I . . .'

'Well, there you are. Look, I can't be too explicit, Lestrade. You don't have the necessary clearance, you see.' He patted the side of his strong, square nose. 'Trust me, Superintendent, I'm the Foreign Secretary.' He stood up and shook Lestrade warmly by the hand. 'Thank you for coming,' he said. 'The point at issue, Lestrade, is urgency. The Press is having a field day. They're revelling in all this gore. It's bad for the Foreign Office; it's bad for Scotland Yard. Damn it, man, it's bad for Britain. The Union Flag besmirched. Our Dreadnoughts are the pride of the world. HMS *Indomitable* took the Prince of Wales to Cowes last week at twenty-six knots. Twenty-six! That's a lot of knots, Lestrade. We can't lose this edge. We can't let a lot of brown buggers get the better of us. We'll be a laughing stock. Take my advice. You are looking for a Turk, the Younger the better. Or it may be a Persian.' He shook the bewildered Superintendent's hand heartily. 'I look forward to results in my *Times* any day now.'

'Very good, sir,' said Lestrade. 'And give my regards to Lady Jane.'

Lestrade wouldn't have been seen dead taking a lady to the Coal Hole in the Strand. Least of all Miss Marylou Adams of the *Washington Post*. So it was with something approaching horror that he sipped his warm brown ale only to catch her earnest face reflected in the glass. He scrambled to his feet and whisked her into a quiet alcove, where there wasn't too much sawdust.

'Er . . . would you like a drink?' he asked her.

'What's that?' She pointed to his jug.

'Beer.'

'I'll have one.'

Lestrade clicked his fingers and mine host did the honours. It wasn't many hostelries below street level that could boast a Scotland Yard Superintendent as a regular. He was worth cultivating.

'You're looking well,' he told her.

She took in the tired eyes, the bruised cheeks. 'You're not,' she said. 'The last time I saw you you were lying in a hotel room with an icepack on your head. God, that seems years ago.'

'Actually, it was three weeks.'

'And there's been more killing since then.'

He nodded gravely, the froth curling on his moustache.

'I couldn't get to you before,' she said. 'Your man Bourne told me at the Yard you'd be here. I hope you don't mind. I guess you don't have much time to yourself right now?'

'Any news then, madam?' he asked.

'Look, isn't it about time we got to know each other? My name is Marylou. Can I call you Sholto?'

'Of course,' he said, 'Marylou. Any news then?'

She smiled. 'You guys never give up, do you?'

'We never sleep,' he shrugged. 'Which reminds me, have you met Mr Maddox of the Pinkerton Detective Agency?'

Marylou Adams's smile vanished. She closed her eyes briefly. She looked small. Afraid. 'No,' she said. 'At least, not this side of the Atlantic. But I do know him, yes.'

'He's over here to protect the interests of Carpenter, the American athlete. That means I've got a French, a German and an American copper, all falling over each other's feet.'

'Can't they help?'

He looked at her with horror. But he must make allowances. She was female and she was foreign. That must explain it. 'Did you find a connection between Hans-Rudiger Hesse and William Hemingway?'

'No,' she said. 'As far as I know, there isn't one. I went to Reuters. I sent a telegram to Berlin. Nothing. The problem is that Rudi had been in the business for so long, most of his contemporaries are dead and gone. I remembered something though.'

'Oh?'

'In his earlier days he had something of a reputation as a crime reporter.'

'Did he?' Lestrade's ears pricked up.

'Is that a clue?'

'The Yard doesn't deal in clues, Marylou. Only in evidence. That's what I need. And that's what I can't get. But I'll tell you something. I think you're right. Hesse, Hemingway, Fitzgibbon, all the others, were killed by the same hand. And you were right, too, about the "back-up" as you call it.'

146

'I was?'

'The death of Besançon Hugo taught me that. He got in the way and was shot. He wasn't the target at all – Hilary Term was. Hugo happened to be in the wrong place at the wrong time.'

'So . . .' Marylou was frowning as the pattern unfolded before her. 'The murderer usually kills by . . . what? Poison?'

'Usually. But he didn't in the case of Anstruther Fitzgibbon.'

'Or Rudi – the paper-knife.'

'Or Rudi,' nodded Lestrade. 'But he doesn't fit the pattern for another reason. And it has to do with him coming to see me.'

'Why?'

Lestrade shrugged. 'I don't know,' he said, 'but I may know more after I've travelled to Dorset.'

'Dorset? Where's that?'

'It's a little county in the south of England, Marylou. I have to meet a hero of ours I spoke to not a month ago.'

'Who's that?' she chirped. 'I love heroes.'

He raised an eyebrow.

She tapped him with her handbag strap. 'I thought the idea was we were working together,' she reminded him.

'All right,' he smiled. 'But I don't want to read this in the *Washington Post* in three or four weeks' time. General Baden-Powell. Heard of him?'

'The Hero of Mafeking, wasn't he? I was at school at the time.'

'Yes, of course.' Lestrade had no need to be reminded of his mortality. He had been an Inspector, going on Superintendent. For him, not much had changed.

'Is that where Baden-Powell lives, Dorset?'

'No. He's holding some sort of camp affair on Brownsea Island. With lots of little boys.'

'Is that what national heroes do in England?' she asked.

'This one does, apparently.'

'How is he connected?'

'I'm not sure. But in my experience, if a name crops up more than once in a case, it's significant. Anstruther Fitzgibbon was his ADC . . .'

'His . . . oh, you mean his exec?'

'Er . . . yes, I suppose so. And he was on more than a nodding acquaintance with Hilary Term.'

147

'What will happen to the Frenchman Term was fighting?' she asked.

'Well, at the moment, it's manslaughter. But we'll have to see when the bandages come off.'

She fell silent. 'There's talk in Fleet Street of your resignation,' she said. 'That there's to be a sacrificial offering.'

He patted her hand. 'I may be an old goat,' he said, 'but I'm not out to pasture yet. There's been talk of my resignation in Fleet Street since Domesday. I've got a train to catch.'

She stood up suddenly. Fiercely. 'I'm coming with you,' she said.

'Now, Marylou . . .' He raised a finger.

She grabbed it. 'You can tell Baden-Powell I want to do a story on him for the folks back home. Maybe I'll get more out of him than you would.'

Lestrade sighed. Perhaps she was right. There again, the Hero of Mafeking was camping on Brownsea Island with lots of little boys.

Lestrade ought to have known that if he went down to the woods that day, he was sure of a big surprise. Brownsea Island stands in Poole Harbour, a beautiful tract of sand and woodland in that still and sultry August. They crossed by rowing boat, the detective and the lady, while the gulls wheeled above them in the cloudless blue. He watched her reflection in the mill-pond surface and flicked the guano off his sleeve. She twirled her parasol and smiled at him. The pilot slid his oars into his rowlocks, but he was all right and helped them both on to the white sand.

'You've got an hour,' he growled. 'After that I goes. 'Ow you gets back is your own affair.'

'Charmed,' Lestrade sneered at the man, who suddenly closed to him and whispered in his ear.

'The best place', he said, 'is about three hundred yards that way.' He jerked his head to the west.

'Really?' said Lestrade. 'What for?'

The pilot frowned and looked at him strangely. 'It's none of my business,' he shrugged. 'You're old enough to be 'er father, anyway,' and he clumped back to his boat.

148

Marylou linked her arm with Lestrade's, lifting her skirts over the driftwood. 'Where would he be?' she asked.

'Baden-Powell?' Lestrade shaded his eyes with his boater. 'In the thick of it, I suppose.' He fumbled in his pocket. 'Heads we go left. Tails right.' He flipped a coin. 'Right,' he said. 'Left it is.'

They left the beach and the rowing boat swaying gently with the tide and made for the way through the woods. After a hundred yards, however, it became clear that there was no way through the woods. The path ended in a tangle of brambles whose needle thorns scraped the skin and clutched at clothes. There was a stillness here. Eerie. Odd. Out there was a blazing summer afternoon, but in the woods, under the oaks and the silver birch, all was dark, except where the sun dappled through on the rustling leaves.

'Is that where we came in?' she asked.

'Er . . . I don't know,' he admitted.

'Let's face it, Sholto.' She threw her hands on her hips. 'We're lost. I don't believe it. We only left the boat a minute ago and now we're lost.'

'You're the pioneer, Marylou,' he reminded her. 'Aren't you all backwoodsmen where you come from?'

'It's not particularly difficult to find your way around Washington, Sholto. Or Manhattan. Or Berlin. We could shout, of course.'

'Shout?'

'Why, sure. The island can't be all that big. If there's a camp here, somebody would hear us.'

'If there was a camp here, somebody *should* be visible,' said Lestrade.

There was a ripple. Was it laughter? Was it the wind? Every shimmer of the trees made them turn and wonder.

'Is anybody there?' called Lestrade.

The birches answered, sighing, but no one else. He checked his half-hunter. 'Ought to be tea-time,' he said. 'Show me a British officer who doesn't stop for tea and I'll show you a . . .' but he never finished his sentence. He suddenly jerked backwards as though about to go into a foxtrot with unusual vigour. His right leg came up and his shoulders went down and Marylou sprang back in terror as Lestrade hurtled in the air, with foliage flying in all directions, dangling by a liana from one

149

of the larger elms. His head swung with a crunch against the rough bark and the thud was followed by a groan. Marylou's scream ended in silence as the bushes around her closed in and dragged her down. Lestrade saw nothing but stars at first, then he was aware of the bushes growing out of the ground above him as he twirled upside down. The creaking of the rope finally stopped. He strained his head up but the pressure on his neck was too great and he lolled back again. The rope now began to twirl, uncoiling against his weight. As though on some mad merry-go-round, Lestrade twizzled through three hundred and sixty degrees. His life, as well as Brownsea Woods, flashed before him.

''Ere,' he heard a voice squeak, 'this isn't the General.'

'What?'

'The General ain't got a pair of these. Has he?'

'I sincerely doubt it.' Lestrade heard Marylou's voice, tarter than usual, and it was followed by a slap and an 'Ow'.

There was a great deal of rustling and smoothing down of clothes. 'And give me that!' he heard her demand. 'You disgusting little ruffian. I'll put you across my knee.'

'Sorry, missis,' a ruffianly, but rather shamefaced, voice said.

'So you should be. Now, will you please cut that gentleman down? He's gone a very funny colour.'

'Lor,' giggled another bush, 'so 'e 'as. 'Ere. He's redder than me woggle.'

'Who strung him up?' another voice asked.

'Dibbens.'

'I never.'

'It was Dobson then.'

'No, it bloody wasn't.'

'Well, what sort o' knot is it?'

'That's what I'm trying to apprehend,' said the biggest bush. 'As sixer, it's my duty to keep you lot in place. Who tied the bloody thing?'

'You bushes . . . er . . . you boys,' Lestrade croaked, a little strangulated by now, 'please remember there is a lady present.'

'What I can't understand is why these boys mistook me for a general,' Marylou said.

'Not a general, miss,' Dobson told her. '*The* General. We're woodsmen, we are. We wouldn't mistake you for *any* old general.'

'Dib, dib, dib?' a voice boomed through the verdure.

'Yes, General.' A bush clicked to attention.

'Dob, dob, dob?' The boom came again.

'Here, General.' Another bush stood at the ready.

'Dibbens, Dobson, which one of you tied the knot?'

Lestrade tried to twist himself to see who was talking by clawing at the brambles that brushed his fingertips. All he could see from that angle was the beatific face of Marylou Adams transfixed in disbelief. Her eyes and mouth were equally wide.

'Good God,' he heard her whisper.

With a superhuman effort, he wrenched himself round and saw the inverted form of the Hero of Mafeking, his clipped military moustache and steely eyes contrasting oddly with the sweeping velvet day dress he was wearing above the khaki slouch hat.

'Ah, brilliant,' Baden-Powell said. 'Dibbens. Dobson. Well done.' He glanced admiringly at the purple-faced detective. 'The Mysore Tiger Trap. Excellent execution.'

Lestrade swallowed – an odd sensation when upside down. It wasn't exactly his tiger that was sore. And he seriously doubted the excellence of the whole thing.

'And', said the Lieutenant-General, 'who in fact did tie the knot?'

'It was me, General,' Dibbens admitted. The General cuffed him smartly round the head, so that, with Marylou's back-hander as well, the boy looked like a poppy.

'What was the knot?' Baden-Powell asked.

'A timber-hitch, sir.'

'Nonsense.' Baden-Powell scrutinized it around the trunk of the tree, tantalizingly out of Lestrade's reach. 'Dobson, your views?'

The boy in the foliage peered at it. 'Blackwall hitch, sir,' he said. Baden-Powell slapped him heartily round the head. 'Idiot,' he said. 'Tonto,' he addressed the sixer, 'are you carrying your trusty Swiss Army knife?'

'Yes, sir.'

'Did I ever tell you boys the story of the Gordian knot?'

Lestrade gave a strangled cry.

'Would you please release that man?' Marylou was at her patience' end.

'Please, madam.' Baden-Powell frowned at her. 'There are

important lessons to be learned here. I am going to give these boys the benefit of centuries of wisdom. Besides,' he hauled up his skirts and squatted on his bony haunches, 'tigers last for up to three hours in that position.' He cleared his throat. 'There was once a great soldier called Alexander,' he told the boys. The bushes fanned out to form a circle around him and sat cross-legged at the great man's haunches.

'Was 'e as great as you, General?' Dibbens asked.

'Nearly, my boy.' Baden-Powell patted him on the head. 'Nearly . . .'

There was suddenly a noise Lestrade had never heard before. It was the sound of the snapping of the tether of a full-blooded American lady. Marylou Adams grabbed the Swiss knife from the sixer and hacked at the taut hemp. Baden-Powell looked on in horror as the whole trap quivered and then Lestrade crashed heavily on to his shoulder, the rope flying upward like a whip to wrap itself around the hapless Tonto.

'For the record,' Marylou said, folding up the clasp knife and stuffing it into the lad's pocket, 'it was a clove hitch,' and she stooped to tend the swinging detective.

Baden-Powell stood up and thwacked the bewildered Tonto round the ear. '*That's* for failing to handle the six,' he said. 'Come along, boys. We're late for tiffin. Get that camouflage off now. Last one to get his chow is a cissy.'

And the bushes scrabbled away through the undergrowth.

'Well, well.' Baden-Powell crouched beside the pair. 'We've met, haven't we?'

'Superintendent Lestrade,' said the Mysore Tiger. 'I'd like to ask you a few questions, sir.'

'Can you walk?' Baden-Powell asked.

Together, they found out that he could, but only after a fashion.

'Your little hooligans might have killed him.' Marylou turned on the Wolf That Crouches.

'Now, Marylou . . .' Lestrade tried to intervene.

'Marylou, nothing.' Marylou stamped her foot. 'What are you doing with these children? Teaching them to kill animals and people? And why is a Lootenant-General in the British Army wearing a dress?'

Baden-Powell stood up sharply, stung by the rebuke. 'I don't

152

care for your tone, madam,' he said. 'I would like you to leave this island at once.'

'It's all right, Marylou.' Lestrade patted her arm. 'Look, I can stand – really,' and he toppled over sideways.

'I'm getting you out of here, Sholto.' She began to haul him upright.

'No, no,' he said weakly. 'The General is only scouting for boys.'

'We have a law against that in Washington DC.' She scowled at him. 'And we don't have officers who wear frocks.'

'Oh?' sneered Baden-Powell archly. 'I've heard one or two things about John Pershing, I can tell you.'

'Marylou.' Lestrade snatched her arm before the steam came out of her ears. 'Perhaps you can find your way to the boat? I'll join you in a few moments.'

'I'm not sure I ought to leave you alone with this degenerate,' she said.

'I'll be all right,' Baden-Powell assured her, 'though I'm grateful for your concern.'

'General,' Lestrade sat up as best he could, 'could you point Miss Adams in the right direction for the beach?'

Baden-Powell crossed his arms over, fingers pointing everywhere. 'Which one, Lestrade? We're on a bally island don't you know?'

'Don't bother!' Marylou said, abandoning all hope of setting her hat on straight. 'I'll find it myself,' and she crashed off through the undergrowth, pulling leaves from her hair.

'Sorry about that, Lestrade.' Baden-Powell squatted beside him. 'Woodcraft, you see. These boys, Lestrade, most of 'em are from your neck of the woods – the East End. Never seen a blade of grass in their lives. I've seen thousands of them – boys that is, not blades of grass – hunched-up, miserable specimens, smoking endless cigarettes, many of them gambling. I've got 'em trekking, rubbing sticks together, signalling with flags and so on. Seeing old ladies across the road.'

'Why did they pounce on Miss Adams?' Lestrade asked.

'Ah, yes. Obviously, in the gloaming, mistook her for me. Easily done at a distance. I remember old Squeaky Auchinleck in India. Completely mistook the shape of a charging Brahma bull. Well, you only get the one chance, Lestrade.'

Both men nodded sagely, combining as they did one hundred and five years of experience.

'Well,' said Lestrade, 'might I have a word before . . . er . . . tiffin?'

'Of course. Something more about poor young Fitzgibbon?'

'Not exactly. Poor young Term this time.'

'Term? Lord, yes. I read it in the paper. Young Tonto swims across every day to get one from Poole. Bally odd, that. Poor bugger buying it in full view of everyone.'

'Young Tonto? Isn't that usually how you buy newspapers?'

Baden-Powell looked at him oddly. 'No, young Term. Getting killed, I mean. Of course, I hadn't seen him for some time. But I'd heard he was quite a good fencer. Still, there it is. No cavalry training, you see. Gets 'em all in the end.'

'In the throat, sir.' Lestrade was a stickler for accuracy. 'The wound was in the throat.'

'Quite, quite.' Baden-Powell leaned back against a handy trunk.

'Rather odd that *two* young men of your acquaintance should die by violence in the space of two months, sir?' Lestrade ventured.

'Hmmm.' Baden-Powell nodded in agreement. 'Did you get back to old Bolsover as I suggested?'

'No, sir.' Lestrade had to confess that it was the last thing on his mind in the helter-skelter of the past weeks. 'But I understand he is at death's door.'

'Oh, at least,' said Baden-Powell. 'Probably half-way through it by now. Have you tried the Circle?'

'Many times, sir,' Lestrade told him. 'Although of course since that fire in Moorgate Station . . .'

'Eh? No, no, my dear chap. I mean the Poetry Circle. Can't abide the bally stuff myself. Namby-pamby, but young Term was a member.'

'Really?'

'I remember his pa telling me about it. Neither of us approved, of course.'

'Was this at Cambridge?'

'Probably began there. Namby-pamby bally place. But I think they hang out in Bloomsbury now. There's another namby-pamby place, by the way.'

'Thank you, General.' Lestrade staggered to his feet.

'Has it been of use?' Baden-Powell asked.

'I don't know,' he said. 'I hope so. In the meantime, you aren't planning to leave the country, are you?'

'What?' He of the Big Hat winked. 'In this dress?'

That Friday was damnably hot. The flags hung limp in the stillness below the giant bastion of Windsor Castle. Fifty-six men, trim and eager in the sporting combinations of their nations, strained at the leash. The King himself mourned the fact that he was not to run with them. Perhaps forty years and fifteen stone ago. Now he could barely make the rostrum. A roar went up from the crowd as he raised the handkerchief – an old one of Mrs Keppel's – and brought it down with a sudden gesture. The marshal squeezed the trigger and the Olympic Marathon began.

Through street and lane the race meandered, elbows nudging elbows, sweat streaming down foreheads, spittle splashing on moustaches. The pride of Europe ran under the blazing summer sun to the enthusiastic cheers of the crowd. Little boys and dogs scampered with them, snapping at the heels of the runners. Some of the dogs were just as bad. Cyclists pedalled alongside, roaring encouragement, passing canteens of water and refreshing, invigorating cigarettes. Flags and bunting fluttered on the route, toffee apples and candy floss and popcorn wafting on the little breeze that blessed the moment.

Price and Lord took the lead in sunny Southall, fifty yards ahead of the appallingly unpleasant South African, Hefferson, and a diminutive candy-maker. Lord glanced back.

'Don't rate the Eytie, Price.'

Price glanced back.

'Rank outsider. What about the African?'

'Amateur written all over him. Cigar?'

'No, thanks, I've just put one out. I say, what a cracking gel back there. Chest like a rolltop.'

'Now, now, old man. Keep your eyes on the road. Still sixteen miles to go, you know.'

'It's not the sixteen miles that bothers me,' Price admitted. 'It's the three hundred and eighty-five yards the blighters have tacked on the end.'

'Wasn't like this in St Louis, was it?'

'Lord, no,' said Price. 'Mind you, they had bloody Kaffirs running in that one, didn't they?'

'Yes, I seem to remember they did. This chappie behind's probably had them shot. Athens was a bit much though, wasn't it? The damned Greek cavalry as escort.'

'Yes. The running shoe hasn't been made that can stand up to horse shit.'

They high-stepped up the High Street to the cheers of the crowd.

'Good old Pricey!' shouted one.

'Lordy, Lordy!' cheered an American.

They waved back. 'Did you hear about poor old Tyrrwhit?' Lord asked.

'Tyrrwhit Dover?' Price began to squeeze his waist to ease the stitch.

'Yes. He was found dead this morning, you know.'

'No.' Price didn't break his stride. 'Well, I never. Accident?'

'Shouldn't think so. Had an arrow in his back.'

'Good Lord.'

'Yes.'

'Suicide?'

'Tricky, I would have thought.'

'Oh, I don't know. He was a damned good shot, you know.'

Hefferson suddenly loped alongside, his jaw set firm, his arms sawing through the Southall air.

Price nudged Lord and nodded in his direction. 'Kronje was a stinker!' Lord shouted.

'Baden-Powell wears a frock!' Hefferson countered.

The British athletes fell silent. It was fair comment, really.

Hefferson loped through Ealing, his lungs agony inside the huge brawny chest. And the little Italian was at his heels the whole way, a cyclist wobbling beside him.

'Eh, Dorando,' the cyclist called, 'my bum, she hasa gone to sleep.'

'I gotta my own problems,' the little candy-maker hissed and, with a supreme burst, trotted past the South African.

'Hey,' Hefferson grunted, 'King Victor Emmanuel sleeps with his mother.'

'*Basta!*' hissed Dorando, flicking his thumb with his teeth. 'President Kruger hasa the personal body odour.'

And in the streets of Willesden, it was true of many of them.

The little man with the huge eyes and ludicrous cap couldn't believe it as the stadium of the White City rose like an elephant before him. He glanced back. Hefferson had gone. Price and Lord had gone. Only the dogged American Hayes was on the skyline, but he looked a long, long way away. Dorando's pacemaker wheeled with his deadened derrière into the stadium and swung his machine to the left under the archway to begin the final lap around the track.

'That'sa it, Dorando. We'ra nearly there. Only a few more metres. Dorando? Dorando?' He screeched to a halt in the dust and his jaw fell as he glanced back. The little candy-maker was running the wrong way. The crowd were on their feet, whistling, stamping, pointing.

'And Dorando's down, ladies and gentlemen.' Kent Icke took up the commentary over the loud-hailer. 'Like a latterday Philippides, he's fallen over. And he's not wearing armour either. But you don't want to know about my enormous classical background. There are people rushing to him, officials, doctors. He's up. Somebody's dousing him with water. I think . . . Yes . . . I see his shoes smouldering in this intense heat. We're all glowing rather, this afternoon. He's up. Dorando's up. This is astonishing, ladies and gentlemen. We are seeing history made here, today, this very afternoon at the White City. Remember where you heard it first. Oh no, he's down. Dorando's down. They're carrying him now. I've never seen such enthusiasm in a crowd. Come on, Dorando! Come on, you little Italian bugger . . .' And the loud-hailer suddenly hiccupped, but the roar was too great for the *faux pas* to be noticed.

So they carried him across the tape, newspapermen jostling with straw-boatered officials and sprinting policemen. The little knees buckled and he went down for the last time.

It was the American, Hayes, of course, who got the gold. Unfortunate that the officials had been over-zealous and not a little partisan in their aid. But Dorando was sponged down, fanned with towels and given a bottle of Chianti to keep his pecker up. Then they put him into his suit and hauled him back out to the Royal Podium for a special accolade. Twice that day, Dorando passed into history. And Mr Irving Berlin sat down at his tinkling ivories and wrote a song about him.

*

'So, let me see if I've got this straight, Paddy me boy. This wop – what's his name?'

'Pietri. Dorando Pietri. Only those wonderful sports commentators of ours persist in calling him Dorando as if it was his surname.'

Lestrade shrugged.

'You can shrug, Lestrade.' Superintendent Quinn was ever one for putting colleagues at their ease. 'But it buggers up my files no end. Do I put his dossier in D for Dorando or P for Pietri?'

'Hmmm,' Lestrade nodded. 'Life is full of little ups and downs, isn't it, as the calligraphy expert once told me.'

'It's not a laughing matter, Sholto,' Inspector Gregory told him.

'No, Tom,' Lestrade sighed. 'I suppose it's not.' Nothing Tom Gregory said ever was. 'So you arrested Pietri or Dorando or whatever his name is because he ran the wrong way in the Marathon?'

'No, no, Lestrade,' snapped Quinn, reaching for his hip flask, 'you haven't been listening. I arrested him because of his irrational behaviour in front of Her Majesty this afternoon.'

'Really? What did he do?'

Quinn bridled. 'I'm sorry, that's classified.'

'Superintendent,' said Lestrade quietly, 'I have spent most of the evening and night on a very crowded train, jolting and rattling all the way up from Poole. I get to the Yard to check my mail and what do I find? A note from Mr Henry insisting that I work closely with you on a brand new case. Well, let me tell you, Mr Quinn, that I am up to my braces in cases at the moment and I need another one like an orang-utan bite. And will you please tell me how what happened in a stadium full of people can possibly be classified?'

Quinn screwed up his moustache. His nose was still a dull cherry colour from its close encounter with the dapper boots of Mr Mervyn Tiny-Teeny and it was three in the morning. 'Very well,' he muttered. 'As it happened, my stenographer, Constable Venables, was on the spot. Got a mind like a mynah bird. Able to repeat everything anybody says.'

'Get to the point, Patrick.' Lestrade tried to make himself comfortable in Quinn's exceedingly spartan furniture.

'Right. Picture the scene. The wop is disqualified because he's virtually carried over the tape by officials. Oh, and one of Gregory's bobbies here.'

'I've had a word with him, Sholto. He won't do it again.'

'Since they don't intend to hold another one here until 1940, Tom, I don't suppose he will. Go on, Quinn.'

'But the Queen – God Bless Her – took some sort of shine to him. Plucky little bleeder et cetera. Et cetera. So she decided to present him, there and then, with a gold cup.'

'Well, after he'd washed and dressed, of course,' Gregory observed, a stickler for orthodoxy.

The others withered him with their glances.

'Her Majesty said, "You brave little Italian. Please accept this gold cup in gratitude for a valiant feat." The wop then looked at his feet. He was shaking all over. It was the damnedest thing. He took the cup. Then he gave it back. "No, no," said Her Majesty, "you don't seem to understand. That's for you."

'Dorando: "No, I cannota accept it. I killed Dover."

'Her Majesty: "Yes, I know you keeled over, but it doesn't matter. We only count falls in wrestling. Don't we?"

'Here she turned to her equerry for advice. He obviously wasn't very up on wrestling because he had to ask somebody else.

'Dorando: "No, no, Your Majesty. You don'ta understand. I did it."

'Her Majesty: "Indeed you did, you plucky little man. Congratulations. That is why we are giving you this cup."'

'Then what happened?' Lestrade asked, on the edge of his seat with boredom.

'The damned Eytie started blubbing. He grabbed the Queen's hand screaming hysterically.'

'What did you do?'

'Poleaxed the little bastard, of course. My boys were on him like a ton of bricks. He was pretty wobbly after the race, anyway. And of course, he's virtually a midget.' Quinn stroked his nose at the mention of the word.

'What did Her Majesty do?'

'Well, if you knew the Queen like I do, Lestrade, you wouldn't ask that question. Her Majesty just smiled graciously and sipped her afternoon tipple from the end of her cane. But you could see as she signed the autographs, she was totally overcome by it all. I asked her how she felt and she said it must be almost four o'clock. Well, it's the heat and the strain.'

'I still don't see why I'm here,' Lestrade said. 'Deranged Italians are quite rightly your providence, Quinn. As I said, I've got my hands full already.'

'Don't you read the papers, Lestrade?' Quinn snapped, hurling the *Evening Standard* at him.

Lestrade saw it. 'Oh, I'm sorry,' he said. 'I thought you meant newspapers.'

'There!' Quinn tapped the item. 'Famous Archer Found Murdered.'

'Archer?' Lestrade asked. 'Any relation to the Archer-Shees?'

'Bless you, Sholto,' Gregory chimed in.

'Sorry, Tom,' Lestrade said, 'I'd forgotten you were there.'

'Dover,' said Quinn. 'Tyrrwhite Falconhurst Dover. One of the British toxophilites.'

'A poisoner?' Lestrade must have misheard.

'An archer, damn it!'

Lestrade had misheard. 'Ah, I see. You interest me strangely. Go on.'

'Well, that's where Gregory comes in. That's his case.'

Lestrade reached for his half-hunter. The lights never seemed to have burned so late at the Yard. Or was it his half-century and a bit beginning to take its toll? 'Go on then, Tom,' he said.

Marylou Adams stood in the moonlight, framed by the French windows. He crossed to her, still holding the wine glass, though its contents were gone. He reached her in a few strides and took her hand, whispering her name.

She turned from him slowly. 'I'll be going home soon,' she said.

'Will you?' he asked and turned her face back to him.

She nodded. 'When I've found the man who killed Rudi Hesse.'

He shook his head. 'You're a newspaperman to the core,' he said, smiling. 'How is Lestrade doing?'

She sighed and wandered into the garden. The rhododendron bushes were bright under the fullness of the moon and they cast sharp, blue shadows across the lawn. 'I don't know,' she said. 'He seems to think he's looking for a mass murderer. He thinks whoever killed Rudi killed all the athletes as well.'

'Isn't that what you think?' He strolled beside her to the rose-garlanded archway. 'I thought you gave him the idea in the first place.'

'I've changed my mind,' she said. 'It *is* a woman's prerogative, you know.'

'But not a newspaperman's,' he reminded her.

'Lestrade spent most of today dangling upside down from a tree. I just don't think he's the man for the job.'

'Well,' he said, 'let's forget him, then.' He looked up at the clear sky and led her into the bower formed by an angle of the privet. 'The night is young, Marylou,' he whispered.

'No, it isn't,' she argued, smiling. 'That's a cliché that a writer like you ought not to be using.'

They laughed in the stillness. From somewhere, an owl swooped and hooted, ghostly white against the woods. 'I'm glad you came,' he said and took both her hands in his. She gazed into his eyes and saw there sadness like her own.

'Richard,' she said, 'I'm not free.'

'Are any of us?' He rested his forehead on hers. 'Are any of us free?'

'There's something I haven't told you,' she said, closing her eyes. 'That man Maddox. The Pinkerton man . . .'

He placed a finger on her full lips. 'And there are a few things I haven't told you,' he said. 'The world is wide, Marylou Adams. We have room for little secrets.'

Under the branches he felt her cheek, wet with tears, rest on his and he heard her whisper. 'I love you, Richard Grant. I love you. I love you.'

He broke away, holding her at arm's length. 'Better not,' he said. 'The world is a cruel place, Marylou. We must find our way in it alone.'

She looked up at him. 'Always?' she whispered.

'I'm married already,' he said and caught her frown. 'No, not to a woman. To a machine. A machine that hums and throbs all through the night. Listen. If you keep very still, you'll hear it now. The presses, Marylou, the rush and the bustle. That's my life. The only one I know.'

'Always,' she whispered again.

8

The Coxless Eight

'Are you sure this is the way, Tom?' Lestrade was spitting leaves out of the corner of his mouth as he and Gregory trudged upwards through the foliage. 'Only I've seen rather a lot of woods recently and I sort of hoped there'd be a road.'

'Yes, I think there probably is, Sholto,' Gregory grunted, disentangling his lower limbs from the creeping ivy. 'I certainly don't remember coming this way yesterday.'

'Marvellous! Ugh!' Lestrade's boater crunched into an oak bough seconds before his head did.

'Ah.' Gregory's bovine face lit up. 'Here's a clearing. Come on.'

He groped forward through the bushes on to a broad, green sward. As he did so, there was a hiss and a thump and he pitched forward on his head. Lestrade hurtled after him, crashing through the undergrowth, and he crouched over him, the switchblade flashing in his fist. He saw no one, other than the poleaxed policeman, and he hauled the body over. Gregory looked pale, only marginally less animated than when he was upright. Lestrade bent over him, listening at his chest. All he could hear at first was the ticking of his regulation half-hunter. Then he caught a heartbeat.

'Good God!' a voice suddenly boomed above him and he looked up to see a giant man in Lincoln green blotting out the sun. 'You perverted swine! Avert your gaze, Millicent. There are two men here engaging in unnatural practices.'

Lestrade stood up, his parting reaching the bowman's biceps. 'The only unnatural practice here, sir, is that!' He snatched the bow and snapped it over his knee with a strength and dexterity which momentarily surprised him.

'How dare you!' the giant roared, looking helpless with the broken bits stuffed back into his hand.

'Is it all right, Freddie?' a female voice called. 'May I look now? Are the gentlemen decent?'

'One of the gentlemen could well have been dead, madam,' Lestrade said as an elegant lady in muttonchop blouse and long skirts hove into view. 'Thanks to this man's appalling aim.'

'Appalling aim?' Freddie had turned bright crimson above his doublet of green. He looked like a Christmas tree. 'There is the target, man.' He pointed to the circle of straw behind him. 'I was only inches off. At one hundred and thirty yards, that's entirely permissible. Besides, the sun was in my eyes.'

'Tosh, Freddie!' Millicent said and stood beside the fallen Inspector. 'You're below par this morning. Have been for days. Good heavens, isn't this the Scotland Yard chappie who was here yesterday?'

'It is, madam,' Lestrade said. 'And I am the Scotland Yard chappie who is here today. Superintendent Lestrade.'

'Oh, Freddie, it's Mr Lestrade. You remember. He was on the Wild Goose Case in Nottingham a few years ago.'

'Have we met, madam?'

'Millie Blanchard,' she said. 'No. But I read all about you in the *Sagittarius*. Issue Number 34. This man is quite brilliant, Freddie.' She took Lestrade's arm. 'Freddie will sort out your chappie there. After all, it was his shaft that laid him low.' She paused. 'Where did you get him, Freddie?'

Freddie crouched over Gregory, muttering. 'Right shoulder, I think. He obviously hit his head when he went down.'

'Right shoulder? A black,' she said scornfully. 'Only three points, I'm afraid, Superintendent. Oh, but of course you know that.'

'I believe I remember the scores on a circular fixed target, madam . . .'

'Millie.' She nuzzled her quiver against him.

'. . . Millie, but on a man?'

'Well, Mr Lestrade.' She led him away across the green where a line of archers were taking aim in the glorious morning sun. 'Oh, good shot, Jeffrey! We're everyday countryfolk here, Mr Lestrade, we don't deliberately aim for passers-by, you understand, but these woods round here do have a certain amount of wildlife, jays, partridge, even the odd . . .' and she ran her fingers over his lapel, '. . . courting couple.'

'I see,' he said. 'How many points for a courting couple?'

She tapped him playfully with her finger stall. 'Saucy!' she said. 'It depends where precisely the shaft lands.'

He stopped strolling. 'And where precisely did the shaft land on Tyrrwhit Dover?'

'Ah.' She let go of his arm, noting the steely glint in the eyes under the battered brim of the boater. 'Poor Tyrrwhit.'

'I must ask you a few questions, Millie,' Lestrade said.

'Of course. Although we all gave evidence to that gentleman now over Freddie's shoulder.'

Lestrade glanced back to where the giant was wandering across to the clubhouse with Tom Gregory dangling over his back like one of the King's deer.

'Yes,' said Lestrade, 'but that's rather like talking to a wall, so could you please tell me?'

'But of course.' She took his arm again. 'You know, you have a bowman's bicep?' she commented, squeezing the muscle under the serge.

'Well, I promise I'll give it back when I've finished with it,' he smiled.

She trilled a high-pitched giggle completely at odds with her fulsome figure. 'Lemonade?'

They sat under the spreading boughs of an oak at a little circular table and she was mother, pouring the cooling glass for him and fanning herself with her score card. The morning was alive with bees, their murmurings punctuated now and then by the thump of arrow on target and some desultory clapping from the perimeter fence.

'Tyrrwhit Dover,' said Lestrade, suddenly feeling a delicate toe tickling his stockings below his trouser leg. 'Can that be his real name?'

'Of course not, you silly,' said Millie. 'No one would be christened that. His real name was D'Abernon Falconhurst.'

'D'Abernon Dover?'

'Yes. He was called "Tyrrwhit" here at the Lincolnshire Poachers for onomatopoeic reasons.'

'I see,' lied Lestrade.

She sensed that he did not. 'The sound of the shaft, you see. He could equally have been called "Whoosh" Dover, I suppose.'

'Or Eileen?' suggested Lestrade.

She looked at him oddly.

'In what capacity did you know him?' he asked.

'Not very well, really. We were not what you would call . . . intimate.' She fluttered her lashes at him. 'He was a cold fish, Mr Lestrade. He lived for his sport.'

'Archery?'

'Toxophily,' she corrected him. 'The Greeks had a word for it, you see.' She leaned towards him. 'But then, they had a word for everything, didn't they?'

Lestrade really didn't know. If it was not in the first declension in Latin, then it was beyond him. And that left a great deal beyond him.

'How long had you known him?' he asked.

'Let me see, about two years I think.'

'Financial worries?' he asked.

'You impertinent fellow,' she scolded him. 'We hardly know each other.'

'I mean, Millie, did Dover have any financial worries?'

'Well, I suppose since death duties none of us are as socially secure as we once were, are we?'

'Indeed not,' sighed Lestrade, whose salary placed him so far below the paying of death duties that it was off the scale. 'Do you know who found the body?'

'Didn't your man tell you?'

'My man?'

She jerked her head in the direction of the clubhouse.

'Ah. Inspector Gregory. No. His report didn't mention it.'

'I see.' She looked resolutely ahead at the archers practising. 'Well, if you promise this will go no further,' she said.

'Millie,' Lestrade leaned across to her, 'you seem to forget I am conducting a murder enquiry. I am not in a position to promise anything.'

She looked at him out of sultry eyes. 'Very well,' she said. 'I suppose you'd find out eventually. I did.'

'When?'

'Night before last.'

'Where?'

She raised a finger tentatively before pointing it. 'Out there,' she said, 'on the butts.'

'What time was this?'

'Oh, let me see. I got here about eleven. Perhaps ten minutes past.'

'So it was dark.' Lestrade was drawing on years of experience.

'Why, yes, Mr Lestrade. It often is at about that time of night, I've noticed.'

He paused. 'Do I gather you had an assignation, Millie?' he asked.

She looked him full in the face. 'If you mean did I come here for Tyrrwhit Dover to make love to me the answer is . . . that's none of your business.'

'I fear it is my business,' he told her, 'if you hit him in the back with an arrow. What would that be on the score card? Nine for the gold?'

'Your chappie said the shaft pierced poor Tyrrwhit's heart, Superintendent. That makes it . . . approximately seven for the red, I'd say.'

Lestrade edged his chair closer, putting down the lemonade. 'Millie,' he took her hand, 'I'd like you to tell me all about it.'

She glanced at him. 'If I must,' she said. 'You must realize, Mr Lestrade, that I . . . what I am about to tell you does not happen all the time.'

'Of course not,' he nodded comfortingly.

'Tyrrwhit and I had been close. A long time ago, it seems to me now, though it can only have been months. He'd found someone else, you see. And indeed . . . well, so had I.'

'The name of this someone else?' he asked.

'His or mine?'

'Either,' he said. In entanglements like these, he knew it was wise to have as many facts as possible at his disposal.

'Mine is a gentleman named Willie Dod, a fellow toxophilite. His was a trollop named Lucy Trundle.' She scowled. 'Anyway, a lady has her good name to uphold, Mr Lestrade. Tyrrwhit was gossiping, right here in the club, dragging my name through the mud. Willie – Mr Dod – threatened to box his ears, but I planned to settle his hash my own way. I went to have it out with him.'

'Again?' Lestrade checked.

She ignored him. 'It was a moonlit night, the night before last. I knew he'd be here.'

'On the butts?' Lestrade asked. 'At that hour?'

'Oh yes. Whatever else Tyrrwhit Dover was, he was a

166

damned good shot. He could put the light out on a glow-worm at sixty paces.'

Lestrade shook his head, clicking his tongue in amazement.

'He often practised by moonlight. Many's the times we . . . only on dry nights, of course, because of the undergrowth.'

'Of course.' For a copper, Lestrade made a damned good father confessor.

'There he was, half-way through a quiver.'

'He was alive?' Lestrade blinked incredulously.

'Of course he was,' she said. 'I challenged him. Told him where to get off.'

'Did you hit him?'

'I certainly did. Caught him a beauty round the side of the head with my riding crop. Why?'

'That would explain the mark on the face,' Lestrade said. 'My chappie Gregory told me about it.'

'Well, there you are. Anyway, I was ashamed of myself for losing my temper. I'd intended to stay calm, you see. He just laughed. Told me not to be a silly little thing and said he had to practise. The Olympic Tournament takes place in two days.'

'Then what?'

'I walked away, crying. I could have . . .'

'Killed him?' Lestrade saw his opening.

'Yes.' Her eyes flashed fire. 'Yes, cheerfully. But I didn't. I went back to the road.'

'Is that where you'd left your horse?'

'Yes. It was then that I heard a cry.'

'Oh?'

'No, it wasn't like that. It was more an "Ugh".'

'What did you do?'

'I turned round.'

'And?'

'I could see Tyrrwhit standing by the target. He'd gone to fish out his shafts.'

'Who had cried out?'

'It must have been him. I called, "Are you all right?" Though why I can't imagine. I didn't really care.' She shrugged. 'It was for auld lang syne, I expect. He didn't answer. I went over to him. I could see that he was pinned to the target with a shaft through his back. It was horrible.' She shuddered so that her ample bosom rippled.

'He was dead?'

She nodded.

'Forgive me, Millie,' he said, steadying her forearms and feeling the muscles at the same time. 'Do you remember how far in the arrow had gone?'

She looked at him, her eyes frightened with the sudden horror of it all. 'I don't know,' she flustered, then collected herself. 'About a third of the way.'

He helped himself to an arrow from her quiver. 'Show me,' he said.

She took the shaft and held it between thumb and forefinger at the point where it had embedded itself into Tyrrwhit Dover.

'Was the arrow the same type as this?' he asked.

She nodded. 'Yes, parabolic flights.'

'And length?'

She nodded again. 'There was one other thing,' she said. 'When the police pulled poor Tyrrwhit down, I saw the arrow head.'

'And?'

'It had been sharpened to a needle point.'

'I see.'

'An ordinary shaft wouldn't kill, Mr Lestrade. Rather like your chappie earlier. It merely knocked him off balance.'

'What strength bow do you use, Millie?' He studied the yew weapon, lying against the tree.

'Standard,' she said. 'Twenty-five pounds.'

He stood up and led her towards the clubhouse. 'Show me where you were standing,' he said.

'About here,' she said, when they reached the spot.

'That was when you heard the cry?'

'Yes.'

Lestrade stood with her and looked to the butts. 'Which target was Dover using?'

'That one,' she pointed. 'Third from the end.'

He looked to his right. The low clubhouse was some yards away. 'Tell me,' he said, walking her towards the target, ignoring the "Look out there's" from practising archers, 'would the clubhouse have been open at that time of night?'

'Yes. I made a telephone call from there.'

'The clubhouse has a telephone?' Lestrade was surprised.

'Of course,' she told him. 'This is the twentieth century, Mr Lestrade. Which reminds me, are you married?'

'Er . . . no, Millie, I am not.' He allowed the surprise of the question to break his stride. 'What was Dover wearing on the night he died?'

'Um . . . let me think. A pair of Lincoln green trousers – the colour of the club – and a white shirt.'

'A white shirt under a bright moon.' Lestrade was talking to himself. 'Would I be right in assuming that there are bows and arrows in the clubhouse?'

'Oh, yes. We all have our own, of course. But there are spares in case one of us breaks a string or snaps a bow.'

He turned back from the target, impervious to the madly waving archers a hundred and fifty yards away. The clubhouse stood alone with lawn all around it. Beyond it he could see the line of the hedge that marked the road. Whoever had killed Tyrrwhit Dover had crept into the clubhouse, carefully honed down an arrow, and had picked him off in the presence of Millie, from her blind side of the building. Dover's white shirt would have been an easy target, particularly if the man was an accomplished archer. And man he certainly was. Lestrade had handled a bow in the Wild Goose Case, albeit years before. A man's bow stood six foot and had a draw weight of forty-eight pounds. No mere lady's bow could have pierced Tyrrwhit Dover and pinned him to the target.

Freddie came lumbering over the green. 'Your chappie's coming round,' he said. 'Look, I didn't realize who you were earlier. I mean, you won't be pressing charges, will you?'

'That rather depends,' he said. 'Thank you, Millie, you've been very helpful.' He kissed her hand.

'I should have told all this to your chappie,' she purred. 'I'm sorry.'

He shook his head.

'Perhaps,' she looked deep into the tired eyes, 'perhaps we could meet again?'

He glanced at Freddie and leaned towards her, whispering, 'I'm not sure Willie Dod would be very pleased about that,' and he stepped away as three arrows thudded into the target where his head had been.

*

Inspector Tom Gregory sat dazed in a darkened room inside the clubhouse. Lestrade mechanically checked the equipment. Rack after rack of arrows. Row upon row of bows. No problem in obtaining a murder weapon there. And if he'd judged his man aright, no point in checking for fingerprints, either. He'd have worn his gloves.

'What's going on, Sholto?' Gregory blinked. 'What the blazes am I doing here? I've got a corker of a headache.'

'You fell down on the job, Tom, I fear,' Lestrade explained.

'Listen,' said Gregory, 'what's the matter with that big feller in green, the one who looks like Little John?'

'Why?'

'Well, when I came to a minute ago, from . . . wherever it was I've been, he was in a sorry state. Muttering apologies and carrying on. Then he made a bolt for the door.'

Lestrade felt the prickles rise on the back of his neck. 'What did he do, Tom?'

'Er . . .' Gregory had difficulty in remembering. 'Made a bolt for the door, Sholto.'

But Sholto Lestrade had done that himself.

Back to the old places. Where it all began. And all the way, he kicked himself. It was always the obvious things. The things that stared you in the face. He caught the underground train despite the fire at Moorgate. After all, lightning didn't strike twice. Only boilermakers did that. He caught a cab to Berkeley Square. There was no Inspector Bland now. There hadn't been time. He toyed with shoulder-barging the door, but it appeared to be made of solid granite and, anyway, passers-by might call a policeman. Softly, softly, then. But first, a little something for the weekend.

He hailed another cab and spent several minutes arguing directions with the growler. And while he did so, he carefully removed several hairs from the hackney's tail. The surly beast turned to look at him reproachfully and snorted in the hames, but other than that, let him carry on. Luckily, he had found the only masochistic cab horse in London. As the growler flicked his whip, Lestrade turned again to his first obstacle. One click of the switchblade in the right place and the great door swung back. He closed it behind him with a heavy click. Here the hall was cool in the August noonday. He pocketed the knuckle blade and made for the stairs, twisting the greasy hairs as he went. By the time he reached the door of the apartment of the late Anstruther Fitzgibbon, it was ready. Here was the second obstacle, less formidable than the first. But it was no obstacle. The door swung wide under the weight of his fingers. Odd. Bland's information was that Fitzgibbon lived alone save for Botley, the manservant. There appeared to be no manservant. No one at all, in fact. Yet the front door to the apartment was open. Had the Bolsover brood sold up? Was Lestrade now breaking and entering into the premises of someone else? Unlikely. Bolsover was a living vegetable, according to the papers. And his only surviving children had scattered to the winds. Who could have sold it?

Lestrade reached the bedroom door. He placed his fingers against the brass knob. He turned it once. It rattled. But it stood. He wound the horsehair into a little loop, fixing it half-way down its length with a knot which would have pleased Baden-Powell. Then he placed his nose against the woodwork. Its flat tip might have been made for the purpose as it roamed over the surface. Like a demented bloodhound on its hind legs he sniffed the panel. Then he felt it. Too fine for his fingers to have detected, his nose recoiled and he plucked the tiny splinter from it. He took off his boater, snapping the rim still further so that a sharp piece of straw stuck out. He poked it in the appropriate place, routing out the resin with the spike. The damn thing broke at first then he realized it slid right through the door without difficulty. He didn't think it would be that easy. Why had he missed all this when he was here before? He poked the horsehair loop through the tiny hole. A perfect fit. He jiggled it first this way and then that. Then he had it and he jerked sideways. He heard the bolt slide back and he breathed again. Just to make doubly sure, he stayed where he was and slid it back. He heard it snick shut. He was right. Thank God for boring old Tom Gregory and his chance remark. He flicked the horsehair strands again and the bolt shot free. He turned the knob and the door opened. But wait a minute, he reasoned, if the door opened . . .

A hand snatched his tie and he was yanked into the room. He felt a powerful thump across the back of his head and he nosedived on to Fitzgibbon's bed. With a mouth full of eiderdown, he was aware of his right hand being twisted behind his back. Rolling sideways, he threw his assailant over and hit him with a pillow. Feathers flew in all directions and the room appeared full of snow.

'You're under arrest,' two voices chorused fluffily and two men knelt upright on the bed, one with a pistol cocked and extended, the other with a switchblade catching down.

'Inspektor Lestrade,' said one, a little crestfallen.

'Inspector Vogelweide,' said the other. 'Two minds with but a single thought, eh?' Lestrade retracted his blade. 'Would you mind?' He gingerly pointed the German's revolver muzzle elsewhere.

'Ach, zorry,' Vogelweide apologized. 'Does zis mean vot I sink it means?'

Both men eased themselves off Fitzgibbon's four-poster and produced their identical loops.

'Znap!' said Vogelweide.

'Not exactly,' said Lestrade. 'Yours appears to be made of wire.'

'Ja. It is faster. Goes through ze wood easier.'

'Which is why my straw went in so easily. And why the hole was easier to find. You'd beaten me to it.'

'Ach,' Vogelweide blushed modestly, 'only by a few zeconds. No zooner had I zlid back ze bolt zann I heard your straw in ze lock. How did you vork it out?'

'We have our ways at Scotland Yard.' Lestrade remained inscrutable.

'Ach, so,' said the German, 'a lucky guess. I, of course, vas vorking from virst prinziples.'

'Really?' Lestrade refused to be impressed.

'I hev to confess it vas an Englishman who pointed ze vay, ztick in my craw to admit it zough it doez.'

'An Englishman?'

'Ja.' Vogelweide crossed to the barred window. 'John Radcliffe. He wrote a novel called *Nena Sahib*.'

'Don't you mean *Nana Sahib*?' For Lestrade some of the pieces were starting to fit.

'*Nein*. I mean *Nena Sahib* Viz an "e", not an "a".'

'So that's why Jones couldn't help.'

'Excuze me, please?'

172

'Nothing. Go on. What has this to do with the death of Anstruther Fitzgibbon?'

'Viz Fitzgibbon, very little. I am only conzerned viz ze death of Hans-Rudiger Hesse.'

'In that case,' Lestrade began pulling fluff from his hair, 'you're in the wrong room in the wrong part of London.'

'*Nein.* Zis case is most material to ze death of Hans-Rudiger.'

'Would you like to enlighten me?' Lestrade was never too proud to ask for help. Even from a Kraut.

'Of course. Are you zitting comfortably? Zigar?'

'Havana?'

'*Nein.* Turkish.'

'No, thank you. Someone once told me not to trust them.'

'Ach, vell, you are probably right,' but he lit up anyway. 'I understand zat Hans-Rudiger came to visit you at Zcotland Yard?'

'Yes. I was out.'

'Do you know why?'

'No. But apparently he left a message for me.'

'"Nena Sahib",' the German said.

'As I now realize, yes. How did you find this out?'

'Zat lanky *schwuler* in ze funny clothes who passes for a detective. Ze one who was following me viz all the subtlety of an airship.'

'Constable Bourne.'

'*Ja.* Before I brought him back to his ztation in life, I extracted zome information.'

'I'll have his balls for that,' Lestrade commented.

'I fear it may be too late,' Vogelweide said ruefully.

'At very least, he's going back to Lost Property.'

Vogelweide nodded. 'I regret zat Hans-Rudiger did not zee you. If he had he might have been alive today.'

'And I regret that he was so cryptic. What did the message mean?'

'Ach, zese journalists. He obviously thought that the novel *Nena Sahib* would be known to you. Let me explain. Many years ago, Herr Hesse made his name as a crime reporter.'

'Yes, I know.'

'In 1881 he covered one of Germany's most zelebrated crimes – ze Beck case in Berlin.'

'Yes?'

173

Vogelweide sensed Lestrade's ignorance. 'Ze detective vorking on ze case vas Commissioner Heinz Hollman.'

Lestrade remembered that name. He'd heard it at the Art Forgery class. Hadn't he painted Henry VIII?

'Konrad Beck was a . . . how do you say it . . . costermonger. He sold costers for a living.'

'Is that a crime in Berlin?' Lestrade asked.

'*Nein*. But ze hanging of your wife and children, zat is a crime.'

'Beck did that?' Lestrade was horrified. Thank God the British just knocked their families about.

'*Ja*. It looked like zuicide. Frau Beck and her children were found hanging in a locked room. How, Hollman wondered, could a mother ztring up her own children like zat?'

'Was she highly strung?' Lestrade asked.

'Ze answer was zimple. She didn't. Beck killed his entire family and greased ze bolt zo zat he vas able to lock it from ze outside by inzerting a loop of horsehair through a tiny hole. I used vire to test zis case. Unlike you I had no aczess to horsehair.'

'I don't understand where *Nena Sahib* comes in.'

'Hollman noticed zat in Beck's apartment zere vas a German translation of zat novel. It fell open at a page vich described ze locked room murder exactly as Beck carried it out.'

'So when Hans-Rudiger read about the death of Fitzgibbon, he immediately realized the significance.'

'*Ja*. Und came to zee you.'

'So someone came to see him.' Lestrade stroked his chin thoughtfully.

'Prezisely.' Vogelweide leaned back, his exposition complete.

'Who?' asked Lestrade.

Vogelweide's complacency vanished. 'I haven't ze faintest idea,' he said. 'I am ezzentially ze zort of policeman who deals in ze "how" of murder. I leave ze "who" to others.'

'Thank you, Inspector,' smiled Lestrade.

You could probably count on the fingers of one hand (and policemen habitually do) the number of times a Superintendent of Scotland Yard had walked into that establishment carrying a bow and arrow. He got some odd looks from passers-by and some odder ones from the uniformed men who saluted him. Was this it? Had the legendary Lestrade cracked at last? He was at a very funny age.

'Right, Imbert,' he snapped at Special Branch's latest desk man on the shady side of the building. 'Is your boss in?'

'No, sir. I'm afraid Superintendent Quinn and Chief Superintendent Abberline . . .'

'. . . are not up to snuff. Yes, I know. Never mind. The Italian this way?' He brushed past the bewildered twigs of Special Branch who were loafing around looking for someone foreign to arrest.

'I'm sorry, sir, but you can't go . . .'

But Lestrade had. He helped himself to keys dangling from the peg and let himself into the tiny cell in the quiet corner of the Yard. Behind him was the ominous steel door that led to Quinn's Quadrangle. Only once had he entered that room and the objects therein made the Holy Inquisition look like a Sunday school. He glanced at the ripped and bleeding fingers of the Italian.

'How did that happen?' he asked.

The little man with the huge eyes and upside-down moustache stood up feebly at his arrival. 'I fell on the tracka, sir,' he said.

Lestrade looked at the manacles around his ankles and the heavy iron ball rolling ponderously between them. 'Imbert!' he roared. The constable of that name popped his head round the corner. 'Undo these things now.'

'I can't do that, sir.'

Lestrade left the cell, ostentatiously leaving the door wide. He placed an avuncular hand on the man's shoulder. 'Constable, do you know a man by the name of Richard Grant?'

Imbert thought for a moment. 'No, sir. I don't believe I do.'

'Well, he is a newspaperman. Or at least he works for the *Daily Mail*. If I were to have a word in his ear about the state of that prisoner and that cell, you and Mr Quinn would be out of a job.'

'I can't help that, sir.' Imbert stood to attention.

'All right,' sighed Lestrade, 'let me try the more direct approach. If you don't take those manacles off I'll smear you all over the wall.'

Imbert's composure cracked. There was something in the

Super's eyes. He dived to the ground and in the twinkling of those eyes, the chains were gone.

'Thank you, thank you, Inspectore,' the Italian jabbered, kissing Lestrade's hands as he re-entered the cell.

'Not at all.' Lestrade stepped back. 'And that's Superintendente, by the way. Now, Mr Dorando, is it?'

'*Si*, Pietri, *signor*. Dorando Pietri. Ata home in Italia, I maka da candy.'

'Yes.' Lestrade perched on the iron bedstead and patted for the plucky little runner to sit down. 'Now Mr Quinn – he's that nice gentleman with the bald head who has been lighting the matches under your fingernails – Mr Quinn tells me that you say you killed Tyrrwhit Dover.'

'*Si*.' The Italian burst into tears. 'I did. I ama guilty. Confessa me, Superintendente, for I hava sinned.'

'Yes, of course. Imbert, have you a handkerchief? I always like young constables to carry handkerchiefs.'

'Here, sir.' Imbert was still watching those eyes carefully. Lestrade passed it to the Italian much to Imbert's silent disgust and Dorando blew his nose like a howitzer going off.

'There now,' said Lestrade. 'Suppose you tell me how you did it?'

'Ah, *si*. I shotta him with a bow and a arrow.'

'Why?'

'Whadda you meana why?'

'Well, you must have had a reason for killing him.'

'Ah, *si*. He . . . er . . . made fun of the gloriousa Italian team.'

'Really?'

'*Si*. First, he pooh-poohed our gloriousa band. He said we didn'ta have enough instruments. "Just onea cornetto," he said, witha the contempt. Third, he laugheda at our water polo, say we didn'ta have gooda enough horses. Thingsa like that.'

'Well, yes,' Lestrade humoured him. 'Motive enough there, certainly. How did you do it?'

'I tolda you. Witha the bow anda the arrow.'

'Could you show me?'

Dorando hesitantly took Lestrade's bow. Then he took the arrow.

'You wanna me to fire it in here?' he asked.

'No, no,' Lestrade said, 'that won't be necessary. Thank you,

176

Mr Pietri. I'll make arrangements for you to be moved to more comfortable quarters. Good-day.'

'Wait,' Dorando called after him. 'Don'ta you want to know how Ia killed your Queen Victoria? Youra Lord Nelson? Youra . . .' and Imbert slammed the cell door shut.

'I'd like to know more about that Lord Nelson business, sir,' he said to Lestrade.

'What's the meaning of this, Lestrade?' Superintendent Quinn had returned.

'Let him go, Paddy.'

'Let him go? Have you been drinking? He killed Tyrrwhit Dover.'

'Look, if you suggested it, he'd say he killed Cock Robin.'

'Aha.' Quinn's eyes lit up. 'With that bow and arrow. Yes, I see. Is that it? Is that the murder weapon?'

'Possibly,' said Lestrade, 'except that if Dorando used it on Dover, it was nothing short of a bloody miracle.'

'Why?'

'Because when I asked him to show me how he did it just now, he didn't even string the bow.'

'So?' Quinn had clearly missed the Medieval Warfare lecture.

'So it won't work, Paddy. It can't be fired that way.'

'Well, his fingers . . .'

'Yes.' Lestrade's eyes flashed cold again. 'I was going to talk to you about that. This isn't the damned Dark Ages, man. We've got a Liberal Government. This is 1908. Dorando, apart from anything else, is an Italian subject. Do you want a war with Italy?'

'Yes, why not?' Quinn shrugged. 'We'd win.'

'Of course we'd win, but that isn't the point. With or without fingernails, if a man has used a bow to kill someone, he has the rudiments of how to fire the thing. Now, I don't know whether it was the sun or the strain of the Marathon or whether friend Dorando is a few ice-creams short of a bicycle. But I do know this. He didn't kill Tyrrwhit Dover. Now get him into a hospital, for God's sake, before a lot of consulates get pretty plenipotentiary with you.'

Quinn threw his hat at Imbert. 'I told you, constable,' he roared. 'Next time I give you an order to release a suspect, you bloody well obey it.'

But it didn't fool Lestrade. He'd heard it all before.

*

177

The hubbub in the room died down as Mr Edward Henry and Superintendent Sholto Lestrade took their places on the rostrum. There was only one room at the Yard big enough to hold a Press Conference. And this vestibule was it.

'Gentlemen,' said Henry, 'we are here today to discuss certain facts with you in the light of recent events in connection with the Olympic Games here in this great city of ours.'

The smoke curled thicker as the gentlemen of the Press and the one lady leaned forward.

'Could I have a photo before we start, Mr Henry?' a muffled voice came from under a black curtain.

'No.' Henry waved his hand disapprovingly. 'This is not a circus, gentlemen. A number of people are dead.'

'How many this morning, exactly?' a journalist asked.

Guffaws in the auditorium.

'Eight, Mr . . .'

'Hart, *Daily Mail*. Is it true that the Italian Dorando has confessed to all the killings?'

'Well . . . er . . . Superintendent?' Henry was a master at buck-passing.

'No, sir,' said Lestrade, who enjoyed these occasions less than his chief. 'He has confessed to only one.'

'So it was a copycat killing, so to speak?' A crusty old Welsh voice rose from the ranks. 'T. A. Liesinsdad, the *Globe*.'

'No, I don't think so,' answered Lestrade. 'Mr Tyrrwhit Dover was killed by the same hand as all the others. That hand does not belong to Signor Dorando.'

'To whom then? Dorian Vine, *Sportsman's Weekly*,' another voice piped up.

Remarkably grammatical, Lestrade thought, for a sports commentator. 'When I know that, sir, you may rest assured that you gentlemen will be among the second to find out.'

There was uproar, papers waving and tongues lashing.

'Eight people are dead. Countries are pulling their teams out. We're losing money. What are you people doing at the Yard?' someone called out.

'Is it a question of sport? Jimmy St James, *Ball's Weekly*.'

I'm sure he does, thought Lestrade. 'That would seem to be the link, yes,' he said.

'When are you going to get answers?' Richard Grant was on his feet. 'Never mind the questions.'

The cries of 'Here, here' were deafening. Henry raised his hands for quiet. 'Gentlemen,' he said, 'we can only say we are doing our utmost. My force is stretched to capacity . . .'

'We're not talking about the Tug o' War team,' someone shouted. There was braying laughter.

'I have absolute confidence in Mr Lestrade. A more thorough-going professional I have yet to meet . . .' and Henry's sentence was drowned in hilarity. 'What I would ask, gentlemen, nay, beg, is that you stop this perpetual sniping at the Metropolitan Force in your articles. You are the voice of the people. If the people lose faith in their police force, then the writing is surely on the wall.'

'Like it was in the Ripper case,' Liesinsdad shouted. 'Lestrade didn't catch that bugger either!'

The policemen made their getaway. As he reached the outer lobby, Lestrade was stopped by two people.

'Sholto.' It was Marylou, the only woman in the room. She held his arm. 'They were pretty rough on you in there,' she said. 'I'm sorry.'

He looked at her. 'Hello, Marylou,' he said. And then at her companion. 'Goodbye, Hart.'

'No need to adopt that tone, Lestrade. Just doing my job.'

'Well, that's a first.' Richard Grant rounded the corner.

'Bitch!' sneered Hart.

'Better get back to the Remington, Sam. Old Harmsworth got out of bed the wrong side this morning. He's screaming for fresh blood. Woe betide the hack who isn't chained to his stall by eleven,' and he watched him go. 'Mr Lestrade, I'm sorry too,' said Grant. 'Couldn't let the chaps down, though. Ink's thicker than water and all that.'

Lestrade wasn't sure that it was.

'Well, it seems we've all drawn blanks,' said Grant. 'Marylou and I are no further forward. I've turned Fleet Street upside down looking for a connection. Just *something* that ties these victims together. You must be at your wits' end. At least for Marylou and me it's just a job. There'll be another story tomorrow.'

'You forget, Richard,' she said, 'Hans-Rudiger is personal. And I mean to get my man.'

She hooked his arm through hers. 'Mr Lestrade,' he said,

'would you join us for lunch? There's a little proposition I'd like to put to you.'

Mr Edward Henry sorted the mail in a desultory sort of way. Rather the way the General Post Office sorted it, in fact.

'Paper, dear?'

'Yes,' he nodded. 'Tons of the stuff.'

His wife nudged him. 'No, dear. The daily paper. Would you like it?'

'Oh.' Henry filed the letters between the egg cosy and the marmalade. 'Thank you, my dear. Good God!'

Cups jumped in all directions. Little Helen, all cheeks and curls and liberally daubed in egg yolk, burst into tears.

'What is it, dear?' his wife gasped, saving the coffee jug with a lifetime of expertise born of alarums and excursions. 'Mr Lloyd George again?'

'Damn and blast Mr Lloyd George,' snarled Henry. 'There's been another one.'

'Another Lloyd George, dear?' his wife frowned. 'No, surely not. It must be a misprint. After all, it is the *Daily Mail*.'

'Another murder, woman!' the Assistant Commissioner barked.

'Daddy,' piped up Hermione, mechanically mopping up her little sister, 'why have you gone purple?'

'Mrs Henry,' he said to her, a sure sign his temper was fraying when he forgot her Christian name, 'take your children away. Don't they have lessons to attend to?'

'Not today, dear, it's Saturday.'

'Well, then, a walk. Perhaps thirty laps around Hyde Park. I must have time to think.'

'Of course, dear.' She poured him more coffee. 'But Hermione's right. You do look a little mauve. You must watch your blood pressure.'

Henry ignored them all and scanned the lines feverishly. 'Discus. Greek Style. Tragedy Struck. Horrified Bystanders. American Athlete Martin Sheridan Killed Outright. Kent Icke's Sports Comments on Page . . .' *American* athlete,' he said.

'Yes,' mused his wife, 'it is rather a contradiction in terms, isn't it?'

'What? Oh, do stop prattling, woman. Don't you see? It's

180

broken the pattern. This fellow – Sheridan – he's the first actual athlete to have been killed who isn't British. Hesse and Hugo were repulsively foreign too, but they weren't athletes. At least, not any more. Hugo no longer and Hesse never had been. Why wasn't I told?' He sat bolt upright. 'What does Lestrade think he's playing at? I told him I wanted to be informed. I have the Home Secretary on my back. His Majesty is said to be deeply concerned. What?' he suddenly screamed.

Little Helen screamed with him, being patted by her mother and sister.

'What is it now, dear?' his wife asked. 'Have they misspelt your name again?'

'Walter Dew!' Henry roared.

'Oh, now, dear,' his wife chuckled, 'not even the *Mail* could get it that wrong. You're reading the gardening page.'

'Gardening page, my left testicle!' roared Henry. 'Lestrade's put Dew on the case. That's like trying to open a tin with this newspaper.'

'Well, they *do* talk about the power of the Press, Edward,' his wife tried to be helpful.

'Daddy?' Hermione chirped. 'What's a left testicle?'

Henry burst angrily from the room.

'I was wondering that myself, darling,' said her mother.

He unhooked the wire that speaks from the wall. 'Operator. Get me Scotland Yard. Yard,' he repeated. 'Y.A.R.D. Y for yellow. A for aardvark. Aardvark. It's an animal. A for . . .' and he slammed the receiver down. 'I'm going down to the Yard,' he shouted through to his family.

'I'll saddle Rover, Daddy,' said Hermione.

'Haven't time. I'll get a cab.' and he was gone.

'Well, dears,' sighed Mrs Henry, 'how about those laps around Hyde Park?'

Chief Inspector Walter Dew stalked the corridors of power, his shadow dancing on the green and cream of the institution paintwork. About now he wished he was back in the sergeants' stews again, in the basement. He even wished he was a damned constable, shivering in horror outside the dingy slaughterhouse at Miller's Court where they had found the last of the Ripper's victims. He had risen at Lestrade's elbow. The same elbow that had dug him in the ribs the day before and whose owner had said, 'Come on, Walter, what do you say? For old times' sake, eh?'

Yesterday, it seemed like a good idea. Now, he wasn't so sure.

'Luv a duck, guv.' Constable Hollingsworth hove into view, looking curiously like the least comforting of the men around Job. 'What a boat race! Come on, it's a nice sunny morning. Cheer up.'

'I'll swing for you, Hollingsworth,' Dew muttered. 'Is Mr Henry in yet?'

'Oh, the Policeman's Policeman, is it? Yes, he went through the Rory O'More in a cloud of smoke. Got up the wrong side of the skein of thread if you ask me.'

'Hollingsworth, I wouldn't ask you the time of day. Haven't you got any criminals to catch?'

'Oh, I wanted to ask you about that, Insp. This Martin Sheridan bloke, knocked brown bread with that discus . . .'

'The day you learn to speak English, Hollingsworth,' Dew swept on along the gloomy passageway, 'I'll discuss cases with you. That and when you've made Detective Inspector. Which will be about the same time as Hell freezes over.'

'Dew!' The Chief Inspector's polished boots skidded to a screeching halt on the polished floor. He knew the Assistant Commissioner's voice of old. The wrong skein of thread indeed. He knocked on the frosted, bevelled glass.

'Come!' The response echoed through the second floor. 'Well, well. Walter Dew.'

'Sir.' The Chief Inspector stood erect.

'They tell me in the canteen, Dew, that you have a certain literary flair.'

'Oh, it's nothing, sir,' Dew chortled, shifting his feet uncomfortably.

'Yes, I'm sure that's right.' Henry emerged from behind the huge mahogany desk with its leather and brass and memoranda. 'But of course, here at Scotland Yard, we are detectives, aren't we? Our job is to detect.' He circled his man several times, then stopped abruptly. 'Do you know you're going grey, Dew?' he asked.

The Chief Inspector shifted uneasily again. 'It has been pointed out to me, sir,' he said, 'on more than one occasion.'

'Yes, well, our line of work gets you like that, doesn't it? Especially if there are no results. Why did Lestrade put you on this discus case?'

'I don't know, sir.'

Henry turned to the window where the morning sun streamed across the gilded towers of Westminster. 'Come on, Dew. You've known Lestrade man and boy. What's he up to? Something smells!'

'Oh, I'm sorry, sir. It *is* August.'

Henry spun back to his man. 'Right,' he sighed. 'Martin Sheridan. What happened?'

Dew fumbled for his notebook.

'Without notes, man!' Henry insisted.

'Righto, sir.' Dew cleared his throat. 'Martin Otis Sheridan, aged twenty-eight. Found dead at the corner of Bayswater High Street yesterday morning. His head had been bashed in by a blunt instrument. Viz and to wit . . .'

'You sound like a bloody owl, Dew. Get on with it.'

'A discus, sir.'

'A discus.'

'Yes, sir. You know, those round things. Apparently the hancient Greeks used to practise by throwing plates at their wives.'

'Yes,' murmured Henry, 'not a bad idea. They knew a thing or two, those Greeks. How can you be sure it was a discus?'

'It was lying next to the body, sir. Covered in blood, it was.'

'Prints?'

'Stockley Collins is working on it now, sir. But it doesn't look good. Gloves, we think.'

'We?'

'Mr Lestrade and I, sir.'

'Which brings me back to my earlier question, Chief Inspector. Why did Lestrade pass this case to you?'

'Oh, I was first senior officer on the scene, sir. I discussed it with Mr Lestrade, naturally.'

'Naturally,' said Henry, sitting heavily in his highback chair. 'The point at issue, surely, is that this is one of the series. It's another athlete. It *must* be part of the same case. And yet . . .'

'Yet, sir?'

'Yet this time the victim is not British. Where is Lestrade?'

183

'I don't know, sir. The last I heard he was following up a lead in the Dover case.'

'All right. Look, Dew, no offence to you, old chap, but I want Lestrade on this discus business. Understand?'

'Of course, sir.'

'Right. If you see him before I do, you might tell him that.'

'As you will, sir.' Dew all but saluted and, transferring his regulation boater from one hand to the other, marched smartly to the door.

As he rounded the corner, he suddenly felt his sleeve being yanked sideways and he found himself nose to nose in a broom cupboard with his guv'nor.

'Hello, guv'nor,' he said. 'Cramped in here, isn't it?'

'Well?' Lestrade asked. 'Did he fall for it?'

'I believe so, sir. He said he wanted you on the case. I must confess, I find it a little hurtful.'

'There, there, Walter.' Lestrade patted the man's cheek. 'You'll get over it.'

'Can't you tell me what all this is about, sir? Why do you want Mr Henry to think I'm on this case?'

'Not just Mr Henry, Walter,' Lestrade whispered. 'Everybody.'

'Who's in there?' a voice shouted from beyond the door. Lestrade released the catch behind Dew's left buttock and the door swung open to reveal a rather puzzled Detective Constable Hollingsworth.

'And this, Dew, is where we keep the brooms at the Yard,' said Lestrade. 'Now, come with me and I'll show you the ablutions.'

Dew smiled weakly at Hollingsworth, who stood there with his mouth open. He watched them saunter down the corridor in earnest conversation.

'Would you Adam and Eve it?' he asked himself.

The nightjars called to each other in the low woods and the last heron flapped noisily from the reeds. The gold of the day had become a livid burning crimson, paling now as night came. A boat wound its way through the reeds, out past the yards and locks, under the five-arched bridge, watched by the silent stones of Father Thames and Isis which Anne Damer carved a hundred years ago.

Against the dark of the river edge, two men walked their dogs that late August evening.

'Here's a boat, George. It looks adrift.'

'Hang on, we'll hook her up. Must have come loose from upstream somewhere.'

They crouched by the path and grabbed at the prow, snatching the rope that trailed in the water, and they pulled it to the bank. Then they both stood up sharply and the dogs scampered away. In the boat, lay a dead man, propped half upright, as though he were cox for a sculling team of ghosts. The oars were gone. The rowlocks slid silent. Only he lay there, strapped in by a rope that had slipped, staring intently ahead, as if to guide the oarsmen along the Henley straight.

'Good God,' whispered George. 'You'd better call the police. This is no boating accident.'

9

Nine Men's Morris

'The guv'nor and the guv'nor?' Bourne asked incredulously.

'As I live and breathe,' nodded Hollingsworth.

'Lestrade and Dew?' Bourne was making sure there could be no misunderstanding.

Hollingsworth nodded.

'Get away.' Bourne took off his pinny and sat down with the nearly-brewed tea. 'In the same broom cupboard? Well, I never.'

Hollingsworth wasn't so sure of that. 'Bloody weird, I call it,' he said. 'Pretending to show the Insp around like he doesn't know the place like the back of his German band.'

'Of course,' Bourne crossed his knee to reveal just a hint of mauve sock, 'there isn't a Mrs Lestrade, is there?' He sipped the nectar daintily.

Hollingsworth shook his head. 'There's a Mrs Dew though. Rumour has it they're crawling with kids.'

'Well,' Bourne tapped him with the napkin his Bath Olivers were wrapped in, 'don't believe everything you see. Anyway,' he pursed his lips, 'they're both at a very funny age.'

The door crashed back and an ox of a man stood there.

'Yes. Can I help you?' Bourne asked.

The man looked him up and down. 'Where's Lestrade?'

'I'm afraid Superintendent Lestrade is not here at present. Can I help? I'm Julian Bourne.'

'You're a faggot,' the man growled.

'I don't believe you've met.' Hollingsworth stood up. 'Julian, this is Mr Maddox. He's an animal from Washington. To be precise, a Pinkerton Animal.'

Maddox's hand shot out, but Hollingsworth was faster and he brought his boot smartly into the American's shins. Maddox

186

snarled and his coat flew back as in one fluid movement he drew a heavy-looking Colt from his shoulder-holster.

'Tsk, tsk,' Bourne said. 'Temper, temper. Now why don't we all have a nice drink?' He proffered a cup to Maddox, nudging the revolver's muzzle with it.

'What is it?' snapped Maddox, not taking his eyes off Hollingsworth.

'Mint-flavoured tea,' said Bourne.

'Varmint-flavoured, more like,' Maddox growled. 'Touch me again, Yard man, and you'll be brushin' your teeth with your balls.'

Hollingsworth unleashed the truncheon strapped to his out-side leg. 'Come over here and say that, son, and you'll have to change places in the choir.'

'Now, boys, boys,' Bourne intervened. 'Tadger, you put that truncheon away and Mr Maddox, please. We don't carry firearms in this country.' He gingerly moved the barrel aside. 'They're so messy. Mr Lestrade is on a case at the moment. You'll find him in Bournemouth.'

'Bournemouth?' Maddox blinked.

'That's down south, shitface,' Hollingsworth explained. 'You know, below the Mason-Dixon line.'

Maddox uncocked the revolver. 'Bournemouth,' he said. 'Ain't got no time for no cockroaches now. But when I get back, asshole, you and me's goin' to have a little spat.'

'Any time, son,' Hollingsworth said casually. 'Don't forget your handbag.'

But Maddox had whipped in his revolver and crashed back down the stairs. He didn't hear Bourne and Hollingsworth laughing hysterically above him.

While Maddox was catching a cab to go south, Sholto Lestrade sat in an imposing front parlour in a house in Bloomsbury Square.

'Anyone for Tennyson?' a voice called from the french windows.

'Shouldn't that be "Tennyson, anyone?"?' the hostess retorted. 'Do go away, Giles, we have more pressing concerns at the moment. Another cup, Mr Lestrade?'

The Superintendent eyed the hostess with something akin to

hatred. It wasn't so much the *taste* of the contents of the cup he'd just somehow managed, it was the things floating in it. 'Thank you, no,' he said. 'Now, Lady Rivers, about Hilary Term.'

'Ah, yes,' she said. 'A dear boy.' She adjusted her lariat of pearls. 'A little effete perhaps, as these young men will be nowadays.'

Lestrade made a mental note. It was obviously Term's little feet that made his balance so good for lunging. 'How long had he been a member of the Circle?'

'Oh, let me see, about three years, wasn't it, Gervase? Gervase!' She tapped a young man with her fan.

'Sorry, Lady R.' He stopped sprawling on the *chaise-longue*. 'I was just soliloquizing to myself.'

'Of course you were,' she said. 'One cannot, in my experience, soliloquize any other way.' She bowed her grey head closer to Lestrade. 'Thank God he was doing it silently.'

'Did Mr Term have any enemies?' Lestrade asked. 'Anyone here, perhaps?'

'I really don't know what you mean,' another young man bridled from the far corner of the room.

'Indeed, Mr . . . er . . .'

'Bell. Clive Bell. I merely dabble, as we all do, in poetry. It is of course the mirror of the soul.'

'Of course,' nodded Lestrade. 'So you wouldn't say that you and Mr Term were rivals.'

'In no sense. But you might ask Giles . . . Giles!'

'Hello.' The voice came again from beyond the french windows. A tall, elegant young man with a full beard and carefully coiffured moustache swung casually into the parlour.

'Lytton Strachey.' He bowed to Lestrade.

'Haven't we seen you somewhere before?' Lestrade's eyes narrowed.

'I shouldn't think so,' Strachey said. 'I am a writer. I don't do Police Reviews. Not even for ready money.'

'Oh, come now, Giles, your "Ballad of Reading Gaol" is legendary,' another young man piped up from a corner.

'It's merely average,' sighed Strachey, lolling in a chair so that his feet were virtually up the chimney. 'And besides, it's someone else's.'

'Oh, I haven't introduced you,' Lady Rivers said of the last unidentified young man in the room. 'This is John Maynard Keynes.'

Lestrade nodded.

'I'd be grateful for your views on the cost-effectiveness of the Metropolitan Police Force, Mr Lestrade,' the moustachioed young man blurted. 'In quintessential terms of supply and demand, of course.'

'Of course,' said Lestrade, 'I'd be delighted to oblige, but now, I fear, I am on a case.' He turned to one of the two young ladies, both of whom appeared to be wearing hammocks. 'Did you know Mr Term?' he said to the prettier of them.

'Indeed,' she answered. 'He was always very kind about my canvasses.'

Lestrade took in the paint-daubed hair, the thumb with the red ring from habitual gripping of the palette, the teeth slightly worn in the centre from clamping on a brush. Or perhaps it was a pipe. 'You are a painter, Miss . . .?'

'I merely dabble, Mr Lestrade,' she said. 'My name is Vanessa Bell. This is my sister, Virginia.'

He turned to the gawky one, with a long nose rather like a violin case. 'And you . . . Mrs . . . er?'

'Stephen,' she said. 'Miss. Yes, I knew Hilary. He was a charming young man. He would visit us occasionally in Gordon Square and here.'

'Did any of you join him on the athletics field?' Lestrade asked the roomful. 'Did any of you fence?'

Lytton Strachey shuddered. 'What a bestial thought, Super-intendent,' he said. 'We here are pledged to the pursuit of truth. We despise conventional thought processes and the use of biceps.'

'Yes,' said Lady Rivers, 'I am a great believer in natural childbirth.'

'I think you're thinking of forceps, Lady R.,' said Bell, struggling with a pipe.

'I jogged with him once at Cambridge,' said Keynes. 'He was a King's man, like myself. I do not share my friends' fear of the sports field, Mr Lestrade, but I'm afraid that two years in the India Office . . . well, you know how the Civil Service grinds a man down?'

Lestrade nodded. He knew only too well. 'When was the last time any of you saw him?' he asked.

189

Strachey looked at Bell. 'You had luncheon with him, Clive, last month I believe.'

'That's right. At the Trocadero.'

'Did he seem . . . strange?' Lestrade asked. Looking at the group before him, the question seemed superfluous.

'In what way?' Bell asked.

'Well, I don't know. Worried? Frightened, even?'

'Lord, no. Hilary didn't know the meaning of the word,' Bell told him.

'I can't believe that,' said Lady Rivers. 'I mean, I know Cambridge isn't what it was.'

'But then,' said Virginia suddenly, 'what is the meaning of worry? Of fright? Indeed, of life itself?'

There was a silence.

'Well.' Lestrade cleared his throat. 'I must be going. Thank you, Lady Rivers, ladies, gentlemen. If anything else about the late Mr Term springs to mind, perhaps you'd contact me at Scotland Yard.'

'I'll see you out, Superintendent,' said Lady Rivers.

When he had gone, Lytton Strachey stretched out his endless legs still further. 'What a repulsive little chap,' he said. 'Not a very eminent Victorian, is he?'

'Wasn't Hilary one of Bolsover's Boys?' Maynard Keynes asked.

'Good Lord, I believe he was,' frowned Bell. 'Still, Lestrade must know that already.'

Virginia hissed, 'People! When are we going to get out from under the voluminous skirts of Lady R. And meet *when* we want to, *where* we want to, and to discuss what *we* want to discuss – the enjoyment of beautiful objects, the pleasures of human intercourse?'

'Yes, yes, of course,' said Bell. 'It's so difficult, isn't it? We're all so wretchedly busy. At least we're agreed on Thursday evenings. As to when we can start, Lord knows. How about 1922?'

In the passageway, as Lestrade and Lady Rivers reached the front door, the doorbell rang. Lady Rivers did the honours and standing there, in a very fetching pelisse and bonnet, was a lady who looked rather familiar.

'Ah,' beamed Lady Rivers, 'our newest recruit to the Circle. Something of a poetess in her own country, I understand.

190

Superintendent Lestrade, I'd like you to meet Miss Marylou Adams.'

The pair of policemen sat huddled in the office, the green lamps burning far into the night. The weather was cooler, the night air over the city still and silent. A breeze wafted in from the river.

'Autumn, guv'nor,' said Dew. 'I can smell it on the wind.'

'It's just Mungo Hyde's river, Walter,' Lestrade said. 'Tell me, how long have we been together now? Forty years?'

'Twenty, sir. Ever since the Ripper case.'

'Yes. I remember. And you're still calling me "sir",' Lestrade chuckled.

'I wouldn't have it any other way, guv'nor,' Dew said.

'Neither would I, Dew,' the Superintendent answered. 'So read the wall to me. Not forgetting the shoeboxes.'

Dew looked up at the noticeboards, cluttered with diagrams, photographs of corpses, pencilled jottings. He couldn't bear to look at the hundreds of depositions stacked up in the cardboard boxes to right and left.

'Murder number one,' he said, 'Anstruther Fitzgibbon, eldest son of the Marquess of Bolsover. Shot to death with a horse pistol in a classic locked-room mystery.'

'Now, Walter, you've been reading Conan Doyle again.'

'Sorry, guv'nor,' Dew smiled.

'What do we know about our man from that?'

'He's careful,' ruminated Dew. 'He wears gloves. He is at least passably familiar with old guns. He's handy with a wire or horsehair loop. And he read a book called *Nena Sahib* that gave him handy hints on how to do it.'

'Which brings us', Lestrade lit himself another cigar, 'to murder number two.'

'Murder number two,' Dew peered through the curling haze, 'Hans-Rudiger Hesse, German journalist.'

'Crime writer,' Lestrade reminded him.

'Yes, sir. Over here to cover the Games. He called here, having read that you were on the Fitzgibbon case, to tell you how it was done.'

'And perhaps by whom, Walter.' Lestrade blew smoke rings

down his nose. 'That's the maddening thing. What happened to him?'

'Stabbed with his own paper-knife.'

'Because he had to be shut up. That's why this one isn't as clever as the others. Our man had no time. He knew Hesse. Otherwise, he wouldn't know he'd been to see me and why. And that's why Hesse breaks the pattern. He's not an athlete. And he's not British. He just happened to have the bad luck to be an old hack who remembered an old case. Murder number three.'

'William Hemingway. Upper-crust sort of bloke who was poisoned over three days almost certainly by eating prunes.'

'Given to him by person or persons unknown prior to the start of the eight-metre class boat race.'

'Yacht,' Dew corrected him.

'What does this one tell us about our man?' Lestrade ignored the correction.

'He's back on track, now. Hemingway is an athlete of sorts and he's British.'

'And?'

'Er . . .'

'Our man knows his poisons. And he knows the customs of these sailors exchanging gifts with each other.'

'And he knows Hemingway's personal dereliction for prunes.' Dew thought of that all by himself.

'Right you are, Walter. Murder four.'

'Martin Holman. Down on his luck. Involved in a pretty amateur bit of embezzlement as well as running. About to tell his boss all when he drops dead at the White City.'

'Again, poison. Again British. Again an athlete. Murder five.'

'Ah, now the break of pattern again.' Dew rocked back, clutching his knee. 'A woman this time – Effie Jennings.'

'But still athletic – in all senses of the word – and British.'

'And we have an eyewitness this time. The chauffeur – whatsisname. . . Mansell – saw her with a man the night before she died. A man who might well have brought her that poisoned unmentionable.'

'Which tells us what about our man?' Lestrade asked.

'Er . . . he goes like a train, sir.'

'Yes, well we've only got Mansell's word for that. But we know he understands the rough and tumble of the fives court –

192

and he's a whizzo at mixing his lethal compounds. Tell me about Besançon Hugo.'

'The pattern broken again. Our man messed that one up, guv'nor, if you ask me.'

'I do ask you, Walter. In what way?'

'Hugo was a Frog and not actually an athlete. And he was shot – harking back to the first murder, perhaps, but it showed all the signs of panic.'

'You'll go far, Mr Dew.' Lestrade was impressed. 'Our man was actually preparing for murder number seven when he was interrupted. He couldn't risk Hugo checking the blade he'd fixed. And I'll tell you something else.'

'What's that, Guvnor?'

'Our man got lucky the next day.'

'In what way?'

'It's my guess that he intended to smear the tip of the Frenchman's blade with poison, not merely sharpen it to a lethal point.'

'Still, the result was the same.'

'It was indeed. Murder number eight.'

'D'Abernon "Tyrrwhit" Dover. Shot in the back by an arrow.'

'Difficult shot?'

'Not really. White shirt under the moon. Less than fifty yards away. He's British. He's an athlete, but the weapon's odd.'

'Poetic, though, wouldn't you say?'

Dew shrugged. Poetry wasn't his strong suit.

'It's the victims, Walter.' Lestrade slammed the flat of his hand down on the depositions on his desk. 'That's what really gets me about this case.'

'In what way, sir?'

'They're so bloody ordinary.'

Dew frowned. 'Is that so unusual?' he asked.

Lestrade turned to the window and watched the black barges trailing in the mauve and crimson of the river. 'Yes, damn it, it is. You and I have investigated more murders than Edward Henry's had hot dinners, Walter. We know the hidden rule of violent death. The only people not inviting it are the poor buggers who stop a bullet or a maddened ox by accident; who just happen to be in the wrong place at the wrong time. For everybody else – and I mean *everybody* else – there's always a reason. There *has* to be a motive. We know that at least Hans-Rudiger Hesse and probably Effie Jennings knew their killer. Besançon Hugo saw and may well have recognized him before he died.'

'But that Effie Jennings . . .' Dew began.

'Oh, yes, I know her morals may have been looser than a llama with diarrhoea, Walter, but this is 1908. You and I have got to move with the times.'

'What about Martin Holman?'

'You said it yourself, Walter. An amateur. Amateur artist. Amateur embezzler. He wasn't in the right league to be in somebody's way.'

Dew fell silent. 'Anstruther Fitzgibbon!' he suddenly shouted. 'Not as other men. Talk of unnatural practices with chaplains and regimental mascots and things.'

'Yes, I'll grant you odd, but unless a flock of outraged goats engineered his death, it still doesn't give us a motive.'

Dew was speechless again. 'What about one murder?' Inspiration shone hopefully on his brow. 'One intended victim and the others merely a blind?'

Lestrade nodded. 'All right, Walter, I'm game. Which one is it? Shall we toss a coin? Stick a pin in the wall? You see, the only thing wrong with that theory is the risk. It's risky enough to kill once, but to kill eight times only increases the risk eight times. It needs meticulous planning and a hell of a lot of luck.'

'Perhaps that's what he had, sir,' Dew said. 'After all, the bugger's still at large.'

Lestrade nodded grimly.

'Hang on, guv'nor.' Dew frowned again, a sure sign that his old grey cells were working overtime. 'You said eight murders.'

'That's right,' said Lestrade.

'But the latest one, Martin Sheridan. That makes nine.'

'Let's leave that, Walter.' Lestrade had dropped his voice.

'But it doesn't fit. Sheridan was an American.'

'It's probably a copycat killing, Walter,' Lestrade said quickly. 'Let's go back. We must have missed something.'

'But the Sheridan case may give us a clue, sir,' Dew persisted. 'Perhaps the one we need.'

'Walter, there's something I ought to tell you . . .' Lestrade began, but before he could finish, the door crashed back and a flushed-looking sergeant Valentine dashed in.

'Sirs,' he blustered, 'there's been another one. Henley. Can you come? There's no time to be lost.'

'Of course not, sergeant.' Lestrade reached for his battered boater. 'There never is. Number nine,' he muttered under his breath.

'Well, well,' said Dew, grabbing his jacket. 'Number ten.'

In there?' Lestrade shrank back from the duckboard.

'Well, of course,' said the captain. 'We're racing on Friday, Superintendent. We really have to practise. If you want to ask us questions, you'll have to do it as we're going along. Rowed before?'

'Well, no, I . . .'

'Never mind,' the captain grinned, 'you'll get used to it. Hop in.'

For a moment, Lestrade was thrown. Did the man mean that literally? Was it vital for the weight distribution? Would he upset the whole damned apple cart? In the event, he reasoned that two legs were better than one and he clambered aboard.

'Steady!' the little man at the back – or was it the front – called out. 'You'll have us over.'

The boat rocked alarmingly and the upright oars wobbled from true.

'Hope your slide's greased,' the man behind Lestrade mumbled. 'Steady your rowlocks.'

Lestrade thought they were reasonably steady, all things considered, and he sat down.

'Er . . . excuse me,' said the man in front of him, 'I think you'll find there should be one of your feet on each side of me. Not two. Unless you've got four feet, that is?'

Lestrade shifted accordingly and an oar fell heavily on his shoulder.

'Watch out, there,' the captain called. 'Right, gentlemen. May I explain the presence of this . . . oarsman . . . in our midst. Superintendent Lestrade is from Scotland Yard. He wants to ask us a few questions about dear old Lin.'

'Poor old Lin,' a few of them chorused.

'I'd be grateful, gentlemen, if you could help me,' said Lestrade.

'You're going to end up pretty far downstream, Mr Lestrade,' the little man in front of him said. 'Would you like your chappies there to accompany you?'

'Good idea, Reggie,' said the captain.

'Is there room?' Lestrade's knees were wedged under the rim. The whole thing seemed rather snug to accommodate Dew and Valentine.

'No, no, they can follow the coach along the towpath. Help yourselves to bicycles, gentlemen,' the captain called. 'By the way,' he passed his right hand under his left armpit, past the man between him and Lestrade, 'I'm Harry Blackstaffe, of Blackstaffe's Blades.'

'Delighted.' Lestrade leaned forward.

'Look, old chap.' The man behind him nudged him. 'I think you'll find that jacket and those braces will be a bit of an encumbrance once we start.'

'Keep your thole clean,' the little man reminded him. That went without saying, really.

'Blades,' commanded the captain. 'Over to you, Reggie.'

'On the feather,' called Reggie. 'Could you bend a bit lower, Mr Lestrade, only the wind's rather high this morning. I fear you'll be blown backwards if you sit like that.'

Lestrade did his best. His knees were either side of his elbows and his arms were locked straight.

'And . . . pull!' shouted Reggie, clamping a loud-hailer to his mouth. 'And . . . pull. Blade. Feather. Blade. Feather. Steady, W.A.L. Steady. That's the way. Pull. Pull.'

Lestrade couldn't believe it. The boat hurtled away from the landing place like a hare out of a trap and the brown water of Mungo Hyde's river sprayed past, lashing them all, but especially him, with brown foam.

'Put your back into it, Mr Lestrade. It's all about leg thrust and body swing in this business.'

Lestrade could second that. But already he sensed his body thrusting and his leg swinging. The left one, that was. He'd lost all feeling in his right.

'We've got a windage problem, gentlemen. Come on, Fairbrother. Catch the beginning from the stretcher. Throw the weight from feet to blade. Now, slide back. Body swing. No, no. Missed it again.'

'There's an imbalance in the centre,' Fairbrother called.

'Yes, I know. It's the Superintendent, but he can't help it. We have to face it. Things aren't going to be the same without dear Lin.'

'Poor Lin,' Blackstaffe said. 'He was a sculler and a gentleman. What can we tell you about him, Superintendent?'

Lestrade's chest was rattling like an old kettle. 'Well,' he wheezed, 'what indeed? Who saw him last?'

'Blade. Feather. Blade. I suppose I did,' said Reggie, leaning back to do something or other to the wind. 'Last Thursday.'

'That would be . . . the day before he died.'

'Yes, I suppose it would.'

'How . . . did he seem?' Lestrade gasped.

'Happy. No, not happy. Elated. Yes, that's the word.'

There was a honking sound from the right bank. The coach was pedalling like a man possessed and calling incomprehensibly through a loud-hailer.

'What's he saying?' Blackstaffe asked.

'Don't know. Can't make it out,' said Reggie. 'Harry, I know one wants to do one's bit for the disabled, but did we have to have a coach with a cleft palate?'

'Bear with him, Reggie. Horace knows what he's doing.'

'Not a lot of good if he can't tell us, though, is it? Yes, Mr Lestrade, elated.'

'Wasn't he normally, then?'

'What? Elated?' Reggie asked. 'Rather more of a taciturn disposition. Wouldn't you say, Benjie?'

A man at the front grunted.

'Takes one to know one, you see, Superintendent.'

'Poor as a church mouse, of course,' said Blackstaffe.

'Oh?' wheezed Lestrade, reduced now to monosyllables.

'Will you get your nose out of my backside, sir?' roared the man in front of Lestrade. 'It's like being back at Uppingham again.'

Lestrade was happy to oblige. The flannel was chafing anyway. But it put him off his stroke and his oar banged into the one behind. 'Sorry!' he hissed through gritted teeth.

'Yes,' said Blackstaffe. 'Scruffy beggar, was Lin. We called him the Sculler Gypsy.' Everybody but Lestrade laughed. 'What's Horace saying now, Reggie?'

The cox put his mouthpiece to his ear. Any port in a storm. 'Bridge,' he said. 'Is one of you chaps due to play bridge with Horace tonight?'

'No. He's saying Bilge,' said Blackstaffe. 'We *are* veering a little, Reggie. Do get a grip.'

'Is there anyone', Lestrade forced his tortured lungs to manage a complete sentence, 'who would want to see him dead?'

'Horace?' Reggie frowned. 'Just because a chap has a speech defect, Lestrade . . .'

'No, no.' Lestrade hacked and spat. 'Lin.'

'Ah, I see. Blade. Stop tickling it, Fairbrother. You aren't at Magdalen now, you know. Pull. That's it.'

The honking from the bank grew urgent. Lestrade glanced sideways to see Valentine vanishing down the path. Horace the coach was gesticulating wildly, while Walter Dew struggled in the rear, his front wheel wobbling under duress.

'Phew, what a scorcher!' somebody grunted on the boat, but he couldn't have been referring to Walter Dew.

'May I remind you, gentlemen, that we are supposed to be averaging forty strokes a minute. Harry's getting there, but Fairbrother, you're a joke. Benjie's on form. Mr Lestrade's getting in three or four, but he's shipping a lot of water. Feather. Feather.'

Horace was now positively screaming, but they all steadfastly ignored him as the pace increased.

'Listen to that,' said Reggie. 'For a man with a cleft palate, he's got a magnificent pair of lungs.'

'Yes,' nodded Blackstaffe, 'what fervour. Makes a chap proud to be an oarsman. Eek!' He glanced up as the bend bared the river beyond the Henley Straight. 'My God, what's that?'

'It's a pontoon bridge,' shrieked Reggie.

'As I was saying,' panted Lestrade, his knuckles white around the oar, 'can any of you think of anyone who wanted to see Lin dead?'

'Blade! Blade! Blade!' Reggie roared. Lestrade was hit in the mouth by the head of the man in front. He glanced to his right because that was the way his neck had been wrenched. He saw Valentine, Horace and Dew, standing astride their bicycles akimbo, staring in horror.

'They've got no right to be here. Who the bloody hell are they?' Blackstaffe was hauling frantically on his oar, pulling it out of the water.

Lestrade saw a moving flotilla of little boats roped to the bank at one end and little boys in long shorts and loose scarves scurrying hither and thither. And in the centre, he saw a wiry little Lieutenant General in a big hat, issuing commands as though in the breach at Mafeking. Thank God, he mused as he heard the crunch and felt his spine jar, thank God he wasn't wearing a frock.

The apparition in splints hobbled down the mortuary corridor. 'Sholto Lestrade as I live and breathe,' a voice hailed him.

'Dr White, I'm not sure I do. I'd shake your hand, but I can't feel my arm.'

'Good God, you look as though you've gone down with the *Abercrombie Robinson*.'

'Whoever he is, I probably did.' Lestrade eased himself into a chair.

'Not there, Lestrade. My sandwiches.'

The Superintendent grunted and removed his highly polished trousers from Mrs White's bloomer.

'Well, well. I know why you're here. Linlithgow Morris.'

'The same.' Lestrade tried to turn his head above the surgical collar. 'What can you tell me?'

White pulled off his green, smeared apron. 'Poison. Quite nasty. Want a look?'

'Why not?' Lestrade staggered across the room. 'I couldn't feel worse than I do now.'

'No,' said White and he studied the Superintendent carefully. 'And actually, he looks a bit better than you do. You'll have to hold your nose, though. What with the heat and the blasted crane flies, I'm afraid things in the garden aren't exactly rosy.'

He slid back a trolley and pulled back a grey sheet. The dead man was naked but for a pair of rowing shorts. His skin was a pale flesh colour, the hair long and still lustrous.

'Arsenic,' said Lestrade.

'Correct. Except for the shrunken face, there's not a mark on him. I cleaned up the vomit, of course.'

'Thanks. Administered?'

'Oh, definitely.' He put back the makeshift shroud.

'No, I mean how was it administered?'

'Oh, I see. Well, his last meal seems to have been prunes. Keeps one regular, I understand.'

Lestrade nodded. 'Is there a family?'

'Elderly grandparents, I believe. Live at Pancho Villa here in Henley. The local bobbies have broken it to them. Pity, he was a damned good oarsman, I understand.'

'Yes, so do I. I saw his cups at the boathouse.'

'So? I know you of old, Lestrade. Once the Yard's been called in, it's all hands to the pumps. What's your theory?'

'This is one of many,' Lestrade told him, turning away in a desperate search for a chair.

'Aha!' White chortled. 'I *do* love a mystery.'

'It's no mystery.' Lestrade winced as his numb buttocks hit mahogany. 'Some maniac is going around killing athletes. The Press have had the story for weeks. I'm surprised there are any of 'em left in London.'

'So it *is* the Turks.' White twirled round another chair and straddled it before tucking avidly into Mrs White's bloomer. 'Bite?' he said.

'No,' said Lestrade, shifting slowly. 'Blister. Do you know the Foreign Secretary?'

'Sir Edward Grey?' White asked. 'Good Lord, no. Should I?'

'No.' Lestrade shrugged, his most volatile movement. 'It's just that you and he have the same theory.'

'And what's yours? From the horse's mouth, so to speak.'

Lestrade tried to laugh, but the effort beat him back into a hollow wheeze. 'I deal in evidence, doctor, not theories. Did you know the deceased?'

'No. Heard of him, though. He's a local legend here in Henley. Always opening public urinals and so forth. Nice chap, they say.'

'Yes, that's just it. I've got seven other nice chaps, not to mention one nice woman, lying in assorted graves and slabs all over the country. Oh, and two of them out of the country I expect, by now. Now, you tell me, doctor, who kills nice ordinary people?'

White reflected for a moment. 'Another nice, ordinary person who has something to gain from their deaths,' he said.

Mr Edward Henry toyed with the marmalade, the extra thick sort to which he was so partial. He flicked the paper over on to the back page. His eyes fell on the small print, tucked away discreetly at the bottom of Kent Icke's column.

'Where's today's paper, dear?' he asked his wife.

Mrs Henry looked a little alarmed. All those years arresting people in the hot sun of Ceylon and all those years scrutinizing the tiny lines at the ends of people's fingers. Perhaps they were beginning to take their toll.

'It's there, dear,' she said.

'Where?' He looked bemused at the array of breakfast things before him. Little Helen's crushed and scattered boiled egg, her toast soldiers looking as though the square had broken, the gleaming silver of coffee jug and tray.

'In front of you, dear.' Mrs Henry instinctively reached for the thermometer in her chatelaine. 'You're looking at it.'

'No, no,' smiled Henry, 'it can't be today's. There's a tiny article here about Martin Sheridan winning a gold medal.'

'Well, if it's in the *Mail* dear, it must be true.'

Henry turned the paper over. He read, incrdulous, that day's date.

'Damn and hell fire!' he thundered. Little Helen burst into tears and slightly bigger Hermione began to hose down the milk that had gone everywhere.

'Not again, dear.' Mrs Henry looked up at him, pleadingly. 'I thought you'd taken Mr Dew off the Sheridan case?'

'Don't you understand, woman?' he roared. 'There *is* no Sheridan case. Unless, that is, a dead man can throw a discus further than a lot of live men.'

'Let me see, dear.' She adjusted her reading glasses. 'It says "Greek Style",' she read. 'Perhaps that's some kind of posthumous award. Rather like the Queen – God Bless Her – gave that cup to that plucky little Italian chappie.'

'The only thing posthumous about all this,' snarled Henry, 'is the obituary I'm going to write on Sholto Lestrade. Will you shut up?!' he screamed at his younger snivelling daughter and dashed for the door. 'I'm off to the Yard.'

Mrs Henry rose to comfort the hysterical child. 'Never mind, darling,' she said. 'Daddy's rather upset this morning because that nice Mr Lestrade has died. But don't worry. He can always get another rat-faced, sallow, rather limited Superintendent.'

*

There was no doubt about it. Linlithgow Morris, like all the others, was essentially a nice chap. One or two of the Henley people to whom Dew and Valentine spoke when they had hauled their mangled, waterlogged guv'nor from under Baden-Powell's raft of boats, had said he was something of a bore and it was generally agreed that Inspector Tom Gregory was the man to follow up that lead. Others found him rather taciturn. Morris's parents had died of the diphtheria when he was a baby and he had been raised by his paternal grandparents, kindly old folk who had scrimped and saved to buy a good education for the boy and who had stood and cheered along with everybody else at the water's edge as he rowed his way to certificate after certificate, medal after medal. All very exciting if you liked to spend your time eight and a half inches above water with someone else's body between your knees. What was it, Lestrade wondered for the umpteenth time as the cab dropped him outside the Wig and Pen Club, what was it that people saw in sport? It was cheaper than Maxim guns, he supposed, to trounce the foreigners in the field. That must be it. A cheap war. And, he thought darkly, as he tottered up the steps, his surgical collar large and gleaming in the street lights, a bloody season.

He shuffled past the doorman, snoring at his post. Faithful unto death, mused Lestrade, and padded down the deserted halls. He caught his reflection in the mirrors that twinkled in the candle-light – a bizarre apparition in lint and gauze, his face shiny with bruising, his lips bulging and split. From somewhere he heard the desultory smack as the last balls of the evening kissed the cush.

'Mr Grant.' Lestrade saw his man sprawled out in the leather-bound corner of the dining-room.

'Mr Lestrade.' The newspaperman struggled to his feet, extending a hand. 'You'll have to forgive me,' he said. 'I'm afraid I've had rather too much to drink. Brandy?'

'I am still on duty sir,' Lestrade reminded him. 'Though I fear not for much longer.'

'Well, then,' Grant steadied the decanter, 'one for the road. Thank you for coming. Cigar?'

Lestrade accepted and the two men sprawled on either side of the table. 'The message was that you wanted to see me,' he said.

'Yes.' Grant downed his brandy and poured another. 'It didn't work,' he said.

'What?'

'The ruse about the murder of Martin Sheridan. It didn't work.'

'I know,' said Lestrade. 'I read Mr Icke's report in the newspaper.'

'The silly bloody idiot!' said Grant. 'I begged him, Mr Lestrade. I even told him why. I said,' he leaned forward, whispering earnestly, 'I said we needed to fool our man. I said that if he thought we were playing with him – inventing a murder he hadn't committed, taking you off the case and putting Dew on it – he'd come out of the woodwork. He'd write to the paper. He'd ring the Yard. Something. Maniacs are like that, Kent, I told him. Vain. This fellow thinks he's damned clever. This will draw him out. You know what he said? Icke, I mean?'

Lestrade shook his head.

'He said, "Over 'ere, son. On me 'ead." '

'What does that mean?'

'I've no idea. Absolutely no idea. These sports commentators, they're a bloody race apart. No pun intended. As journalists, they make damned good lavatory attendants. Good God.' Grant frowned in the dim half-light. 'You're pretty banged up, aren't you?'

'It's nothing,' said Lestrade, 'that a fortnight flat on my back wouldn't cure. And please, don't feel badly about the Sheridan idea. It was a good one. It might well have worked. What will Mr Harmsworth say?'

'Who?' Grant grunted. 'I don't give tuppence for that bugger, Lestrade. There's more to life than working for a halfpenny trash sheet.'

Lestrade could believe that.

'Anyway,' Grant dropped his head into his hands and played with a cigar butt absent-mindedly, 'it couldn't have worked.'

'Why not?' Lestrade asked, wincing as the brandy passed his lips. 'Because Martin Sheridan is still alive?'

Grant looked at him. 'No,' he said and his eyes were rimmed with tears. 'Because there is one person, in this whole, wide world, apart from you and me, who was in on our plan from the beginning.'

Lestrade straightened slowly. 'You mean . . .?'

Grant stood up, collecting his brandy balloon and quaffing the last of its contents. 'And you can't prove a thing,' he said. 'Perhaps you can understand why I'm glad about that,' and he wavered towards the door.

Sholto Lestrade was fifty-four years old. He stood in the warm night air under the black turrets of the Temple Law Courts. Here he stood thirty-four years ago, a green copper on the beat. And on his first day, a photographer had parked his tripod in front of him and snapped him there and then for posterity. In years to come, perhaps, they'd look at that photograph, yellowed and cracked, and look at that eager young face under the helmet and say, 'What a funny-looking bugger he was, that Sholto Lestrade.'

Now it was time to do it one last time. To go on the last beat. But the years and the pontoon bridge had taken their toll. He couldn't even manage the steady pace of two and a half miles an hour this evening. He'd take a cab. Mr Edward Henry must have seen the paper by now. Or someone with promotion in their eyes at the Yard – there were plenty of those. Or Abberline or Edgar-Smith or any one of them would have pointed it out to him. It wouldn't take him long. Henry was sharp as a razor. He'd know it was Lestrade. Falsifying evidence. Obstructing police in the course of their duty. Not to mention casting another slur on the *Daily Mail* – but then, who would notice that?

Well, he'd beat him to it. He'd go to see the Policeman's Policeman tonight. He checked the half-hunter. One o'clock. The Temple Bell confirmed it. He looked down the dark alleyway to the Crusader Church where he had walked with a lovely lady only weeks before. He'd go to the Yard and write out his resignation. In triplicate, of course. And he'd put it into one of Edward Henry's blasted 'In' trays.

'Are you good-natured, dearie?' a hopeful street-walker called to him from the Temple Arches.

'Not any more, ducks.' He clicked his teeth and hailed a rattling hansom.

*

He did not go to the Yard. Something in him rebelled, recoiled like a dying cobra. He was a Yard man. Long in the tooth, maybe. Short of time and patience and salary, without doubt. But no newspaperman threw him a murderer and said, 'You can't prove it.' There *had* to be proof. And he had one last place to go to find it. What was it old Bolsover had said? That first time they had met, when the old aristocrat had come to the Yard? He had been talking – briefly, for that was his fashion – about his son. 'Nimbler than all my boys.' *All* my boys? But Bolsover only had one and he was dead. Even with another one the wrong side of the ticking, that only made two. So what did he mean by 'all my boys'?

'Cabbie!' Lestrade jabbed the roof with his stick. 'Grosvenor Place. And step on it.'

10

Crossing The Tape

The little old man lay propped on a pillow. His breathing was sharp and erratic. The last of the Bolsovers had a journey to go. His Master called him. He probably couldn't say no.

A large woman with a bust like a scullery ushered the ailing Lestrade into the aristocratic presence. She folded her arms and tapped her foot, much after the manner of the late Queen Empress.

'I told you it was pointless,' she shrilled, smoothing down her dressing-gown and adjusting her curlers. 'Lord Bolsover has not stirred for nearly five weeks.'

'You've never left his bedside, Miss . . .?'

'Sister!' she corrected him stridently. 'Never. Except of course to sleep and attend the usual offices.'

'Has he regained consciousness in that time?' Lestrade asked, finding it increasingly difficult to tilt his head to the necessary angle to establish eye contact with the sister.

'Four times,' she said.

'Did he say anything?'

'Let me see.' She whipped a thermometer from nowhere and inserted it into the recesses of the bedclothes. A less comatose man would have been dangling from the chandelier. 'The first time, he asked me who I was. I told him I was Sister Plinlimmon of the Hospital for Rectal Disorders.'

'That must have comforted him no end,' Lestrade observed.

'I like to think so,' she smiled, whipping out the thermometer and shaking it vigorously. 'Aha, I thought so.' She flicked open Bolsover's eyelids and pushed an extraordinary length of rubber tubing up his left nostril. 'The second time the old so-and-so had the temerity to tap my posterior.'

'And what did he say then?'

'I'd rather not say.' Lestrade fancied he saw her blush in the candle-light. 'Except that in his condition what he proposed was medically impossible.'

'The third occasion?'

'Yes. That was only the other day. He said, "Bugger Buccleuch. He's tied me laces together."' She dived under the covers again and wrenched out another length of tubing. 'Aristocrat's Friend,' she explained the gadgetry to Lestrade. 'A boon to the incontinent.'

Lestrade wasn't remotely surprised. He felt sure you couldn't buy that sort of thing in Britain. 'His fourth comment?' he asked.

'Yes.' Sister Plinlimmon frowned and sat down beside the four-poster. 'That was very strange. He was quite lucid yesterday – for a vegetable, that is. He began to call out for his boys.'

'His boys? Aggh!' Lestrade jarred his neck anew with the shock of the moment. He closed to the woman, as far as he was able with the huge starched frontage between them. 'Is that all?'

'Yes. The rest of it was rambling. Incoherent. The ramblings of old England.' She looked down at him, affectionate in her own, psychopathic way. 'Poor old boy. It's astonishing he's held on this long, you know. Something's keeping him going, but I'm bothered if I know what. The breed, I suppose. They say a Bolsover rode up that hill with William the Whatsisname.'

'It was probably him,' mused Lestrade, looking at the yellow face and pinched features in the yellow half-light. 'Bolsover!' he suddenly shouted.

'Are you mad?' Sister Plinlimmon shrieked. 'You'll wake the dead.'

'That's the idea,' said Lestrade. 'Lord Bolsover!'

She tugged his sleeve. 'Desist, sir,' she snapped. 'I won't have the poor old man bullied.'

'Do you know me?' Lestrade did his best at a military sneer, though it had to be said he lacked the Big Hat and the frock. 'It's Bobby. Bobby Baden-Powell. Remember the Fifth? In India? What a fine body of chaps, eh? Are you listening? Bolsover? I'm talkin' to you, don't you know!'

The little old Marquess stirred, rolling sideways, his eyelids rolling.

'Leave him alone, you boundah!' Sister Plinlimmon roared, the massive forearms flexing as she grabbed the bedpan.

'Madam,' hissed Lestrade, 'I'm up to my surgical collar in corpses. And this patient of yours is the one man in England who can help me. I'm desperate.'

'I can see that,' observed the nurse contemptuously, 'but I cannot allow you to abuse a dying man by pretending to be General Baden-Powell.'

'Baden-Powell?' a scarecrow voice rattled from the corner. 'Come closer.'

The Superintendent and the sister rushed to him, one to each side. He looked at her first. 'God, Bobby. You've put on weight. Breasts! Curse on Vishnu! Serves you right.'

'My lord,' Sister Plinlimmon sobbed, 'my lord. It's a miracle.'

'Miracle, my arse.'

'My lord,' Lestrade shook the old man's cadaverous shoulder, 'do you remember me?'

Bolsover's filmy eyes flickered again. 'Remember you?' He smiled and patted Lestrade's hand. 'Of course, vicar. Place in the Abbey. All dug? Not too near Poet's Bally Corner, remember.'

'No, no, my lord. Lestrade. Scotland Yard.'

'Scotland Yard?' Bolsover frowned. 'Don't want to be buried there, damn it. Too far north.'

Sister Plinlimmon sat sobbing, tears splashing liberally on to her heaving bosom. 'I knew it was too good to be true,' she wailed. 'He's going, Superintendent.'

Bolsover scowled at her. 'Stop that snivelling, Bobby. Never gone superintendent in me life. Won't start now.'

'Your boys.' Lestrade grabbed both the old man's shoulders.

'My . . .' The old aristocrat tried to focus.

'Your boys. Tell me about your boys.'

'Where are they?' he asked.

'*Who* are they?' Lestrade would settle for that at this stage.

'Anstruther chose them. All athletes. All my boys. Even the girl.'

'The girl?' Lestrade's head pounded. 'Do you mean Effie Jennings?'

'That's her.' Bolsover chewed his tongue. 'From Derbyshire.'

'What's the connection?' Lestrade shouted. 'Why are they your boys?'

208

'Select group,' said Bolsover. 'Get it all when I go. And when Anstruther goes.'

'Anstruther's gone,' said Lestrade.

Bolsover hiccupped and raised himself up. 'Gone?' He turned incredulous to the nurse. 'Bobby. Is that true?'

She nodded with quivering lip.

He fell back on the pillow. 'My God. Muffed it. Had my chance. Goes to them then.'

'All of them?' Lestrade asked.

Bolsover nodded.

'They're all dead,' Lestrade said levelly.

Bolsover's face darkened. Then his fingers clutched the air. He caught Lestrade's sleeve. 'As ye sow, vicar,' he whispered, barely audible now, 'so shall ye reap.' He turned to Sister Plinlimmon. 'You've got to stop it, Bobby,' he said softly. 'This frock business.'

And he died.

Sister Plinlimmon let out a wail and stood up, sniffing. 'Well, there it is,' she said. 'So passes the last of the Bolsovers. Who'll inherit now, I wonder?'

Lestrade looked at her. 'Is there a will?' he asked.

'I've no idea,' she said. 'There's no safe in the house.'

'Who are his solicitors?'

'Doesn't have any. Legend has it he shot the last one to offer his legal services. He doesn't – didn't – approve of lawyers.'

'Very wise,' Lestrade concurred.

'What was all that about his boys?' Sister Plinlimmon asked. 'And one of them being a girl?'

Lestrade stood up with a suddenness that brought tears to his eyes. 'Sister Plinlimmon,' he took her hand, 'if I wasn't in splints, I'd kiss you.'

She looked appalled. 'No, you wouldn't,' she said.

Sholto Lestrade went walkabout. He saw dawn come up over Mungo Hyde's river and nodded to the postman and paperboys who trickled out in the gold of the dawn. A policeman saluted him as he hobbled down the Embankment. He had sat for an hour in the snug of the Coal Hole, sipping brandy with mine host long after hours as the bobbies patrolled the pavements above. He had written out his resignation and he passed it now, in its Yard envelope, to the beat man.

'Mr Edward Henry,' Lestrade had said. 'On your way past.'

'Very good, sir,' the constable had answered. 'Mind 'ow you've been.'

At the top of the steps, he saw her. A vision in white, gold curls dancing as she ran towards him. She threw herself into his arms, jarring his neck and back, and she kissed the bruised and battered lips.

'Daddy, daddy.' She buried her face into the lint of his collar.

'Emma,' he whispered, 'little Emma.' He lifted her down. Not so little now, I see.'

She looked at him, tears trickling down her face. 'Daddy, you're hurt.'

'No,' he said, 'it's nothing. How have you been? Tell me all about yourself. How are things at Bandicoot Hall?'

She squeezed his hand and pressed herself against his good arm as they strolled along the Embankment. 'Harry and Letitia and the boys and I are going home today. They told us at the Yard you'd been seen wandering about. What is it about this dirty old city of yours?' she asked.

'This one?' asked Lestrade. 'I don't know.' He smiled. 'It's all I know, Emma. Apart from you,' he held her to him, 'it's all I love.'

'I saw you at the fencing,' she said. 'How awful about that man.'

'Yes, it was,' he nodded. 'Awful.'

'Are you on a case, daddy?' she asked.

'Yes,' he nodded, 'I'm on a case.'

'Is it a difficult one? A very difficult one?'

He shrugged. 'Do you ever have a problem?' he asked her. 'At Monsieur Le Petomaine's Academy? Do you ever have a problem and you've nearly solved it, but you can't quite get the answer?'

'Oh, yes,' she beamed, 'almost all the time. I'm not very bright, daddy,' she confessed.

'Now,' he said sharply, 'don't ever say that. You've got your mother's looks and your mother's brains. That's a winning combination, I'd say. What do you do?'

'When?'

'When you can't quite get the answer.'

'Well.' She screwed up her freckled nose and sucked her teeth. 'I really *think* about the last bit. The bit I can't get.'

'Do you?'

'Yes. What's your last bit?'

'Mine?' he said. 'It's a quotation from the Bible I think – "As ye sow, so shall ye reap."'

'Silly, daddy,' she scolded him, 'that's Galatians.'

'Sorry,' he apologized, 'I thought it was the Bible.'

'It actually says, "Be not deceived; God is not mocked; for whatsoever a man soweth, that shall he also reap."'

'And what do you think that means, Emma?' he asked.

'Well,' she giggled, 'it means that if you've done something naughty, retribution will catch up with you.'

'Retribution?' His eyes widened. 'That's a good word for a little girl.'

'Less of the little.' She nudged him in the ribs so that his eyes watered. 'Oh, sorry, daddy. But you said so yourself, how I'd grown. This naughty thing.' She nuzzled into his shoulder. 'Is it something to do with sparking?'

'With what?'

'Sparking,' she said. 'Old Jem at the Hall said it was what made the world go round and when I was bigger I'd enjoy it. What did he mean, daddy? He wouldn't tell me.'

'I should hope he wouldn't,' said Lestrade. 'I must have words with Harry about Old Jem.'

'Is that what your case is all about, then?' she asked. 'Sparking?'

'No,' he laughed, 'no, it isn't . . .' and he stopped short, the hairs on the back of his neck rising to brush the collar. 'Emma Bandicoot-Lestrade,' he held her shoulders, 'did I ever tell you you're the best girl a man could have?'

She beamed with pride. 'Thank you, daddy,' she said. Then she twirled him round and linked her arm with his. 'Now, about this sparking business . . .'

'Oh, look,' said her father quickly, 'there's Harry, waiting for you. Come on. Race you to the steps.'

'Don't be silly, daddy,' she scolded him, ignoring the physical wreck that staggered beside her. '*Ladies* don't race.'

'Good,' he said. 'Besides, the sparking in my case happened rather a long time ago.'

*

The White City Stadium lay bare and gaunt under the moon, peeping now in, now out of the clouds. The only sound was the patter of a thousand legs as the crane flies flitted here and there over the terraces and the gnats teased silently over the limpid waters of the pool.

The five policemen spread out across the track, walking along the strings as though in some grotesque parody of a race. The one with the stick and the white collar was trailing and the one in the chiffon scarf took an early lead. Then they stopped. A solitary figure approached across the turf, her step light, her pace measured.

'Sholto.' She stopped in front of them, and then, more warily, 'Gentlemen.'

'Marylou,' he said. 'Thank you for coming.'

'You know us newsmen,' she said. 'Never could resist a cryptic note like yours. "Come to me by moonlight." Alfred Noyes, isn't it?'

Lestrade thought it was rather quiet. 'I don't know,' he said. 'Chief Inspector Dew here found it written on the back of a matchbox. He thought it rather appropriate.'

'What is it all about?' she asked.

Lestrade leaned against his stick. 'It's about murder, Marylou,' he said. 'Murder and money.'

She let her hand and her clutch bag fall to her side. 'So you know?' she said darkly, the sorrow heavy in her voice.

'We know,' he said. 'But I'd like to hear it from you.'

She sighed and walked closer. 'Sholto, I'm still not entirely sure of my facts. Perhaps we could compare notes. I'm not as good at this as you are.'

He chuckled. 'Oh, come now, Marylou. You've had nine lots of practice.'

'Excuse me?' she blinked, thrown by his line.

'All right,' he said, 'if you want to play it that way. For the benefit of these young impressionable policemen here, let's play it by the book. Or would you rather do all this at the station?'

'No.' She glanced around her. 'Here will be fine.'

'Anstruther Fitzgibbon,' Lestrade began, circling her slowly, the ferrule of his stick gouging holes in the Olympic turf. 'He was your first obstacle.'

'Mine?' She straightened.

He nodded. 'Correct me if I go astray on this one. You picked him up on some pretext and went to his room in Berkeley Square. You had your "back-up" as you called it – careless of you to drop that in conversation at Yelf's Hotel. You were a little too cocksure of yourself there.'

'Now, just a goddamn minute . . .' She began. And he recognized the steel he had heard in her voice on Brownsea Island.

'Please.' He held up his hand. 'This is my patch. Washington's . . . over there,' and he pointed in the wrong direction. 'But you decided not to use the pistol – yours, that is. You decided to use his. It appealed to the romantic in you. The poetess. You saw Fitzgibbon's antique guns and you loaded one. Coming from pioneer stock you managed the mechanical gubbins and you forced your victim to sit at his desk. That threw me, at first, but it was, what? Nerves? Is that why you fired from that angle, because you were nervous?'

'You're telling the story,' she said coldly.

Lestrade was in full flight. 'It certainly didn't bother you later, when you shot Besançon Hugo and when you hit Tyrrwhit Dove with the arrow.'

'They say it gets easier,' she said, 'with practice.'

He nodded. 'Then, you worked your way through Bolsover's boys,' he said. 'But there was a problem, wasn't there? Ironic, really, that the one man who could have proved your undoing was an old friend. That's what sickens me most, Marylou. That you were prepared to kill someone close to you to get what you wanted.'

'Sholto, I . . .'

'Perhaps you'd forgotten where you'd heard about the Beck case. Or the book *Nena Sahib*. It was from Hans-Rudiger himself, when you learned all there was to learn about journalism from the great man. Or perhaps you didn't expect him to turn up in London for the Games. It was a little inconvenient for you, wasn't it?'

She shook her head sadly.

'Somehow, you heard he'd been to see me. You told me you hadn't seen him recently. That was a lie. He must have told you of his visit to the Yard. And it was either then or sometime later – are you taking notes, Valentine? I'm sorry if I'm not going fast enough for you. You had the luck of the Irish, then. Gilbert Chesterton may be a brilliant man, but he doesn't know what day it is. He thinks Napoleon lived in Notting Hill. And the only other neighbour was deaf as a diving board. You visited Hesse and stabbed him. Bloody, that. Not very nice, Marylou. Not very ladylike. But I remember Lizzie Borden.'

'She didn't do it,' Marylou said.

'She wasn't *convicted* of doing it,' Lestrade reminded her. He hobbled closer. 'Then you went south. To cover the boat racing.'

'Yacht, Super,' said Hollingsworth.

'It was you who gave William Hemingway the prunes, via Captain Overland and Philip Hunloke, relying on the confusion at the start of the race so that no one would remember who'd done it. It took nerve, to hang around like that. But as I said, you were too cocksure. That business in the bedroom in Yelf's Hotel . . .'

He felt four sets of colleagues' eyebrows rise at the admission, but he ploughed on regardless. 'You showed me the back-up weapon and you owned up to knowing about poisons, implying you'd doctored my brandy.'

'Oh, come on, Sholto,' she said. 'Wasn't that a little obvious of me?'

'I thought so,' he nodded, 'but not, I confess, at the time. You told me you hadn't been there since the start of the race. That was a lie. But you said you'd been spending time with the Ladies' Team. One lie merely compounded another. While my head was mending in the Isle of Wight, you went north.'

'What the hell,' she said. 'It was all on expenses.'

Valentine continued to scribble feverishly.

'You visited Martin Holman of Worplesdon Harriers. He wasn't much of an artist. And he wasn't much of an embezzler. But he was a damned good runner. That is, until you noticed the colour of his mushrooms. He had a weakness for a pretty ankle, did Holman. The confessions of Miss Fendyke in the cab to Bow Street were very revealing. The till wasn't the only place his fingers had been.'

Walter Dew gasped involuntarily.

'What did you do?' Lestrade asked her. 'Cook his breakfast?'

'My hash browns are the stuff of legend,' she said.

'Your next problem was a tough one. The Bolsover Boy who was a girl. Perhaps you'd seen the metal whatsits the Ladies' Team wore under their thingies. After all, on your own admission you'd spent time with them. Ingenious to smear Effie

Jennings's thingummies with chrome. Running a risk though, weren't you, playing squash with her?'

'It was early morning, wasn't it?' she asked. 'No one around.'

'Then, of course, Hilary Term went badly wrong, didn't it?'

'You tell me.' She shrugged resignedly.

'I will,' he said evenly. 'You got as close as you could to the fencing teams, but there was no opening. So you broke into Prince's Club the night before the bouts, intending to smear poison on Leotard's sword. You knew in advance which was his. Each fencer has his own favourite weapon. That you'd already checked. You filed down the point. Probably carried the file in that bag there.' He pointed to it. 'But the coach, Hugo, surprised you. You shouldn't have been there at that time of night. He probably recognized you from the previous days. How could you explain your presence? You couldn't, so you used your "back-up" for the first time – that natty little pistol you carry – and you shot him. The poor old Besançon did his best to let me know who'd done it. He wrote the letter "J" in his own blood.'

'Is Miss Adams Jewish then, sir?' Dew asked.

'No, Walter,' Lestrade said. 'Miss Adams is a journalist. "J" for journalist. Only he died before he could write any more. The irony of course was that Term would have died the next day anyway, because Leotard's sword broke. Which brings us to Tyrrwhit Dover.'

'And how did I kill him?' Marylou asked.

'Again,' said Lestrade, 'by poetic means. Oh, you had your little pea-shooter just in case, but you'd filed down a sword already. Why not an arrow? You who'd written a thesis on crusaders. All very romantic, really. You'd visited the archery club and talked to Dover and the other Lincolnshire Poachers. You knew he often practised late, even on moonlit nights. Fleet Street is full of almanacs. You picked your night and arrived. But it's my guess you didn't expect Millie Blanchard to turn up. That was a little peccadillo your newshound's nose hadn't dug up. Still, with her there, inspiration came to you. By killing Dover in her presence you might be able to implicate her. You overheard their argument. The woman was an archer. Fragrant and radiant no doubt, but a woman scorned. What more natural than that she should pin him to a target for jilting her? You little old romantic, you.' He clicked his teeth.

'And then?' she yawned.

'Then, Richard Grant had a bright idea. He tried to catch our murderer by tricking him, by printing a false murder in the paper in order to draw out the murderous – what is it you Americans say, "Son of a gun"?'

'Bitch,' she corrected him. 'Son of a bitch.'

'Well,!' Bourne bridled.

'That's where you finally slipped up, Marylou,' Lestrade said. 'You should have played along with it. You should have faked a letter from a maniac, ranting on about copycat killings or why that idiot Dew should be put on the case – sorry, Walter . . .'

The Chief Inspector shifted uneasily.

'But you didn't. You let it go. And only three of us in the world knew the false story about Martin Sheridan. You, me and Richard Grant.'

She nodded slowly. 'I see,' she said. 'You're right.'

'Linlithgow Morris was a bit of an anti-climax, really, wasn't he? I haven't even finished investigating him, but I've got enough on the others. You had to kill him because he was the last of Bolsover's Boys. You poisoned him – rather dull of you to choose prunes again – and put him in a boat. Like that woman. The lady with the onions. These little poetic, female touches. They'll get you every time.'

'Well,' she said, 'have you done?'

'For now,' he said. 'Constable Bourne here will accompany you to the station.'

'What about motive?' she asked. 'You've got your method – right, I'm sure, in all cases – and I'll concede I had the opportunity. Why did I do it?'

He closed to her so that they stood face to face. 'That's what threw me,' he said. 'All your victims, with the possible exception of the first, were too damned ordinary. *So* ordinary I overlooked the most obvious thing.'

'Which was?'

'The oldest motive in the book,' he said. 'Financial gain. Bolsover's Boys weren't worth much alive, but dead, the entire Bolsover fortune would be yours. As long as they died before he did – that's why you had to work so fast. The papers carried regular bulletins on old Bolsover's health. He couldn't last long. Half Berkshire, town houses wall to wall, a gallery full of

216

priceless paintings, objects of virtue one of which alone would keep Bourne here in fol-de-rols for ever.'

'And how was I supposed to collect this amazing fortune?'

Lestrade stepped back. 'Tell her, Walter.'

Dew flipped open his notebook, but unlike the eagle-eyed Valentine he couldn't read it by the light of the moon, so he had to rely on that rare companion of the policeman, his brain. 'We've been sending telegrams all day, miss,' he said. 'And receiving a few, too. Constable Hollingsworth here has been up to his armpits in Somerset House. Between us we've come up with a few interesting facts.'

'Such as?'

'Such as, your real father was the late Marquess of Bolsover.'

'What?' she faltered.

'Come on now, miss,' Hollingsworth said. 'No use coming the wide-eyed innocent. You're in this up to your Princess of Teck.'

'Bolsover?' she repeated dumbly. 'Wait just a second. You're telling me that the Marquess of Bolsover is my father?'

'Was,' said Lestrade. 'He died last night. Ironic that, Marylou. You very nearly made it. You were born out of wedlock, it's true, but your natural father was prepared to finance you eventually – but only after his Boys, his chosen athletes. It was a silly notion of his dotage – to leave his vast fortune to a group of young hopefuls who only had one thing in common: they were good sportsmen. Oh, and one woman. Only after that would you inherit.' He closed to her again. 'It's funny,' he said. 'Whatever I saw in your eyes, it wasn't pounds. Or dollars.' He straightened. 'Marylou Adams, I am arresting you for the murders of . . .'

'No!' A voice rang around the stadium, echoing and re-echoing through the rows of empty seats. From the darkness of the Royal Podium, a shadow dashed across the lawn. 'You can't do it, Lestrade. I can't let you.'

'Mr Grant,' Lestrade said, 'please stay out of this.'

'You can't prove a thing,' he said, holding the uncomprehending Marylou to him.

'Yes, you've told me that,' Lestrade said, 'but you're wrong. I've got enough here for a conviction. And if not, I can always hand Marylou over to Superintendent Quinn. He's got a way with women.'

'Sonofabitch!' Another voice rang through the dark. Marylou screamed and flung herself sideways as a shot rang out. She was thrown backwards into Grant's arms and he toppled with her. 'Christ, no!' The voice sounded again.

The policemen flung themselves to the ground, Lestrade landing on his good arm.

'Where is he?' Valentine hissed, his nose in his notebook.

'*Who* is he?' Dew panted, scrabbling for his boater.

Hollingsworth looked up. 'Bugger me,' he said, 'it's that American bastard.'

'Maddox?' said Lestrade. 'Well, gentlemen, that's one reason I asked you all along tonight. I must admit I half expected our constabulary colleagues from France and Germany as well.'

'What the hell's goin' on, for Chrissake?' Maddox snarled, jabbing the gun back into the holster. 'Who the hell's that?' He pointed to the sprawled form of Marylou.

'You've just killed a fellow countryman of yours, Mr Maddox.' Lestrade staggered to his feet. 'Congratulations.'

Maddox's eyes narrowed. 'I didn't mean it,' he said. 'My finger just sorta . . .' He went closer. 'Marylou? Marylou?'

'You know her?' Lestrade asked.

Maddox nodded as Grant rolled clear and laid the matted head down carefully. 'She's my wife,' he said. 'I wasn't over to cover no goddammed Games. I came over to find her. She left me. I was following Lestrade 'cos I figured he knew where she was. I came for what's mine.'

'Well,' said Hollingsworth, 'you've got 'er now, ain't you, shitface? You see,' he crouched next to the kneeling Pinkerton man, 'that's the reason we don't carry guns in this country. They tend to go off too bloody easy.' He stood up and, without warning, brought his boot back and drove it hard into Maddox's head. The big American went down as his lights went out. 'Sorry, Super,' said Hollingsworth, tending his throbbing toe, 'but he had it coming.'

Lestrade nodded. There was a moan behind them all and Marylou Adams stirred on the grass. They ran to her. Lestrade, for all his paraplegia, got there first. He lifted her head. 'Well, I'm damned,' he said. 'Bhisey's Improved Bust-Improver.' He tapped the metal thingummies and Marylou breathed again. 'Are you all right?' he asked.

'I . . . I think so,' she said.

218

'It's all right,' he told her. 'Your husband's bullet knocked you off your feet. You've got a little Indian gentleman to thank for being alive.'

'And I'll thank you,' she said, 'to take your hand off that.'

'Oh, I'm sorry.' Lestrade hastily withdrew it. 'Now then, Miss Adams, if you're ready. Constable Bourne?'

They helped the newspaperman to her feet. Bourne flicked out the handcuffs. 'No,' said Lestrade, 'I don't think so.'

'Richard?' she held a hand out to him. 'Richard . . .'

He shook his head. 'I'm sorry, Marylou,' he said, 'I can't help you now. But we'll fight this. We will. I'll have all Fleet Street on your side. Wait for tomorrow's editions.'

She let her hand fall.

'Bourne,' said Lestrade, 'it's back to Lost Property for you tomorrow, remember.'

Bourne smiled. 'I know, guv'nor,' he said. 'Actually, Betty's rather pleased.'

'Who?' asked Lestrade.

'Betty, Superintendent. My intended.'

'Your what?' Four policemen had asked the question simultaneously.

'Well, actually, I've named the day.'

'Have you?' blinked Lestrade.

'Well, what with the three boys and all, we thought it was about time, really. You know what people are like.'

Lestrade nodded, then remembered to close his mouth. 'Tell me,' he said as Bourne took Marylou away, 'Betty is . . . er . . . a woman, isn't she?'

'Lord love you, Superintendent, of course she is.' Bourne smiled. 'Who do you think I make all those frocks for?'

'Oh,' said Lestrade, 'I thought for a moment it was General Baden-Powell.'

Valentine hauled up the unconscious form of the Pinkerton man and carried him from the field. Dew and Hollingsworth walked a little way behind. Lestrade and Grant brought up the rear.

'I'm sorry, Mr Lestrade,' the *Mail* man said, 'I shouldn't have come.'

'I guessed you would,' the Superintendent answered. 'In your position, I'd have done the same myself.'

'Will she . . . what will happen to her?'

'Marylou?' Lestrade stopped, leaning on his stick and fumbled for a cigar. 'Oh, she's pretty and she's American. If she can find an old crusty judge . . .'

'Don't patronize me, Lestrade,' Grant said, standing still.

The Superintendent puffed, looking straight ahead. 'All right,' he said. 'She'll hang.'

There was a silence. 'I should never have invited her over,' Grant said.

Lestrade turned slowly, a wry smile on his face. 'Thank you, Mr Grant,' he said. 'I thought you'd never admit it.'

'I shouldn't have said that, should I?' he said.

Lestrade shook his head. 'No more than you should be wearing those gloves in this sticky weather. I'll wager they're covered with traces of black powder. You see, wiry as Marylou probably is under that newspaper exterior, she couldn't have pulled a bow back with the force to pin Tyrrwhit Dover to a target.' He watched Bourne and Marylou disappear through the gates where Dorando had staggered a fortnight before. 'Neither could she make a convincing enough man to make love to Effie Jennings in the woods the night before she died – the one that Mansell, the chauffeur, saw. That man was you, Mr Grant. You gave Effie that contraption. Pity for you that the Ladies' Team gave Marylou one as well. Fitting, really. Everyone else was giving Effie one, after all.'

He heard the click of a safety catch near his ribs. 'Ah,' he said, 'your little back-up. The same calibre, I'll wager, as Marylou's. That's where you were really clever, wasn't it?' He saw Valentine vanish at a jog into the darkness, the prone Pinkerton over his shoulder.

'Was I?'

'Yes.' Lestrade turned to face him. 'You heard me explain the murders to Marylou just now. It all fits equally well for you. You had access to all the athletes, just as she had. I daresay that if I put you into an identity parade, and could persuade Captain Overland to pay a visit from Norway, he might pick you out as the man with the prunes on Ryde Pier. Mansell might even identify you as the man wrestling with Effie Jennings. If Besançon Hugo were here, he'd certainly finger you as the journalist he was trying to warn me about. It's poor old Hesse I feel sorriest for. He liked you, didn't he? Well, I suppose we all did. He confided in you, about the Beck case? The locked room?

Nena Sahib? Ironically, he was confiding in the very man it was fatal to confide in. Tell me, where did you learn your poisons?'

'Imperial College, London.' Grant positioned himself between Lestrade and the exit. 'Before my career in Fleet Street took off, I tinkered in laboratories. It was there I learned to play fives.'

'Hmm,' mused Lestrade, 'you're pretty good. At poisons, that is. I can't speak for your game. But then you were playing the deadliest game of all, weren't you? That's why you called yourself Victor Ludorum when you bought Effie Jennings's whatsit – the Winner of the Games.' He glanced beyond Grant as Dew and Hollingsworth passed into the great outside world. His heart sank. Now he was alone with Fate. And Richard Grant. 'You had the whole thing planned from the start, didn't you?'

'Did I?' he asked mockingly.

'Oh yes. You see, what dear old Walter didn't explain to Marylou was that his telegrams yielded something else. You were a Bolsover Boy too. But a real one. You were the son of a servant girl – the wrong side of the ticking. It's my guess the old man didn't acknowledge you. Blot on the Bolsover escutcheon as you were.'

Grant grinned. 'You're right,' he said. 'The miserable old bastard kept me as a boot boy – his own son scraping the shit off his shoes. I couldn't stand it. I ran away. He had me tracked down. I never understood why. Couldn't bear to lose something that was his, I suppose. Oh, he paid for my education – a cheap crammer and Imperial. But alongside his wealth, that was mere loose change. There was more. And I wanted more. So I went to see him. Not as Richard Fitzgibbon, eldest surviving son of the Marquess of Bolsover, but as Richard Grant, of the *Mail*. The old duffer hadn't seen me for twenty years. As I thought, he didn't recognize me at all. He kicked me out as soon as I got there – couldn't stand journalists, you see. But not before I'd got my hands on a very interesting document – the list of Bolsover's Boys. All those bone-headed nonentities who were going to inherit in the event of the death of dear old Anstruther. I don't want to think about what I had to do to get into his bedroom, by the way. Imagine my chagrin, then, when on the bottom of the list, before me – oh yes, the sanctimonious old bastard had put me in his will, except that I'd have been dead before I could reap the benefits – there was the name of a little bitch he'd sired on some American tour when he was still young enough to follow the Games himself. Well, I'm a newshound, Lestrade, and a good one. It didn't take much to find out she was now called Marylou Adams. And, irony of ironies, she worked in that woebegotten country on the *Washington Post*. Naturally, I invited her over to work on the Games. Naturally, she came.'

'And you created the Martin Sheridan story to implicate her.'

'Exactly. It almost worked, didn't it?'

'Almost,' admitted Lestrade. 'I must admit, when I came here tonight, I honestly didn't know which one of you it was.'

'Well,' said Grant, 'now you do. I'm sorry about the histrionics at the Wig and Pen, by the way. In my experience, a few well-timed tears created by sharp squeezing of the crotch can work wonders. That and flagrant challenge.'

'Ah, yes,' Lestrade remembered. 'That I couldn't prove a thing.'

'That's right, and essentially, you still can't. Oh, yes, I've confessed, I know, but that's just between you and me, isn't it? You and me and all this vast arena. Thank you, Lestrade, for the news about old Bolsover. I've been so busy on the final touches I haven't kept abreast of the Stop Press. At least,' he held the muzzle up to Lestrade's head, 'you'll have the satisfaction of being killed by one of the richest men in England. There'll be blood on the tracks tomorrow, Lestrade. And I'll do the story on it. It will say how that madman Maddox – who was in on his wife's onslaught on our athletes – tried to kill us all. Sadly, his bullet found Superintendent Lestrade of Scotland Yard.'

'That won't work, Mr Grant,' Lestrade said, feeling the muzzle cold and clammy on his sweating forehead.

'Perhaps not,' shrugged Grant, 'but you forget the power of the Press, Lestrade. The power that can *prove* black is white and white black. The power that will not in fact lift a finger to help Marylou Adams. Your men heard you accuse her. And she did not deny it. And anyway,' he grinned, easing his finger on the trigger, 'whatever happens, you won't be here to see it.'

There was an explosion and a cloud of smoke. Two men stood upright for a moment in that moonlit stadium, stark terror in the eyes of both. Then one of them lolled sideways and rolled over in the dust.

Mr Edward Henry stood with one hand behind his back, looking out over Mungo Hyde's river. There was a knock on the door and Chief Inspector Walter Dew walked in.

Henry had not said 'Come!' in his usual fashion. He did not turn round. He did not move.

'It's true then,' he said.

''Fraid so, sir,' Dew said.

'He went down fighting.'

Dew felt an iron-hard lump in his throat.

'Still,' sighed Henry, drawing himself up to his five feet four, 'it was the way he would have wanted to go.'

'It was best,' said Dew solemnly. 'At least he didn't suffer. It was all over quickly.'

Henry turned. 'Yes,' he said. 'Two minutes of the first round.' He shook his head. 'The Metropolitan Boxing Team isn't what it was, Dew.'

'No, sir.'

A dishevelled figure in a grubby surgical collar limped in alongside the Chief Inspector.

'Ah, Lestrade. All right, Dew. Tell Sergeant Marciano never mind. And next time,' he fished in his pocket, 'he'd better stay on his feet for a bit longer,' and he reluctantly passed over a five pound note.

'Very good, sir. Thank you, sir,' and Dew actually bowed before he left.

'Well, Lestrade?' Henry raised his eyebrows.

'As can be expected, sir,' said the Superintendent. 'You got my resignation?'

'Resignation?' frowned Henry. 'Oh,' and he passed the man a cigar, 'I think that must have got lost somewhere in my memoranda. Well, I won't keep you, Lestrade.'

'Er . . . no, sir.' He hobbled back to the door.

'Lestrade. I understand there's a rather irate American lady in the cells who is', he looked down at a paper on his desk, '"going to sue the butt off you". How do you propose to handle it? After all, you not only accused her of murder, you stole her Derringer too – the one you stopped Richard Grant with.'

Lestrade opened his mouth, but inspiration failed him. 'I don't know, sir,' he said. 'But I'm very grateful she'd loaded it, this time.'

'Hmm,' Henry nodded. 'It's a bit of a facer. Well, well done, Lestrade, and off you limp.'

'Yes, sir. Thank you, sir,' and the Superintendent closed the door quietly lest his head should fall off with the vibrations.

'Actually, Lestrade,' said Henry to himself, as the tapping of the stick died away along the corridor, 'you should always read the small print. Especially where newspapers are concerned. Miss Adams has written a postscript here. It says, "But I'll settle for dinner."'

A STEAL OF A DEAL

Here's your chance to order more books from the Lestrade Mystery Series at <u>20% off to 50% off, with **FREE** shipping and handling</u>.

❏ Yes, please send my copies from the Lestrade Mystery Series as indicated below.

    ❏ Enclosed is my check or money order.

    or

    ❏ Charge my ❏ **VISA** ❏ MasterCard ❏   ❏ NOVUS

Credit Card # _____Exp. date_____

Signature _____

Phone _____

Please indicate the address to which you would like your copies sent.

Name _____

Street _____

City _____State _____Zip _____

Mail this form to:

Gateway Mysteries c/o Regnery Publishing
P.O. Box 97199 • Washington, D.C. 20090-7199

(fax forms to 202-216-0611)

Qty.	Book	Code	Price	Total
	The Adventures of Inspector Lestrade	LST1	$9.95	
	Brigade: The Further Adventures of Lestrade	LST2	$9.95	
	Lestrade and the Hallowed House	LST3	$9.95	
	Lestrade and the Leviathan	LST4	$9.95	
	Lestrade and the Deadly Game	LST5	$15.95	
	Lestrade and the Ripper	LST6	$15.95	
		Shipping and Handling		FREE
			Total	